My God, he was jealous.

Jealous that Shea was laughing at something his partner was saying, jealous of the man's easy charm. Chance watched the sparkle in Shea's eyes and the dimple that appeared in her cheek as her mirth deepened. Then he looked away.

Chance just couldn't do it; he couldn't look at Shea Austin and see just a job. Not when those wide, thickly lashed eyes made his stomach knot, not when just hearing her laugh made him feel a warmth he'd never felt, not when that slim yet ripely curved figure made his body respond with a fierceness that left him breathless.

You'd better bail out, Chance, he told himself. You've lost your impartiality—you've committed the cardinal sin in police work. You're already so far-gone that it'll rip you apart if she's guilty.

But then Chance looked at her again and knew he wasn't going anywhere.

Dear Reader,

If you have children, it's back-to-school time for them—and that means more reading time for you. Luckily, we've got just the list of books to keep you enthralled, starting with *One Last Chance,* the fabulous American Hero title from Justine Davis.

And the rest of the month is pretty terrific, too, with titles from Suzanne Carey (a bit of ghostly fun to get you set for the Halloween season), Nikki Benjamin, Maura Seger, Clara Wimberly—an Intimate Moments newcomer whose Gothic novels may be familiar to some of you—and star-in-the-making Maggie Shayne. (Look for her next month, too—in Shadows.)

I'd also like to take a moment to thank those of you who've written to me with your thoughts and feelings about the line. All of us—editors and authors alike—are here to keep you reading and happy, so I hope you'll never stop sharing your comments and ideas with me.

So keep an eye out for all six of this month's books—and for all the other wonderful books we'll be bringing you in months to come.

Yours,

Leslie Wainger
Senior Editor and Editorial Coordinator

AMERICAN HERO

ONE LAST CHANCE

Justine Davis

*To Bobbi —
Thanks for
taking a 'Chance'!
Best
Justine Davis
9/93*

Silhouette®
INTIMATE MOMENTS®

Published by Silhouette Books New York
America's Publisher of Contemporary Romance

SILHOUETTE BOOKS
300 East 42nd St., New York, N.Y. 10017

ONE LAST CHANCE

ISBN: 0-373-07517-0

First Silhouette Books printing September 1993

Printed in the U.S.A.

Books by Justine Davis

Silhouette Intimate Moments

Hunter's Way #371
Loose Ends #391
Stevie's Chase #402
Suspicion's Gate #423
Cool Under Fire #444
Race Against Time #474
To Hold an Eagle #497
Target of Opportunity #506
One Last Chance #517

Silhouette Desire

Angel for Hire #680
Upon the Storm #712
Found Father #772

JUSTINE DAVIS

lives in San Clemente, California. Her interests outside of writing are sailing, doing needlework, horseback riding and driving her restored 1967 Corvette roadster—top down, of course.

A policewoman, Justine says that years ago a young man she worked with encouraged her to try for a promotion to a position that was, at that time, occupied only by men. "I succeeded, became wrapped up in my new job, and that man moved away, never, I thought, to be heard from again. Ten years later he appeared out of the woods of Washington state, saying he'd never forgotten me and would I please marry him. With that history, how could I write anything but romance?"

Para Elia de la Cova, mi preciosa suegra—
who with a heart so beautiful
took in a loner
and made her feel loved.

Yo te amo, mamacita.

Chapter 1

"Am I boring you?"

Chance Buckner's hands stilled, and he looked casually sideways at the man in the gray suit who stood before him, hands on where his hips would be if they were detectable.

"You would be," he said lazily, "if I was listening."

Unconcernedly he went back to the informational sheet the speaker had handed out. Almost right, he thought, holding it up for a sighting, then lowering his hand to make a minor adjustment to one of the wings of the paper airplane.

Out of the corner of one eye he saw the livid flush rising above the older man's collar, and had to smother a grin. He heard a cough but didn't dare look at his partner. He knew that if he locked eyes with him, his laugh would break loose; he and Quisto had a way of communicating without words that got them into trouble nearly as often as it saved them.

"Perhaps you can explain to me, Detective Buckner," the man said in barely suppressed fury, "just why you are here?"

In one smooth, fluid movement, Chance levered his lean, muscled body away from the wall he'd been leaning against.

He drew himself up to his full six-foot-two height, topping the shorter, older man by at least six inches.

"I'm here," he said with slow emphasis, "because you guys blew it. I'm here because you guys can't find your butts with a map. I'm here because you guys couldn't make a case on a guy you had under your thumb for two damned years."

"You son of a—"

The man broke off, sputtering. He whirled toward the fourth man who had been sitting at the head of the long table that sat in the center of the conference room, quietly observing.

"If this is an example of this department's discipline," he spat out, "then we haven't got a chance of nailing Mendez!"

"You had *your* chance, in Miami."

The man's red face snapped around to glare at Chance's partner, the source of the comment, a compact, wiry, dark-haired young man with flashing brown eyes who was seated at the other end of the table. Quisto looked back, totally untroubled. The gray-suited man spun back toward the man at the head of the table.

"I was told we would have complete cooperation, Lieutenant!"

A pair of dark eyebrows rose over an inscrutable pair of brown eyes. "I was told," the lieutenant said mildly, "to listen to what you had to say, and do whatever you asked. I don't recall you asking me to maintain order for you."

Chance managed to convert his burst of laughter to an apparent fit of coughing, but at a warning glance from Lieutenant Morgan he stifled even that. Quisto wasn't quite so lucky, and drew another furious glare.

"If you can't control your own men—"

"I have no problem with my men, Mr. Eaton. They know their job, and they do it well. But perhaps we can speed things up by setting down some basics. As a result of your office's investigation—"

"We chased Mendez right out of Miami," Eaton said smugly.

"Yeah," Chance said caustically. "He was so scared he barely had time to pack up his whole operation and move it here."

"Listen, pretty boy—"

"Gentlemen," Lieutenant Morgan interrupted, in a tone his men had come to know meant they were pushing the limits of his considerable patience. "Let's get on with this. As I was saying, as a result of the federal investigation, Paolo Mendez has taken up residence in Marina del Mar. So regardless of how or why, he is now our problem. As is—" he paused and opened the file folder in front of him on the table "—the establishment he intends to open."

Eaton looked blank. "Establishment?"

"He's taken out a lease on an empty building on Marina Boulevard. He's already remodeling. Word is he intends to open a club of some sort."

Lieutenant Morgan handed out a sheet of paper to Eaton, whose crimson face did not fade a bit as he read the report.

When he had finished, he cleared his throat and spoke reluctantly. "Well, er, yes. Good information."

"Thank Detective Buckner. He had it within twenty-four hours of Mendez's arrival, despite the fact that he is using the name Paul de Cortez."

Eaton's expression told everyone in the room exactly what he thought of the idea of thanking Chance Buckner for anything, short of dropping dead. Quisto smothered a snigger, and got a third glare.

"This is obviously going to be his cover for his drug activities." Eaton slapped the report down on the table. "We will begin the surveillance immediately, of course. We already have the necessary court orders."

"You mean *we* will," Chance muttered, knowing all too well that it was unlikely that the federal agents would be the ones doing most of the tedious stakeout work.

"You have a problem, Detective Buckner?"

"Yeah. Something's making me sick." The look Eaton gave him made his glance at Quisto seem like a loving gaze. Chance waited just long enough to make it obvious what—

or who—his problem was, then said easily, "Must have been that burrito at lunch. It was too...heavy."

Eaton's color deepened, but Chance's innocent expression never wavered, and Eaton had to let it pass.

"Why don't you tell us what you have in mind for the stakeout?" Jim Morgan threw Chance another warning glance as he spoke to Eaton. Chance shrugged and, pulling a chair from the table and placing it against the wall, sat down.

The agent's voice hadn't improved since he'd begun. It still had the annoying, buzzing timbre of the fly trapped in the upper corner of the office window. The hum of the insect seemed infinitely more interesting as the man elaborated on procedures any first-year cop would know. And it had been a long time since Chance Buckner had been a first-year cop.

He glanced at Quisto, who rolled his eyes. Restraining a grin, Chance sat back in the chair, fiddling with the rubber band he'd found on the floor. He wound it around his fingers, snapped it a couple of times, and was just wondering how close he could get to that fly when another, much more tempting target presented itself.

Eaton had walked between Chance and the table, inadvertently exposing his considerable backside to attack. Chance drew back the elastic band until it refused to go any further, and zeroed in on the broad expanse of gray.

Quisto suddenly tapped the table in an odd rhythm. Chance glanced up to see his partner's gaze fastened on Lieutenant Morgan, who was looking at Chance pointedly. With a sheepish grin, Chance eased off the tension on the tiny weapon, and with exaggerated conspicuousness dropped it to the floor. Only then did he catch Eaton's last words.

"—expect an improved attitude from your detectives, Lieutenant."

"I'm sure we can handle this investigation in a spirit of mutual cooperation."

Lieutenant Morgan rose, closing the file folder. Seeing the signal they'd been waiting for, both Chance and Quisto got rapidly to their feet and headed for the door.

"Detective Buckner." The lieutenant's words forced Chance to turn back. "My office."

Chance smothered a sigh, then nodded. He heard an odd sound, and turned to see Eaton's face wearing a satisfied smirk. He throttled the urge to deck the man with a well-placed fist, and with an elaborate bow, held the door open.

"So what did he say?" Quisto asked.

"I'm fired."

"Gimme a break, Buckner. The jerk had it coming. What did he want you for?"

"A startling revelation. Eaton doesn't like me."

"Well, that's understandable."

"Thanks a lot." Chance took a swipe at his partner, who dodged agilely away. Quisto grinned.

"Hey, if I looked like him, instead of my classic macho, Latin self, I wouldn't like you, either."

"If his ego was as secure as yours, he wouldn't care," Chance said dryly.

"And who else but someone with a secure ego could work with you? I mean it gets kind of old, my man, watching all those ladies throwing themselves at you all the time."

"They don't throw themselves at me," Chance muttered, although he supposed there was something in what the young Cuban said. He would never understand what there was in the arrangement of his features, in the aligning of the parts that made up Chance Buckner, that made women look twice. He only knew that, to his embarrassment, they did. And often came back for a third look.

"It's those piercing blue eyes," Quisto said dramatically, "and all that sun-bleached California hair."

"My hair's from Iowa, just like the rest of me."

His answer was automatic. They'd been through this teasing routine many times. So was the gesture of his hand as he ran it through the tangled mass of the gold-streaked brown hair. He would be grateful for that if nothing else when he left this assignment to narcotics, he thought. He hadn't had his hair off the back of his neck in four years.

"Besides what are you complaining about? I send 'em all to you anyway."

"Ah, yes, and I teach them that every wonderful thing they've always heard about Latin lovers is true. But you, my friend, don't you think you're carrying this solitude bit a little far?"

"You worried about my social life, Quisto?"

"I'm worried," the younger man said frankly, abandoning the formal tones, "about your libido. You haven't even had a date since Sarah died, let alone anything more...strenuous."

Chance's face closed up in silent warning, but the wiry young man kept on.

"You walk around looking like the poster boy for the wrong side of the tracks, women drool on themselves trying to get to you, and you ignore them all."

"Quisto." His tone was the equivalent of the look that had shuttered his face.

"And you're going to volunteer for all the night shifts on the stakeout, aren't you? Just like last time. Damn it, Chance, when are you going to—"

"Not now."

Chance had stopped dead, turning to fix his partner with a steady, forbidding gaze. Quisto shrugged and gave it up.

"Okay, *amigo*. I was just worried about you." He grinned suddenly, a brilliant flash of white teeth against perfect olive skin. "Hey, maybe that's the secret. Ignore 'em, and they flock to you. I'll have to try it."

"You, ignore women?" Chance accepted the unspoken apology easily. "That'll be the day."

Chance thought of Quisto's words again that evening as he sat in the surveillance van outside the building Mendez had leased. He had been wary of the effusive young Cuban at first, especially after the quiet, laid-back man who had been his partner for his first three years in the division.

But Marty Thompson was gone now, the unruffled exterior having hidden the ravages of burnout that had surfaced abruptly and finally one day beneath the brilliant California sun. That funeral had frightened him as no other, filling him with the eerie sensation that he was looking at himself, and he wondered if someday, somewhere down the hard, sometimes dirty road, he too would walk out onto the golden sand of this paradise and blow his brains out. It was a question he'd always been able to say no to, until Marty. And Sarah.

"All set, Chance?"

He glanced at Jeff Webster, the detective who was monitoring the equipment. The redhead nodded, and Chance looked up at the man who had turned around in the driver's seat of the van.

"Yeah, Todd. Go ahead."

With a nod, the other man turned, slid out of the van and shut the door, locking it from the outside. He would, Chance knew, walk casually toward an expensive shopping area two blocks down, linger there long enough to be sure he hadn't been followed, then pick up the car that was parked in the lot and return to the station. In about four hours he would be back to do it all in reverse, while a few miles away, the driver of a nondescript panel truck that was parked near Mendez's house would be doing the same. The two vehicles would trade places, and then it would begin again.

The system would work until someone realized that the same vehicles always showed up in the area, and perhaps even after, if the drivers could pass themselves off as locals with legitimate business in the area. And when the federal vehicle arrived, that would give them one more to play with, he thought, leaning forward to adjust the recording level on one of the machines.

That was one good thing about working with the feds, he thought wryly. They had a lot more leeway when it came to permits for wiretapping and any other kind of surveillance. And the bugs that Quisto, doing his near-perfect migrant-worker imitation, had planted, were working beautifully.

"You stand out too much," Quisto explained with a superior air. "Me, I just blend, like a chameleon."

"Okay, Mr. Lizard, get on with it," Chance had said, smothering a laugh.

Yes, Quisto had gradually worn down that wall of wariness, mostly, Chance admitted, through sheer persistence and a stubborn refusal to be ignored. He had—

The sharp rapping on the back doors of the van cut through his thoughts. Damn, what the hell? He glanced at Jeff, who shrugged his shoulders in bewilderment. The rapping came again, louder, and Chance scrambled to the back of the van and peered through the mirrored, one-way glass.

"That stupid son of a bitch!"

Jeff jumped, both at the sudden exclamation and at the suppressed fury in Chance's voice. "What . . . ?"

"Eaton," Chance spat out as the pounding came again. "He pulled up in a damned government car, complete with labeled plates."

Jeff gaped at him. "What is he, some kind of a nut?"

"Worse. He's stupid."

The door handle rattled, and they heard a muffled voice. "Come on, Buckner! I know you're in there!"

With a snarled curse, Chance braced himself against the roof of the van and reached for the door. With a swift movement he threw it open, reached through with one leanly muscled arm and yanked the startled Eaton into the van. Despite his bulk, the man flew through the opening as if catapulted, and Jeff Webster stared in awe.

"What do you think you're—"

"Why the hell don't you just hang out a sign?" Chance snapped, cutting off Eaton's protest.

"Get off it, hotshot! Mendez left here an hour ago."

"And just where do you suppose his right-hand man is right now?" Chance bit out. "He's inside and, unless we're luckier than you deserve, calling Mendez to tell him there's a government car sitting in front of his new business. Which means he'll be looking for one at home. Congratulations, Eaton, you may have burned two stakeouts at once."

He opened the door again and practically threw the agent from the van. Chance followed him and shoved the man into the plain gray car that stood out like a sore thumb. "Now get the hell out of here!"

Eaton was furious, but something in Chance's eyes made him stamp down on the accelerator. Staring in disgust as the car sped away, Chance called lowly to Jeff through the door of the van.

"I'm going to see if I can tell if they made us."

The tap from the inside told him Jeff had heard him. He turned on his heel and strode off, still fuming. He'd go to the building next door, he thought. It was a large office building, and they'd discovered a spot on its roof that gave a bird's-eye view of what was apparently being converted into an office.

Damn, he thought, I should have grabbed the binoculars from the van. But I was so damned mad, I didn't even think of it. God, I hate working with the feds. The troops are good, but the generals are just—

"Ouch!"

Chance barely kept himself from going down; he didn't know how the person he'd just crashed into had stayed upright. He flushed as, muttering an apology, he knelt to pick up the book that had bitten the dust—or the concrete sidewalk, in this case.

Poetry, he noted as he lifted the thick volume. He dusted it off and began to straighten up to give it back. And stopped dead before he'd moved an inch.

There before him were the most beautiful legs he'd ever seen. Small feet were encased in short, bright red socks and pristine white tennis shoes, the ankles were slender and delicate, the calves bare, smooth and shapely. Even the knees were lovely, and the thighs . . .

He gulped, aware that he seemed to have forgotten how to breathe. Where the reality of that long stretch of golden leg ended at the edge of a short white skirt, his imagination had kept right on going.

After a long moment he managed to make his reluctant muscles respond and bring him upright by telling them that it was safe; the rest couldn't possibly match those legs.

He was wrong. He knew it the moment his eyes slipped over the white skirt to the fluffy, bright red sweater that topped it. The soft plushness did little to disguise the full, feminine curves beneath the cheerful color, and Chance found himself gulping again. He didn't want to look any further, but he wasn't sure if it was because he was afraid the rest wouldn't be as incredible, or afraid that it would.

He looked anyway. It was.

He didn't realize it at first. Her face was shadowed by the brim of the cheerful red-and-white cap she wore, covering what appeared to be dark silky hair. Then she tilted her head and took his breath away again.

Her mouth was a little wide by classic standards, but her lower lip was so full and soft he barely noticed. Her nose was small and pert, her skin creamy and smooth, but once he saw her eyes he forgot everything else. They were huge, framed by thick dark lashes, and deep, smoky gray. And at the moment, those eyes were looking at him with a mixture of wariness and amusement.

"Uh, sorry," he mumbled again, still staring.

"I hope you're coming from and not going to."

He blinked. "Huh?" Oh, brilliant, Buckner. But damn, what a voice. Husky. Silky. Sexy.

"Whatever turned you into the original raging bull."

He flushed again, then wondered what the hell was wrong with him. "Whoever," he said hastily.

"A whoever I don't envy."

Amusement was winning in the gray eyes, and Chance felt himself responding with a speed that startled him.

"I promised myself I'd wait until tomorrow to kill him. If he's lucky, I won't want to by then."

She looked him up and down consideringly. Contrary to Quisto's earlier comments, he wasn't at all sure the total she came up with was favorable. What he was even less sure of was why he cared.

"Why am I not sure you're kidding?"

His mouth twisted wryly. "Maybe because I'm not sure."

She smiled suddenly, and took his breath away for the third time. The wide, full mouth started a pulse beating somewhere deep inside him, and the sparkle that had turned her eyes to a glittering silver made it begin to race.

"I'll have to remember not to read a paper tomorrow," she said in the silky voice that was a feather up his spine, "in case he's not lucky."

"Maybe I'm not so mad at him after all," Chance said slowly, fascinated by the silver gleam that had lit the gray eyes when she smiled. What would those eyes look like when she laughed? What would they look like hot with passion?

He jerked himself upright and backed up a step hastily. What the hell was he doing?

"Uh, here's your book."

He held it out with an uncharacteristically choppy motion. She reached for it, her hand narrow and graceful, her fingers long and slender. Her nails were gleaming red, but a neat, attractive length and shape instead of the daggers he saw so often in this expensive town—nails that made him think of the old mandarins who had thought long nails a status symbol, an indication that they were wealthy enough not to have to do menial work with their hands.

He realized suddenly that he hadn't released the book and that she was looking at him rather oddly. He let go hastily, pulling his hand back as if the embossed leather cover had burned him.

"Thank you."

He nodded, wondering what had gone wrong with his coordination that made every move he made seem awkward. He decided the answer was not to move at all, and he didn't as she replaced the thick volume in the crook of her arm.

"You . . . like poetry?"

"You get an 'A' for deductive reasoning," she said. Chance suddenly felt as if he'd blushed more in the past five minutes than he had in his entire thirty years. Yet there hadn't been any real sarcasm in the husky voice, merely the sound of an amusement, matching that in her eyes.

Quisto wouldn't believe this, he thought ruefully. He'd figure the real reason I ignore all those woman is because if I try to talk, I'll make a fool out of myself. Hell, maybe he'd be right. "He always is," he muttered.

"What?" She was looking at him quizzically.

He grimaced. "Just trying to remember back to when I could carry on a conversation."

"Maybe you knocked something loose here."

Again there was no sarcasm in her voice, just a touch of the amusement that had been there since he'd first met her eyes. I wish it was only that, he thought, suddenly afraid something had shriveled and died inside him for good.

"Probably permanently," he said wryly.

"Somehow I doubt that."

She glanced at the elegant gold watch that banded her slim wrist, her eyes widening when she saw what time it said. He read her look and moved out of her way. She took a step in the direction she'd been going when he had careened into her, then looked back at him.

"About tomorrow . . . whoever he is, he's not worth it."

He let out a breath, then chuckled as he nodded. "Go ahead and read the paper tomorrow."

The smile came again, even wider this time. He stared after her as she walked away, appreciating the subtle feminine motion of her hips in the short white skirt. He watched her until he realized people were watching him, then he turned around to head toward the other building.

He'd gone only a few steps when he realized he'd never asked her name. It seemed suddenly important, *very* important, and he turned back to see if he could catch up with her. She was nowhere in sight.

His eyes flicked over every person on the sidewalk in disbelief. She couldn't have disappeared so fast, she had to be there. But she wasn't. Damn, Buckner, maybe you hallucinated the whole thing. Maybe she didn't exist at all.

By the time he gave up and headed once more for the office building that they had scouted out earlier, he was half convinced he had dreamed her. He must have, he thought. No real woman had affected him like that in years. Forget it, he told himself. Get moving.

Chance slipped in the side door of the office building. He passed the elevator and headed for the stairway. He took the four flights at a run, thinking that with working on this case, neither he nor Quisto would have the time for the cutthroat games of racquetball that kept them both in shape.

He was breathing deeply but not, he noted with satisfaction, puffing when he pulled the door open at the top of the stairwell and stepped on to the flat roof of the building. He found a spot quickly and crouched down behind the low parapet.

The first thing he realized was that this vantage point wasn't going to be useful to them for much longer; he could see a stack of window blinds sitting on a table just inside the now bare window. But more important, he could see, sitting at the desk, Pedro Escobar, Mendez's lieutenant. Or I guess I should say Pete, he thought wryly. Paul de Cortez seemed to have made some sweeping changes in the names of his employees, as well as his own. I wonder if the Mendezes back in Columbia mind.

The man appeared cool and calm as he worked on something at the desk. Chance's mind was racing. If he'd made them, he would have already had time to call Mendez, but it was unlikely he'd be sitting there so calmly. From what he knew of the man, Escobar had a tendency to go off half-cocked. Maybe, just maybe they might have lucked out.

No thanks to Eaton, he thought as he kept an eye on the figure at the desk. His report hadn't even mentioned Escobar; Chance had called a friend in the Miami office for what information he had. Eaton was a prime example of incompetence rising to the top, he thought, wondering cynically how many good men he'd gotten killed along the way.

Eaton. The whoever that had sent him crashing into that vision in red and white. Unless, of course, she really had been a phantom. He ran a hand through his hair, thinking that it was entirely possible. His mind had been doing some funny things lately. Quisto kept telling him he needed a vacation. Actually, what Quisto kept telling him was he needed a vacation *and* a woman, and not in that order. Maybe he was right.

He knew, of course, that that was the last thing he needed. Or wanted, anyway. Although for a pair of smoky gray eyes, he might think about it....

"Damn," he muttered, a little stunned at himself. Had she really had that strong an impact on him, to make him think of things he'd sworn off for so long? Had she—

Escobar had moved, and Chance jerked his wandering mind back to the matter at hand. The man had risen from the desk and started to walk toward the door. Before he got there it swung open, and a man in a bright red hard hat stood there. About the red of her sweater—

Knock it off, Buckner, he ordered sharply. The man was smiling, and so was Escobar, nodding and shaking the man's hand.

As Mendez's right-hand man turned to walk back to the desk, Chance ducked quickly out of sight. They were safe. They had to be. Escobar didn't have it in him to remain so calm if he knew they were here.

So, I won't kill Eaton. At least not yet. Not in time for tomorrow's paper, anyway, he thought, smothering a grin. Then he settled down to wait until the coast was clear for him to leave.

"Nothing," Quisto said in disgust. "Absolutely nothing."

Chance shrugged. "He wouldn't have all these people after him if he was stupid."

"I'm the one who's starting to feel stupid. He hasn't dealt with anything that even looks like china white, let alone the real stuff. If I didn't know better, I'd swear the guy was opening a legitimate business."

"Maybe he is."

"Sure, and Charles Manson's been rehabilitated."

Chance shrugged.

"Damn it," Quisto said, "all he's done for a week and a half is talk to decorators, food suppliers, and interview chefs."

"Hey, now there's a thought. You could sneak in as a chef. We could close him down in a night."

Quisto scowled. "One little mistake at a home barbecue and they never let you forget it."

"It's your mother who can't forget it."

"It was only one fire engine, I don't see—"

Chance cut off the words with a quick gesture as a silver Mercedes coupe pulled into the driveway behind them. He watched it in the rearview mirror until it pulled into a marked parking stall and Pedro Escobar got out.

"Alone," he said, and settled back down in the driver's seat of the black BMW he and Quisto were sitting in.

The car had been, along with a luxurious motor yacht that was moored down at the marina, the spoils of the biggest bust ever made by the Marina del Mar police, two years ago. Under the Federal Forfeiture Statute, they got a large chunk of the hapless drug dealer's cash in addition to the boat and the car. Chance had been instrumental in that case, and it gave him no small pleasure to know that the man's resources were being used to bring down others like him.

"Speaking of my mother," Quisto said as the vigil began again, "she wants to know when you're coming for dinner."

"Sometime. When there's less than twenty of you around," Chance said dryly. He liked Quisto's family, especially his energetic, vivacious mother, but sometimes they were daunting just in sheer number. For an only child who'd been a loner most of his life, the chaos of seven brothers and sisters, plus assorted spouses and children was a little overwhelming.

"She worries about you, you know."

"She worries about everyone."

"Yes, but when she worries about you, I'm the one who constantly hears about it."

"Tell her I'm fine."

"You know she won't believe me."

"I know." Chance grinned at him. "Why is that, partner?"

Quisto grinned back. "Never mind. What you don't know—"

"—I can't tell your mother, right?"

The grin widened. "Right."

They watched as a truck pulled into the driveway, then looked at each other with raised eyebrows.

"I don't get it," Quisto said. "If he's not going to open for another week, like the ad said, why is he having food delivered now?"

"I don't know. Something private, maybe."

Chance's eyes were fastened on the reflected truck. It was food, all right. And perishable stuff at that, lettuce, vegetables, fruit. He shifted his gaze to Quisto, then his eyes shot back to the small mirror, searching.

She wasn't there. He could have sworn he'd seen her somewhere in the background of the tiny scene the mirror held, but she was gone now. If she'd ever been there at all, he thought wearily.

He rubbed his forehead with one hand, remembering all the times over the past ten days when he'd jerked to attention, thinking he'd seen her somewhere in the distance, or turning a corner, or going through a doorway just far enough away that he couldn't tell where exactly she was.

"Chance? You all right?"

He turned to find his partner's bright dark eyes fastened on him curiously. He let out a long breath.

"Yeah." He shook his head as if to clear it. "Maybe I do need that vacation you're always on me about."

Quisto's gaze sharpened, the curiosity changing to concern. "Chance—"

"Forget it, will you? I'm fine."

Just a minor delusion. Just a strange tendency to jump out of my skin anytime I see a dark-haired woman wearing red. Seeing one woman in particular every time I turn around. Oh, yeah, I'm just fine.

After a moment's hesitation, Quisto accepted it, at least for now.

"Guess I'll go see what I can find out, then."

Although Chance had seen the transformation many times, it never ceased to amaze him. Off came the trendy linen jacket, and the cotton sweater beneath. Quisto reached behind the seat and tugged out a worn plaid shirt that he slid on over the plain white T-shirt he'd had on under the sweater. His hands went to his hair, pulling it down over his forehead, out of its usual smooth style.

His normally straight, proud carriage changed, slumped. His very features seemed to change, flatten somehow, and he was no longer the aristocratic young Cuban with the flashing dark eyes. He was every brown-skinned Latino day worker seen on the streets of California, the kind that the wealthy people in town looked arrogantly past as if they weren't there.

"Pick me up around the corner," Quisto said, and slipped out of the car. He leaned over to look in the window. *"Hasta luego, amigo."*

"Yeah, later."

With an amazed shake of his head, Chance started the car and pulled it away from the curb. Around the corner, as Quisto had indicated, and out of sight of Mendez's building, he parked again. He picked up the portable radio from the seat, letting Jeff, who was still in the van back in front of the building, know what was going on, then settled down to wait.

It was an unseasonably warm January day, even for sunny-year-round California, and Chance found he had to work to keep his eyes open. He hadn't been sleeping well lately, and it was starting to catch up with him. That it was because those gray eyes and that full, soft mouth had come too often to haunt his dreams was something he didn't care to admit.

You've been a fool before, he told himself severely, but that doesn't mean you have to spend so much time mooning over a woman you saw once, for all of three minutes, and will never see again. And it's not like you to be mooning over a woman at all, he thought wryly now. You're out of that market for good, remember?

He shifted in the driver's seat, leaning his head back against the headrest. A mistake, he thought immediately, and tried to lift it. At least he thought he did. When he came awake with a start, he realized he hadn't made it. Still leaning on the headrest, he let his head roll to the side, to check the rearview mirror for any sign of Quisto. Seeing none, he let his eyes drift closed again.

Like a video replaying in his head, he saw the scene in the mirror. The construction crews packing up, the food truck driving back the way it had come, the girl with the great legs walking past the driveway—

He jerked upright, his head snapping around. The narrow street was empty. His eyes flicked over both sidewalks—nothing. A long, compressed breath escaped him, and he let his head loll back on his shoulders, his eyes closed.

Of course, he told himself sourly, she's a phantom, a hallucination, remember? Lord knows, it had happened before.

"Bang, you're dead."

Chance's eyes snapped open, but he managed to keep himself from a startled jump as Quisto slid back into the car.

"Hey, man, you all right?"

Chance shrugged. "Sure."

"You seem a little . . . distracted lately."

"I'm fine," Chance said firmly. "What'd you find out?"

"You were right. Private party. Big wheels only." Quisto eyed his friend and partner for a moment. "You gonna tell me what's bugging you?"

"Nothing."

"Sarah?" Quisto's voice was quiet, suddenly devoid of any of its usual glib slickness.

"No."

For once he could say it and mean it. At least, he thought he could. Maybe this apparition that kept haunting him was no more real than that image had been. It had been nearly two years before Sarah had at last let him rest.

Two years of nightmares, of twisting pain, of reaching for her only to grasp emptiness. Two years of tortured nights spent staring into the dark, staving off sleep, and wondering if the dreams would ever stop. And at last, exhausted, sleeping, only to wake to the ever-present knowledge that he had killed her as certainly as if he had planted the bomb himself.

Chapter 2

"You ready?"

Chance eyed his partner critically. "That depends. Do I have to go in with you?"

"Afraid you're underdressed?"

Chance grinned. "Everything's relative, I guess."

Quisto was looking rather resplendent in a dark, shiny silk double-breasted suit. If he worried about things like that, Chance would have definitely felt underdressed. As it was he was comfortable in the black lightweight wool slacks and thick black-and-tan sweater he had on, which were several steps above his usual worn jeans.

"Let's hit it, partner," Quisto said. "Party time."

They left Quisto's modern apartment that overlooked the marina, heading for the parked BMW. Tonight was the official public grand opening of the Del Mar Club, and they were off to make a survey of the territory.

They'd spent a useless week running every license plate that had showed up at Mendez's—de Cortez, Chance reminded himself again—private party. The man was bent on showing everyone how legitimate he was. The guests ranged from the head of the local chamber of commerce to the councilman for the district. Not a single dirt bag in sight,

Chance had muttered after two hours hunched over the computer readouts. Except for the ones running the place, he had amended wryly. And, he wondered as he scanned the crowd, any of those local community leaders de Cortez might have managed to stuff in his pocket. . . .

If the number of cars in the lot and on the street was an indication, de Cortez had a hit on his hands. Chance and Quisto scanned the crowd, looking for any familiar faces. Other than a few of the better known local high rollers, they came up empty.

They joined the throng at the door, Chance idly looking at the sign on the wall just inside. No checks or credit cards, he mused. De Cortez must be pretty sure of his own success to run a cash-only operation. Then they were inside, going with the flow of humanity that was pouring into the club.

"Nice," Quisto murmured as he looked around.

Although places like this usually left him cold, Chance had to agree. Through the construction of different levels, and clever, careful lighting, the huge room gave the appearance of private, even intimate alcoves. Yet each was angled in such a way as to give a view of the brightly lit stage, where a four-piece band was hammering out a rock number.

He glanced at them—nothing unusual there, just the expected costumes and slightly shaggy long hair. Look who's talking, he muttered to himself, running a hand through the blond-streaked hair that brushed the top of his shoulders.

Continuing their inspection of the clientele, they made their way around the nearly full room, checking the layout of the place. Chance spotted the hallway just to the rear and the left of the stage that appeared to lead to the stairway up to the office, and marked its location on the mental diagram he was making.

He would have preferred to sit somewhere on the outskirts of the room for a better view of the crowd, but when one of the tuxedo-clad ushers led them rather grandly to a table next to the stage, Chance knew they couldn't refuse without drawing attention, and it was too early in the game to risk that. He noticed that the music had changed, softened just a bit, although still hardly tame. He glanced over his shoulder at the band, who had changed position, as he sat down.

The table was small, covered with a spotless white linen cloth. The ashtray was cut crystal, as was the elegant vase that held three red roses.

"Whew." Quisto let out a low whistle. "Three roses per table. That's a lot of change."

Chance grinned wryly. "I wouldn't know. You're the one who has the standing order for three dozen a week."

"Hey, I have ladies to keep happy."

"Rough life."

"You should try it sometime."

They'd been through this routine before, too, and Quisto waited for the standard "No, thanks." His eyebrows rose as he looked at Chance, who had gone suddenly still. The customary answer didn't come; all Quisto heard was the singer who had joined the band.

It had been all Chance had heard since the first clear, crystal notes had begun, more than a match for the now less boisterous backup band. Pure, sweet and powerful, the words washed over him. He couldn't seem to move, not even to turn to look, all he could hear was that voice. And the words . . .

"You wonder when the dreams will stop
Or if they ever will
You wonder if you're doomed to spend
Your life this way until
You end the dreams . . . or you"

A shiver ran through him, an eerie sensation of violation, as if his very soul had been invaded, as if the woman whose voice was sending ripples up his spine had climbed inside his mind and read his darkest thoughts.

It was with a sense of trepidation he hadn't felt in years that he made himself turn. He'd faced armed criminals with less apprehension than he felt when he twisted around in the chair to look at the woman who'd stolen his soul.

Somewhere in the depths of that plundered soul he must have known, because when the slender gray-eyed girl with the wild mane of dark silken hair turned his way, he felt no surprise.

She was in red and white again, this time tight white jeans of some sleek, shiny fabric that molded every taut, trim curve, and a short, bright red leather jacket that came to two points in front where it nipped inward to fit her slim waist. She had on red high-heeled pumps, curving her legs beautifully and emphasizing the delicate ankles. He stared, barely breathing.

The song went on, the words digging deeper, the voice holding every ounce of feeling, every bit of the torture he'd lived with for so long. He was spellbound, completely unaware of Quisto's gaze fastened on him, as she moved around the brightly lit stage with supple grace.

The tempo changed, the driving beat eased, and she slid into the next song with barely a pause. Slower now, husky with a note of longing and pain so real it was almost tangible, that voice enveloped him, plucked at feelings buried so deeply inside him that he'd been able to deny their existence for a long time.

He tried to turn away, tried to tear his eyes from the personification of the phantom that had haunted him since that day on the street. He couldn't do it. He could only stare at her as she was lit by a soft spotlight, as she explored his soul with her sweet, poignant song. Only when the third number began, and she drifted back out of the spotlight to let one of the male band members take over the singing, did the spell release him, allow him to move, to suck in a long, deep breath.

"She's good."

Quisto's voice was loud enough to be heard over the music, and Chance's head snapped around as if he'd forgotten he wasn't alone. He stared at his partner, fighting the lingering haze that seemed to have surrounded him from the moment he'd first heard that voice, those words. From the moment he'd seen her on the street, he thought wryly.

"Chance?" Quisto was looking at him with an expression that changed from curious to speculative as Chance just looked at him, not speaking. "You all right? You look like you've seen a ghost."

Chance let out a short, compressed breath. "If you only knew," he muttered, shaking his head.

Quisto's brows shot up. "You know the lady?"

"Yes." He grimaced. "No."

Quisto's brows lowered in a hurry. Indecisiveness was not a trait he'd ever seen in his rather taciturn partner. Chance saw the look and shrugged. He couldn't explain, not here, not now, maybe not at all. He wasn't sure he understood it himself.

At least now he knew how she had disappeared, where she had vanished to so quickly. Crazy, he thought. All those hours sitting outside, thinking about her, thinking he'd seen her. Hell, maybe he hadn't been hallucinating, he probably had seen her. She'd apparently been here all the time.

And then she was singing again, a powerful, angry lyric, tearing away at the unnecessary, useless pain of life, shouting fiercely at the darkness. Chance knew that darkness, knew it too well. He wished he'd had her words to help him fight it then.

He hadn't even realized he'd turned, hadn't realized the sound of her voice had drawn him as surely as a magnet drew steel. He watched and listened, mesmerized. Each song held words that seemed to reach for something inside him, and her voice held a tremulous note that made his mind, his heart, say yes, that's how it is, how it was.

She moved to one side, toward them, as the lead guitarist moved to center stage for the bridge between verses. The closer she came, the more Chance held his breath. If she came to the edge of the stage, she would be barely two feet away—

A loud wolf whistle from somewhere behind them broke the spell, and its source tossed something at the stage. Chance tensed, every instinct screaming as the object flew past his head. He ducked, hand outstretched reflexively to grab for the gun strapped to his ankle. Then he heard a small sound and caught a flash of movement from the corner of his eye. His rigid muscles slackened, and he let out a rueful breath when he realized the whistler had tossed a rose from the table to the stage.

Then all realization fled, along with most of the rest of his breath, as he began to straighten up. He found himself looking straight into a pair of beautiful gray eyes.

She had bent to pick up the rose, but when their eyes met, bare inches apart, she seemed to go suddenly still. She had begun to smile, the smooth, professional smile of the entertainer, but it stopped abruptly. The gray eyes narrowed, then widened in recognition. When the smile came again, it was soft and warm and real, and it started Chance's heart on a crazy effort to beat its way out of his chest.

The driving sound of the lead guitar ended, and so did the frozen moment in time. She straightened, whirled and was back into the song without missing a beat. More roses hit the stage and Chance leaned back in his chair, wondering why he was having to think so hard about breathing. All he wanted to think about was that split second when something had seemed to crackle between them.

Hadn't it? Or had it just been his imagination that had been so overactive lately? But it hadn't been his imagination, not really. She *did* exist, she was here, she'd been here all along. But had that moment of electricity really happened? Had her smile been that genuine, that full of what seemed like an intimate warmth?

Then, as that number ended and she turned toward the guitarist before he struck a few softer, slower notes, Chance knew it had been real, that moment had been real. She turned back, the gray eyes searching past the lights until she found him, and the smile came again. When she began to sing, everything in her smile was in the warm velvet of her voice, and the new sweetness of her words.

"It doesn't happen often
You can't let it slip away
So when that moment happens
Remember what they say—
You've got to seize the day"

With one driving chord the lead guitarist slammed the song into high gear, but all Chance heard was the soft, silky introduction. His eyes were fastened on her, on every graceful move, as if there were an invisible bond between them. She seemed to feel it, too. Her eyes found him often and he felt, absurdly, as though he were the only one in the smoky room.

"Well, well, that should make things easier."

"Yeah."

Chance hadn't really heard a word of what Quisto said, he was too intent on watching the vision in red and white until she disappeared down the hall he'd seen earlier. Just before she went out of sight, he saw two tuxedo-clad men close in behind her.

He was on his feet before he even realized he'd made the decision. His eyes were fastened on the hallway as he muttered to Quisto that he was going to check it out, so he didn't see the gleam that came into his partner's eyes.

"You do that," Quisto said, a smile quirking his mouth as he watched Chance's progress. The men gave way before his broad-shouldered approach; the women, as usual, were slower to move, as if hoping he would decide to stop. And as usual, it was as if Chance never even saw them.

Except, Quisto thought speculatively, for the lady with the big eyes and the bigger voice. He'd certainly seen her. And had reacted more than he had to anyone in all the time Quisto had known him. His eyes were still fastened on the dimly lit hallway as the tall figure in the black-and-tan sweater went out of sight.

Chance never made it to the first door in the narrow hall. He wasn't sure if the two men who seemed to appear out of nowhere were the same two who had followed her or not. All of the formally dressed attendants seemed to be about the same size. Fifty-two extra-brawny, he thought wryly. At two inches over six feet and a solid two hundred pounds he was hardly tiny, but these guys made him feel inferior.

"Sorry, sir," one of the bow-tied walls said with impeccable politeness, "no guests allowed beyond this point."

"Oh?" Chance tried to look surprised; actually he hadn't expected to get this far. Meanwhile, his eyes were scouring the hallway, noting each door and the barely visible stairway at the end.

"No, sir." They were closing in, subtly urging him back toward the crowded main room.

"Wait," he said, grasping at a reason he told himself was only a cover. "I just wanted to see the lady, tell her how much I enjoyed her singing."

"Visitors aren't allowed, sir."

"But I only wanted to see her—"

"She sees no one, sir."

"No one?"

"No one."

Chance shrugged, as if he were nothing more than a frustrated fan. "I guess I'll just wait until she's done, then."

"I wouldn't bother, sir. She won't see you then, either."

This was starting to irritate him. "Oh? Why not?"

"She sees no one, sir," the left bookend repeated. "Boss's orders."

Something cold crept down Chance's spine. "The boss?"

"Mr. de Cortez."

"Does he own her, or what?" The chill had settled into a frosty knot in the pit of his stomach.

"You might say that. He's put her...shall we say, off-limits?"

The "sir," Chance noticed, was gone.

"I'd say that's for her to decide, isn't it?"

"She does," the right bookend said warningly, "what Mr. de Cortez tells her to do."

That cold lump shifted, changed, spreading out with creeping tentacles, making him fight off a wave of nausea. That lovely vision with the huge eyes and the voice that could melt the most frozen of souls was involved with slime like Mendez?

Get real, Buckner, he told himself fiercely. After all these years, you should know that the most innocent, most beautiful of exteriors often hides the darkest of hearts.

"I suggest you return to your table."

Suggest? Chance almost laughed. He would have, if he hadn't been reasonably certain it would get his arm broken. Realizing that any normal patron would have disappeared long ago, he shrugged and managed a careless grin.

"Can't blame a guy for trying, can you?"

The bookends relaxed a little. "No, sir."

"You guys here every night?" he asked in a joking tone.

"Yes, sir. Every night."

With an exaggerated sigh of surrender, Chance shrugged again. Then he turned and walked casually back into the room, wandering here and there, looking around, until the two wardens apparently decided he was harmless, and disappeared. Only then did he go back to the table.

"So," Quisto said as he sat down, "what's her name?"

"I was checking the hallway," Chance answered in automatic protest.

"Sure. What's her name?"

Chance's mouth twisted in a wry grin. "I never got that far. Two of the those tuxedoed linebackers stopped me."

Quisto's brow furrowed. "They hit you or something? You look a little green."

"No." It was short, clipped. He wasn't about to admit that the thought of the woman who had haunted him for days being connected—intimately—with someone like Mendez made him sick.

"So what's the story? Why'd they stop you?"

He took in a steadying breath. "I gather she's . . . private property."

Quisto's brows shot up. "Oh? De Cortez?"

"So it seems."

Chance could almost see Quisto's quick brain working, reassessing, placing the vibrant gray-eyed woman in a new niche. A niche that was on the wrong side of the line that he had been walking for the past two years, and Chance for four. Four years that seemed like four centuries.

"A shame," Quisto said quietly.

"Yeah." There was a world of bitterness in the single syllable, and Quisto stared at him.

"Chance—"

"Three doors in the hallway," he said abruptly, cutting his partner off. "Two on the left, one on the right. One's got to be a dressing room of some kind. She disappeared too quickly to have made it to the stairs." At least he knew she was real now. "Nothing's labeled, but we know the office is upstairs. There's a door at the bottom of the staircase. From the layout, I'd guess it opens into the alley."

"Lock?"

"Not too tricky, but it's rigged to the fire alarm. Have to take it out first."

"I'll check it out. Just in case."

Chance nodded. "How many men you figure?"

"Twenty, tonight. Let's hope that's just for the big opening. I wouldn't want to have to deal with all of those clowns through this whole thing."

"I'd guess the two I ran into are permanent. I'll check the pictures we got on Mendez—de Cortez's crew from Florida, see if I can spot them."

Quisto nodded. He shifted in his chair to look around the room again, then turned back. For a moment he watched his partner, who sat staring at the roses on the table.

"Red roses," Quisto heard Chance mutter as he reached out and plucked a petal from one of the blooms.

"I'm sorry about the lady, partner."

"Yeah." The petal disappeared, crushed in a tightening fist. "Me, too."

Then, as if realizing what he'd admitted by that answer, by even acknowledging that he knew what Quisto meant, he shut down. His face became stiff and impassive, his voice cool.

"Your turn. Why don't you check for any other exits, or unexplained doors?"

Reluctantly, Quisto went. He knew there wasn't any point in arguing when Chance got like that. When he closed himself off, there was no getting through to him. He wandered around the bustling room, scanning every foot of it as he wondered what had happened, what connection there had been between Chance and the sweet-voiced singer before tonight.

He was still wondering by the next night, when it came time to go back to the club. They planned to establish themselves as regulars, become familiar enough to be overlooked, but as he thought about Chance's reaction the night before, he offered to go it alone, figuring he could check it out and wait and see what happened. Chance only gave him a cool look and asked politely if he was ready to go.

He realized something was up when Chance pulled the car to a stop in front of a small shopping center. Saying only he wanted to get something, he got out of the car. He was back in minutes, empty-handed.

"Closed," he muttered, and stopped again a few blocks farther on. Again he came back empty-handed. Quisto lifted a brow at him. "They were out," he explained cryptically. Quisto rolled his eyes in expressive silence, but when Chance stopped once more, in front of a small row of shops, he finally broke.

"Okay, I'll bite. What the hell are you looking for?"

"The right color."

Quisto blinked. "Of course. I should have known."

Chance shrugged noncommittally and got out of the car. When he came back this time, he had something long and slim wrapped in green florist's paper.

"I thought you didn't buy flowers." Quisto's tone was mild, but his eyes were intently curious.

"It's Election Day."

Quisto stared. "It's not an election year."

"If it was, this would be."

Without another word he started the car and pulled away from the curb. Quisto opened his mouth then shut it again, reminding himself that there was no use prodding Chance when he got like this, he just clammed up more.

There were even more people than there had been last night, and the club was crowded to capacity. They worked their way through the milling groups, Quisto following Chance, who appeared to have a definite destination in mind. They moved slowly, eyes searching the crowd. Neither spoke, so they could hear the bits of conversation around them.

"—bringing Sam here tomorrow—"

"—was here last night. The singer is really good—"

"—sexy as hell—"

"—I heard she signed a record contract—"

"—she turned it down—"

"—a knockout. Great body, and she can really sing—"

"—could eat crackers in my bed anytime—"

By the time Chance came to a stop beside an empty table, his jaw was rigidly set. He'd spent a long time last night determinedly shoving the vision that had haunted him into the category of merely a possible way to get to de Cortez. Unless, he thought grimly, she was doing more than just playing house with that piece of slime.

It came back to him then, the picture he'd built last night. He'd had to, to keep his perspective. He'd made himself think about it, made himself picture them together. The crime boss who thought nothing of ordering a murder along with dinner, and the wide-eyed, crystal-voiced woman who had seemed to slice open his soul with her songs.

It was just an image, he told himself again, as he had countless times last night. It was a front, a facade. Part of the big picture de Cortez was building in his new home, the veneer of respectability he was trying to paint over his activities.

He had to accept, no matter how rotten it made him feel, that she knew what de Cortez was, perhaps even helped him. The only alternative was that she was too naive to realize it; he found that more impossible to believe than her connection with the man.

She was a way in, that's all. A way that might or might not work. Just one facet of a complex investigation. He silently ordered himself to remember that one more time as he tossed the long, slim cylinder of green paper down onto the pristine white cloth covering the table.

"Planning an ambush?"

Quisto had noted immediately the location of the table Chance had chosen. It was farther from the stage, but was exactly where the singer had passed last night on her way to the hallway.

"Sort of."

"Good luck."

Chance shrugged. "If it doesn't work, you're on next. Maybe she likes the machismo type."

Quisto lifted a brow in elegant disbelief. "After the way she looked at you last night?" The brow came down in sudden puzzlement. "Besides, I got the idea you were... interested yourself."

Chance made a low, grunting sound that could have meant anything. "She's part of the job."

"So why do I get the feeling you knew her before we came in here last night?"

Chance had had time now to marshal his defenses. "I ran into her on the street a couple of days ago. I was surprised when she showed up here, that's all."

Quisto backed off, but he wasn't convinced. In the two years he'd worked with this man he'd come to admire and respect, he'd never seen Chance react the way he had last night. Quisto leaned back in his chair, occasionally scanning the room, but just as often watching his partner.

She moved so quietly as she opened the first door on the left in the hallway that she was almost even with their table before they saw her. The other members of the band were both in front of and behind her. Still, she paused for a barely measurable moment when she saw Chance. The smile she gave him seemed so warm, so genuine, that he was already smiling back before he realized. Then she was gone, headed for the stage, and he sank back in his chair as he called himself seventeen kinds of a fool.

"Whatever game she's playing, she's good," he muttered, hardly aware of saying it aloud.

"Didn't seem like a game to me," Quisto observed mildly.

"It has to be. She belongs to de Cortez, remember?"

"For now."

Chance's eyes narrowed as he stared at his partner. "What's that supposed to mean?"

Quisto shrugged as if he'd meant nothing by the comment. "Just that we need to put the heat on without burning ourselves, and I can't think of any better way to give de Cortez one more thing to worry about than messing with his woman."

His woman. Chance's stomach churned. "Yeah," he muttered, and sank into his seat. He turned toward the stage as the beat began, glad when the houselights went down and the spotlight came up, encircling the slender figure on the stage.

She was in red and white again. This time in a short red leather skirt that reminded him sharply and immediately of the first time he'd seen her, and those long, graceful legs that had knocked the breath out of him. Above the skirt was a shimmering white blouse that draped over her body in a demure cowl neck in front, hinting at the full, feminine curves beneath, then plunged into a deep V in the back, baring a stretch of silken skin that made his fingers curl oddly.

She did it again, as easily as before, reaching into his heart and soul and tying him up in knots with her words. She sang of love and loss, of pain and anger, of fear and mistrust, as if she'd known them all as deeply as he had. For Chance it was a constant battle between the heart that heard and believed every clear, shining note and the mind that knew better.

When she ended with an unexpected ballad, a song of anticipation and hope that she made soar as her strong, sweet voice soared, none of it seemed to matter anymore. For those minutes, she was everything she seemed to be, everything he wished was true.

He watched her as she came off the stage, unconsciously savoring her graceful movements. Those legs, he thought, were incredible. They'd be even more incredible wrapped around—

Damn! He barely kept the oath silent as he sat up sharply. He hadn't reacted like this to a woman since...since when? Not even with Sarah had it been so quick, so hot.

Great, Buckner, the only thing worse than your timing is your choice of women. Where the hell was all this libido when there was a willing, unentangled woman around?

He didn't want this, he thought fiercely. Not now, not ever. And especially not with this woman. But he had to deal with her. She was the best chance he had to get close to de Cortez, and if he was going to find out just what de Cortez was up to, he had to take that chance.

She was close now, and with a tremendous effort he forced his mind back to the business at hand. He would think about what he had to do, nothing else. You've had years of practice, Buckner. It'll be easy.

Right, he muttered under his breath as he reached for the green florist's paper and unrolled it.

He waited until the other members of the band had passed, until the moment she couldn't avoid seeing him, then slowly stood up. Everything he'd thought of saying fled his mind the moment the gray eyes settled on him. He'd considered the clever lines he'd heard Quisto use and discarded them all, knowing he'd never be able to get one out with a straight face. Finally, as she paused beside the table, he said the only words that came to him.

"Thank you."

Her eyes shone warmly, then widened as he held out the single flower he'd brought. It was a rose, a beautifully unfolding bud, as perfect and flawless as those on each table that were inevitably tossed to her after every song. But where those were a deep blood red, this one was a pure, immaculate white.

Her gaze lifted from the delicate bloom to his face, a soft smile curving her lips, an acknowledgment of his choice of color in her eyes that was almost a salute. In that moment he would have bet his life that she was for real, that what he saw was the truth. Then one of the tuxedos beside her moved, and he remembered with a dull ache that his life might really be the cost if he didn't keep his head on straight.

She lifted a hand to capture the long stem in slender fingers. He didn't release his grip on it but held it, as his eyes held hers. His fingers flexed slightly with an odd tingling sensation, as if the stem of the rose had suddenly developed the capacity to transmit electricity, a current that had begun the moment her fingers had touched it.

She looked momentarily startled, as if she felt it, too, but before she could speak, the tuxedo to her right did, gruffly.

"Let's go, Miss Austin."

Irritation flashed through the gray eyes. "In a minute," she said without looking at the man.

"Maybe you'd better go," Chance said, a tinge of rancor creeping into his voice despite himself.

"Oh?" She looked puzzled, either at his words or his tone.

"*Now*, Miss Austin," the tuxedo said stiffly.

"I said in a minute." Her voice was cool, her eyes icy as she shot a glaring look over her shoulder.

"You know the boss's rules," the man said.

"And we can't break the *boss*'s rules, can we?" Chance's emphasis on the word drew her gaze sharply back to him.

"He's not my boss," she began, ignoring the grip the tuxedo had taken on her elbow.

"So I've heard. He's much more than that, isn't he?" Chance reined in the irritation he couldn't seem to control. He went on, but still kept his grip on the stem of the rose. "You'd better go. The master awaits."

"Master?" Her delicate brows furrowed below the tousled fringe of bangs that swept forward from the thick mane of dark hair.

Chance shrugged. "He does own you, doesn't he?"

He'd wanted to prod her, make her react, but he hadn't counted on his own reaction to the sudden flare of anger and hurt in her eyes. Contrition flooded him, and before he could stop himself, he said softly, "I'm sorry."

The tuxedo pulled at her arm, forcing her to move, but she hung back for one last moment. The hurt had faded, but not the anger, and as she at last yielded to the pressure of her escort, she yanked at the rose. It ripped free of Chance's grasp, a thorn snagging and tearing at his thumb. He jerked his hand back at the sudden pain, shaking it sharply as blood welled to the surface.

When he lifted his head, she was gone, disappearing down the hallway with her solid wall of an attendant. He stared after her for a moment, then slowly sat down.

"It seems the lady has a temper." Quisto was obviously smothering a grin as he held out a napkin from the table.

"Yeah." Chance took the cloth and wrapped it around his bleeding thumb. De Cortez could afford it, he thought.

"Of course, you did rather... provoke her." He looked at Chance consideringly. "Intentionally, I presume?"

"Of course."

He waited, wondering if Quisto was going to comment on that involuntary apology that had escaped him. But either he hadn't heard it or had decided not to bring it up. Chance gradually relaxed, dropping the guarded, defensive posture he'd assumed.

"You're still bleeding." Quisto eyed the now red-stained napkin. "Do you need—"

He broke off as one of the club's waitresses, dressed in a short-skirted version of the men's tuxedos, appeared at their table with a silver tray.

"From Ms. Austin," she said, and lowered the tray in front of Chance.

Startled, Chance looked at the tray. He stared, then smiled. The smile widened into a grin, then a full-throated burst of laughter broke from him.

Quisto stared. In all the time he'd known him, he'd never heard Chance laugh like that. He shifted his bright gaze to the silver platter and suddenly understood. For there, grandly ensconced on an elegant white doily, sat a thumb-size bandage.

Chapter 3

"He must be on to us. That's why he hasn't made a move."

"If he is," Quisto muttered to Chance, "it's thanks to Eaton."

Eaton's head snapped around, but they could tell by his expression that he hadn't heard the actual words. Chance smothered a laugh.

"You have something to say, Detective Buckner?"

Chance raised an eyebrow. "No. I think you're saying quite enough."

Color suffused Eaton's face. "If you can't treat this with the seriousness it deserves, perhaps we should find someone who can."

"Oh, I'm taking the case very seriously."

"What's that supposed to mean?"

"Was there a word in there you didn't understand?" Chance's tone was innocent.

Eaton sputtered, but no recognizable words came out.

"All right, gentlemen," Jim Morgan interjected sternly, "let's get on with it. What do we have so far?"

"I talked to one of the doormen last night," Quisto said. "He said that about half the crew was hired for this opening week only. That leaves about ten or fifteen that are probably de Cortez's own men.''

''Most of them are from his organization in Miami,'' Chance added. ''We spotted them in the photos they sent out.''

Morgan scanned the papers on the table in front of him. ''It seems he brought only those with clean sheets. No serious charges against any of them in Florida or anywhere else. His right-hand man, Escobar, has a local juvenile record, but as far as we can tell, nothing as an adult.''

''Yep,'' Quisto drawled, ''just a pack of Boy Scouts.''

''Can we get on with this?'' Eaton dropped down on to a chair that creaked ominously under his bulk.

Morgan's eyes flicked to the federal agent, then back to the papers he held without comment. ''We've gotten nothing on the wiretaps,'' he went on as if the man hadn't spoken. ''Only normal business calls, nothing unusual.''

''Unless it's in code.''

Morgan nodded at Chance's comment. ''Yes. But so far every call has proven legitimate. Every call to a supplier has resulted in a delivery of what was ordered. No unscheduled deliveries have been made. No unaccounted-for appointments.''

''And no unknown visitors to the house,'' Quisto put in. ''Only the men we already know about.'' His eyes flicked to Chance. ''And the singer from the club.''

Chance's face remained impassive as Morgan read from a page of the surveillance log. ''The other members of the band are fairly clean. Local. No connections. A couple of arrests on traffic warrants, but no felonies. One marijuana cite, a couple of years ago. Less than an ounce.''

''They may be clean, but the bimbo's dirty as hell.'' Eaton's voice was almost avid in its luridness.

Chance didn't visibly stiffen, but Quisto had come to know his partner rather well over the past two years. He looked from Chance's face back to the agent's.

''You've got proof of that?''

''Proof? If he'd just wanted someone to sing in his club, he would have hired local talent, instead of bringing her in. What more do you need?''

"She's not from Miami," Quisto argued. "Our sources say she came in from Reno. And de Cortez has no known contacts there."

"He obviously has one," Eaton snapped. "The broad. He must have stashed her there when we made it too hot for him in Miami."

"Then why isn't she in the file on his known associates? She's not in any of the surveillance photos, either." Quisto gestured at the pile of black-and-white pictures.

"Look," Eaton snarled, "she's shacked up with de Cortez, isn't she?"

"She comes and goes from the house. Doesn't mean she lives there," Quisto said.

"She doesn't have to live there to give Mendez what he wants," Eaton suggested with a leer.

"That doesn't mean she's part of it." The words broke from Chance as if against his will, and Eaton turned to stare at him.

"She's screwing him, she's got to know. Even if she isn't involved in his operation, she has to know what's going on. Dirt by association is still dirt."

Chance sat up sharply, but when Eaton's beady brown eyes narrowed with a gleam of interest, Chance made himself sit back. He stared at his hands, his eyes fastened on the adhesive bandage that was wrapped around his thumb.

"We can't assume she's involved," Quisto put in quickly. "She may be with de Cortez, but that doesn't mean she knows the details we need."

"She could be the weak link," Morgan said slowly. "Can you work her?" He looked at Quisto.

"Er..." Quisto jerked a thumb toward Chance. "He's already started."

"I'll bet," Eaton sneered. "You pretty boys are all alike."

Quisto moved as if to stop Chance, then stopped himself when his partner never moved, never even reacted, only lifted a finger to run it lightly over the flesh-colored bandage. His dark brows furrowed.

"That's enough," Lieutenant Morgan said. He looked over at Eaton. "Your other men reported in this afternoon. I've assigned them to take over the surveillance so my men can get some rest." Eaton stood up, ready to protest this appropriation of his authority, but Lieutenant Morgan gave him no chance to speak. "Since there's nothing further to discuss, I suggest we all get some rest." He got to his feet. "Detective Buckner, my office please."

Chance's eyes flicked to his boss, then to Quisto. Had he said something? Was he about to get warned about keeping this completely business? Quisto shrugged, eyebrows raised to indicate he knew no more than Chance did.

You're a basket case, Buckner, he told himself grimly. Suspecting your own partner of ratting on you about... about what? What was there to tell? Nothing, he answered his silent question firmly. He'd overreacted to a beautiful voice, a pair of wide gray eyes. And those words. Words no doubt borrowed from whoever had truly felt them and set them to music, he told himself.

He walked into the lieutenant's office, sat down and waited. Morgan dropped the files onto his already cluttered desk, then turned and sat on the edge.

"I know he's a pain, but we've got to work with him."

Chance smothered a sigh of relief. "I can work *with* anybody. But I can't work *for* him."

"You're not. This is our town, and de Cortez is our problem now." Jim Morgan smiled wryly. "The feds always have a problem about local jurisdiction, but his is—" his mouth quirked "—larger."

Chance grinned. "Yeah, it is, isn't it?"

"Try to live with it, will you? It won't be forever."

"It'll only seem that way," Chance said dryly. He slid forward to the edge of the chair. "I'll be good, I promise. Is that it?"

After a split second of hesitation, Morgan answered. "No. Not quite."

Uh-oh. Chance sat back.

"You know this is our number-one priority now."

Chance nodded. "I heard the chief wants the feds out of here as soon as possible."

Morgan nodded. "That's why we've got the go-ahead to table everything else until this is wound up."

"Which could be awhile." Chance grimaced. "It looks like de Cortez is determined to build one hell of a respectable facade here."

"Yes. We may have to do a little prodding, eventually."

"Make him an offer he can't refuse?"

"Perhaps. But for now, our instructions are to just watch."

Chance looked steadily at the man he'd worked for, for over five years. "None of this is news, Lieutenant. We've discussed it all before."

"Yes." Morgan got up and went to sit behind the desk. "But what we haven't discussed is that devoting all our time to this investigation is going to back up everything else we have going."

"I know." Chance was truly puzzled now.

"It's almost November now. We may have to push hard all the way through the holidays to catch up."

Chance's expression changed from quizzical to shuttered.

"I'm sorry, Chance," Jim Morgan said softly, "but I can't guarantee you the time off."

"I understand."

"I know how hard it is for you to—"

"No. I'm sorry, sir, but you don't."

Morgan sighed. "You're right. I don't." He paused. "I wish I could promise you we'll be able to spare you by then."

"You can't. I understand." He got up. "Is that all?"

Morgan hesitated as if he were about to say more, then stopped. He only nodded before adding, "Get some rest. You're looking a little ragged."

Chance gave a short, sharp nod, then turned on his heel and strode out of the office. Jim Morgan shook his head slowly as he watched him go. His expression was sadly compassionate, his mouth compressed into a tight line as he lifted the top folder from the stack on his desk and began to read.

Chance lay sprawled on his bed, trying to blame his sleeplessness on the bright silver glow that filled the room.

He was exhausted, he could feel it in the aching of his head and the grittiness of his eyes, but still sleep eluded him.

He rolled over and swung out of bed in one smooth, controlled motion, and walked over to the sliding glass door that led to the small deck. He'd intended to close the drapes to darken the room and then try again, but instead found himself tugging open the heavy door and letting the chilly night air wash over his naked body.

He stared out at the hillside before him, not really seeing it. He'd chosen this place for its seclusion and remoteness. It was a spacious set of rooms over the garage of a large, expensive house whose owner was more than happy to have a police officer in residence while he spent most of the year traveling around the world for his lucrative business.

The garage wasn't even visible from the street. It backed up to a steep hill, and unless you knew they were there, you might never guess the rooms above it existed. Chance liked it that way, and had gotten to the point where he didn't even think of why every time he came home or left. The gang that had blown his life apart had been put away. But the knowledge that a man in his job made new enemies every day never left him.

He slammed the sliding door shut with a mutter of disgust. He admitted at last, with tired certainty, that sleep was beyond him tonight. He'd lain there for hours, trying not to think about the one thing his mind refused to let go of. When he looked at the clock that glowed atop the old ammunition crate Quisto had jokingly given him to use for a nightstand, it was only to calculate what was happening at the club.

She'd be starting the first show now, he'd thought at nine. Then at ten-thirty, the second. And at eleven-fifteen the last. What then?

And then, he'd told himself sourly as he rolled over and pounded his innocent pillow with merciless force, she'd go home and climb into bed with the boss. An image of them intimately entwined shot through his mind and banished any hope of sleep that night.

Still muttering, he yanked open a drawer and got out some clothes. He picked up the worn pair of jeans he'd tossed across the foot of the bed and pulled them on, then tugged a thick cotton sweater, boldly patterned in shades of blue, over his head as he walked into the living room. He slipped on the leather dock shoes he'd kicked off inside the front door, and grabbed his battered faded-denim jacket from the hook on the hall tree. He locked up with instinctive care and headed down the narrow staircase.

He noted almost absently that the third and twelfth steps from the top still creaked with a satisfying loudness. More than once Mr. Hagan, the house's owner, had offered to have someone come in for repairs. Chance had quietly declined without explaining why.

He skirted the edge of the large pool, the water shimmering from the lights below and the moonlight above, giving the lagoonlike pond an eerie glow. The man-made rocks that surrounded the glistening water looked real and solid yet strangely ethereal in the silver glow. Once he would have appreciated the effect, would have let his imagination run with the slightly unreal setting, let it become the almost fantasy place it appeared.

But the capacity for such whimsical thought seemed burned out of him now, and all he could do was think vaguely that he would have to remember to switch on the waterfall for a while tomorrow, to keep the pump clear of debris. It was one of the little things he did regularly around the place, and while Mr. Hagan had never asked him to do those tasks, he felt it was small enough payment for the low rent and privacy he was getting.

Not to mention, he thought with a wry grin, access to Hagan's small fleet of cars. The wealthy man had a passion for the more exotic forms of transportation, and the contents of the five-car garage were the proof. After Chance had lived there for about six months, Peter Hagan had apparently decided he was reliable, and had entrusted him with the keys to his babies while he was gone for weeks at a time.

"Take 'em out now and then," he'd said casually. "It's not good for them to just sit."

There was, he'd thought ruefully then, enough kid left in him to make it difficult to stifle the little kick of excitement that went through him while driving the finely tuned, powerful vehicles.

He hit the combination on the keypad outside the garage door that disarmed the elaborate alarm system. The big door lifted, and he stepped inside. Like furniture in a house closed up for the winter, the cars were low bulky shapes beneath enveloping covers. Chance's open Jeep sat at one end, quietly unimpressed with its august company. He grinned wryly at himself, at how he'd found himself missing the high, stiff ride of the totally utilitarian vehicle after a few days of that smooth, purring power.

It was a good thing real police work didn't imitate movies and television, he'd thought more than once when behind the wheel of one of the low-slung sleek cars. He could just see himself explaining to Pete how he'd racked up his Lamborghini chasing some crook. No, real life was full of long hours of drudgery and paperwork, with those moments of pulse-pounding, adrenaline-induced frenzy few and far between.

He started automatically for the Jeep, then realized that the odd angle of the vehicle meant it had a flat tire. He looked down the row of covered cars.

Gee, Buckner, that's too bad, he told himself flippantly. Guess you'll have to drive one of these.

He uncovered the one that had been sitting the longest, the blatantly red Ferrari Mon Dial. The tan top was up and he took a moment to drop it, thinking he would need the blast of cold air. It started with its characteristic throaty roar, and within moments he was pulling onto the street, the heavy iron gates swinging automatically shut behind him.

After a run up the coast that did nothing to ease the restlessness that plagued him, Chance at last pulled to a halt near the waterfront, in a spot overlooking the marina that housed boats whose extravagance matched the car he carefully parked. He didn't think about it anymore, the fact that he couldn't afford even the upkeep on the toys that belonged to the people he was sworn to protect. Possessions had come to mean very little to him in the past few years.

He wandered along the waterfront for a while, watching the moonlight play on the water. He tried to keep his mind empty, knowing all too well that moods like the one that had descended on him tonight too often resulted in a flood of memories he didn't want. He wasn't up to dealing with it, not tonight. He walked on.

He wasn't really aware that he had changed direction until a car racing by made him look up. With a little shock, he recognized his surroundings. Had it been an accident, or had some subconscious urge turned his steps in this direction?

He hesitated at the corner, staring up the street. He could see, just beyond the halo of a streetlight two blocks up, the shadowy shape of the surveillance van. There was no movement on the street, only the sound of distant cars passing. A horn honked, somewhere a heavy door slammed, and then silence reigned again. It had to be later than he realized, he thought. No drunks out, no last stragglers leaving the club. He glanced at his watch, shaking his head ruefully when he saw it was nearly three-thirty.

He could go relieve the guys in the van. He wasn't going to sleep anyway. Then maybe he could go home and get some rest before he was due back tomorrow. Tonight, he corrected himself glumly. He and Quisto were set to go back to the club tonight, and then to take over the stakeout on the house afterward.

Approaching footsteps snapped him out of his reverie. Instinctively he drew back into the shadows, watching, waiting. A woman, he thought, listening to the quick, light stride. And then, suddenly, without knowing how, he knew. He fixed his eyes on the circle of light cast by the corner streetlight, knowing she must pass through it.

When she did, it was as if the light had merely been waiting for her presence to come to life. It seemed to dance around her, gleaming on the sleek fall of her hair, glinting in the huge gray eyes.

She was wrapped in a thick red sweater that came almost to her knees, over a white turtleneck sweater, slacks and boots. Her hair was brushed to a smooth sheen, unlike the dramatic, tossed mane she wore onstage. She was carrying what looked like some kind of a notebook in the crook of her arm, and she looked lost in contemplation. Like a butterfly adrift on a puff of air, he could hear her humming a soft, airy melody. It seemed incredible that the power of that voice could be harnessed to anything so fragile, so delicate.

Not a butterfly, he thought suddenly. An eagle maybe. The essence of restrained power. Able to glide effortlessly on the breeze with the most delicate adjustment of feathers, yet in the blink of an eye able to soar and plummet with dynamic grace.

She walked on, into the shadows, and the streetlight's glow once more became merely a circle of light on an empty street. She crossed the street, mere yards away. Chance stepped out of the shadows. She jumped back, every muscle in her slender body tensed to flee.

"At least I didn't knock you sideways this time," he said quietly.

Her gaze flew to his face, and he saw the tension drain away as she recognized him. Still, she looked at him warily, as if too aware of the late hour and the empty street.

"I'm sorry," he said quickly, "I didn't mean to scare you."

"You just startled me." She looked at him for a moment. "I didn't see you tonight."

She'd noticed. He couldn't help the silly feeling of pleasure that gave him. He tried to smother it. "I... couldn't make it." His mouth quirked. "Where are the bookends?"

She looked puzzled, then a grin curved her mouth and put a sparkle in the gray eyes. "Shh," she whispered conspiratorially, "I gave them the slip."

He grinned back. She looked at him rather oddly, then shrugged. "I needed to get away. I told them I was taking a cab home."

His brow furrowed. "Why didn't you? You shouldn't be out here alone at this hour."

"I know, but I wanted to walk. And better now than an hour ago, when they were pouring all the drunks out the door." She wrinkled her nose expressively.

Something twisted inside him. She didn't like drunks, but she was de Cortez's girlfriend? A man who dealt in substances that made alcohol look like Kool-Aid?

"Does the boss know you're out?"

She drew back at the sudden acid in his tone. "I did my shows," she said carefully.

Except for the one that comes later. In de Cortez's bed. His stomach knotted at the image that again flashed through his mind. His voice was as sour as the taste in his mouth.

"I'm surprised he let you out of his sight."

"Look," she said in exasperation, "if all you stopped me for was to have somebody to snipe at, forget it. I've got better things to do."

"I'll bet. I'm sure de Cortez sees to that."

Suddenly the exasperation became anger. "What is your problem? You don't even know him!"

I know him, lady. Better than you could ever guess. "I know his type."

"I don't care what you think you know. He's been good to me, and I don't care to continue this conversation!"

She walked stiffly past him. His gaze followed her automatically, noting her angry stride. He's been good to me. God, the words alone made him sick. He could imagine just how he'd been good to her.

Snap out of it, Buckner, he ordered himself. She's part of this job, and you'd damn well better do it, and now— you'll never have a better chance! Just keep thinking about what she is, about her and de Cortez together. That ugly thought gave him a steadying jolt, and he made himself go after her.

"Wait," he said as he caught up with her. "I didn't mean to make you mad. I'm sorry."

She eyed him skeptically, anger still flickering in her eyes. "But you're not sorry about what you said."

She wasn't going to let it slide. He took a deep breath. "I... Sometimes I form an opinion before I know all the facts." Like I did with you, he added grimly, after that day on the street. "And sometimes I'm wrong." Very wrong. So wrong it hurt. He waited.

She read it as he'd intended, thinking he'd meant de Cortez. After a moment she nodded. "All right."

He breathed a sigh of relief. "There's a café a couple of blocks down that's open all night. Can I buy you a cup of coffee?"

She hesitated.

"Please?" He held up his hands. "No sniping, I promise."

A reluctant smile curved her soft mouth, and he felt the knot in his gut unclench. It didn't make any sense, she was what she was, but that smile still turned his frozen insides to glowing warmth.

"How's your thumb?" she asked, and he knew she'd accepted.

He held up the wounded thumb with a grin. "Okay. Somebody sent me a Band-Aid."

Her smile widened into a grin, and the warmth became a rippling heat.

They walked down the deserted street toward the beckoning light of the café's window. Chance changed position and walked on the inside when he spotted someone pacing in front of the doors, keeping himself between her and the seemingly agitated young man.

"Hey, man, got any change?"

The words were quick, sharp, and punctuated by a swift swipe of one hand to what appeared to be a runny nose. The eyes that looked up at them were wide and dark, and even in the dim light the sheen of sweat on his forehead was visible.

"Sorry," Chance said shortly, guiding her past him and into the café.

She looked back over her shoulder as the door swung shut after them.

"Maybe he's hungry—"

"Save your money. He'd just use it to buy another pop."

"What?"

"Meth, I'd guess."

"Meth?" Her brows furrowed, then cleared. She stared at the man still pacing anxiously outside. "You mean drugs?"

"That's what methamphetamines are, yes," he said more sharply than he'd intended. Damn, if he didn't know, he'd swear she was shocked. She played the innocent perfectly, looking as if she had no idea what he was talking about.

"What a waste."

He stared at her as they sat down in a booth in the small chrome-and-glass diner-style café. This didn't make sense, either. Those soft words had been heated, almost angry. He glanced out the window again.

"Him?"

"Anyone. All the people who waste their lives, and destroy the lives of everyone around them."

He sat back in the upholstered booth, his mind racing. Was she testing him somehow? On de Cortez's orders, perhaps? Or was that harsh, vehement tone for real? But how could it be, when she was involved with a man whose livelihood came from the source she was denouncing?

"That sounded rather personal." He probed carefully.

"It is. Very personal."

She volunteered no more, and her expression told him clearly that he would get nothing by pushing right now. He let it drop, knowing that he had to go slowly, that he didn't dare risk alienating what could be their most valuable source of information. And he reminded himself once more that that was how he had to look at her.

The cups of steaming coffee were in front of them before he spoke again.

"You are out pretty late," he said, careful to keep his tone merely solicitous.

"We were working late. Going over some new songs."

She gestured at the notebook she'd set down on the table. Only now did he notice that the paper sticking out from between the pasteboard covers was lined for music and covered with bold black notes.

"Was that what you were humming?"

"Was I?" She looked surprised. "Yes, I suppose I was. I get sort of . . . engrossed sometimes."

"It was beautiful. Kind of fragile."

Her eyes widened as she looked at him across the small table. Her voice was full of a surprised happiness that he had chosen the perfect word.

"Yes," she said softly. "That's how it was meant to sound. Just like that."

"Who writes your songs?"

She shrugged. "I do."

He stared at her. "All of them?"

She nodded. "The boys just play, mostly, although Eric helps with the music sometimes."

"But the words...?" For some reason he was afraid of the answer he knew was coming. It came.

"All mine. Such as they are."

It couldn't be. How could someone who could do that, who could reach into his very soul with her lyrics, possibly be involved with the likes of de Cortez?

"They're...I...they..." He shook his head sharply, his mouth twisting into a wry grimace. "Apparently they leave me speechless."

She laughed lightly. "Since my ego is fairly secure, I'll take that as a compliment."

"Do," he said, recovering himself. "They're wonderful. And you're amazing."

"Thank you." She accepted it simply.

"Why aren't you doing it professionally?"

One dark, silky brow rose. "Last time I checked, I was. I do get paid, you know."

He couldn't help grinning. "You know what I mean. Records, concerts, that stuff."

"Not for me."

"Why?"

She made a rueful face. "You may find this hard to believe, but I really don't like performing live. I'm not at all how people seem to perceive me. I'm really just a song writer, not a performer, and a little shy, and it's very hard for me to do it. The idea of doing it for a living..." She shook her head.

"But you'd be a big hit. A celebrity. And rich."

"And poor in what matters to me most."

"Such as?"

"Privacy, for one thing."

"Ouch." He winced. "Was that a hint?"

She looked genuinely startled. "What?"

"I got the feeling you meant that rather pointedly. I didn't mean to pry."

"You weren't," she said quickly, smiling at him with a warmth that sent an inverse chill rippling down his spine. "I just meant that I have no desire to subject myself to that kind of exposure."

Of course, dummy, he thought as it hit him at last. The last thing someone like de Cortez needed was a high-profile girlfriend. His kind of work was done best in the dark, not in a spotlight.

"Oh," he said, barely aware that the biting tone had crept back into his voice. "I should have known."

"What?" The warmth faded at that sharp note.

"A man like your...boss wouldn't want anyone looking too close, would he?"

"What is that supposed to mean?"

He knew that he was out of line and out of control, that he was risking blowing the whole investigation, but that image had settled vividly in his mind, of her in de Cortez's bed, and he couldn't stop himself.

"Just that I know what de Cortez is."

Her coffee cup hit the saucer with a clatter. She stood up, her eyes wide and bright, angry. Her delicate jaw was set, her voice icy.

"I don't know what your problem is, but I've had about enough of it."

Chance knew he'd made a major mistake and tried hastily to backtrack. He scrambled to his feet.

"Look, I didn't mean—"

"I don't care what you meant. I'm not going to sit here any longer and listen to you bad-mouth someone I happen to care for a great deal."

Chance winced. Somehow, hearing her say it made it worse. His shoulders slumped. Maybe he should just let it go. There were other ways, and he didn't think he could take this anymore.

"I know you...care for him," he said, in a tone so weary that, despite her anger, she looked at him intently. When she spoke again, her voice was oddly quiet.

"What is it with you, anyway? You don't even know my brother."

Brother? He stared at her, stunned and utterly speechless.

Chapter 4

"Your...brother?"

"Yes," she said rather acidly. "You remember, the guy you've been bashing off and on ever since I met you?"

"He's...your brother?"

Her forehead creased. "What?"

Chance stared at her across the table, his jaw slack with astonishment. His dazed brain couldn't take it in. He barely managed to make himself use the right name.

"Paul de Cortez is your brother?" He enunciated each word with careful precision, as if his life depended on perfect communication.

She nodded slowly. "What did you think he was?"

He took a deep breath, and his eyes flicked away from hers. He stared down at the table.

"I thought he...that you were..."

His voice trailed off, and at last he lifted his head to look at her. She was staring at him.

"Were what?"

"They said he put you 'off-limits.' I thought..."

One arched brow rose. "You thought we were...lovers?"

He nodded, still shaken.

An odd look came into her eyes. "That's why you were down on him so hard?"

Slowly he nodded again. At the moment, with all else chased from his mind by this unexpected revelation, it was the truth, and he was too astounded to realize what he was revealing by that admission.

She sank onto the booth's seat, two spots of color staining her cheeks.

"I suppose I should be flattered."

Something in her voice, a kind of shy pleasure, caused a burst of heat inside him. He stared at her, at the becoming blush, at the innocent gray eyes. It was the innocence that brought him back to reality with a snap. And with that reality came a sinking realization. He sat down abruptly.

"Your name," he said slowly, "they said it was Austin." Was she married, he thought, to somebody else?

"It is. Paul is my half brother, really."

"Then de Cortez is . . . ?"

She sighed. "It's kind of complicated. That's our mother's maiden name. She married my father after Paul's father was . . . killed."

He knew how de Cortez's father had been killed, it had been in the files. He pushed the knowledge aside for the moment. "But he uses her name?"

"He does now." A shadow darkened her eyes. "She died a few months ago. He did it in her memory."

She believes it, he thought in bewilderment. She really believes the guy gives a damn. "I'm sorry," he managed to say.

"So am I," she said softly. "But she'd been very sad for a long time. She missed my father terribly."

Chance's head came up. "He's . . . dead, too?"

"Twelve years ago."

"That's tough," he said quietly. "You must have been just a kid."

"Is that a tactful way of asking how old I am?"

He smiled slightly. "If it was, would you answer?"

"Twenty-six."

"Your brother's a lot older, then." He couldn't quite suppress the twinge of relief using that word gave him.

"Ten years," she said, eyeing him curiously. "You seem to know an awful lot."

"I don't even know your first name."

"That makes us even." A look of surprise crossed her face. "On second thought, it doesn't. I don't even know your last name, let alone your first."

"Chance." If there was any significance to the fact that he never even thought of giving her a cover name, he didn't dwell on it. Her brother hadn't been here long enough to make him, anyway. "Chance Buckner."

"Chance as in 'not a'?"

He grinned. "Nope. As in 'last chance.' My mom had about given up on kids when I finally came along."

"And how long ago was that?" she asked sweetly.

He laughed. "Okay, it's only fair. Last birthday was the big three-oh."

"You don't look any the worse for it."

He smiled, toying with the handle of his mug of cooling coffee. "Speaking of fair, you're still one up on me."

"What?"

"Your name."

"Oh. It's Shea. Shea de Cortez Austin." She laughed. "Quite a mouthful, huh?"

"An interesting combination."

He studied her as she sipped her coffee. They'd been way out in left field on her relationship to de Cortez, he thought, trying to contain the thankfulness that flooded him. Easy, Buckner. You're not that much better off knowing that she's his sister. She still more than likely knows what he's up to. Unless . . .

"Do you live around here?"

A legitimate question, he thought, for a man interested in a woman, as she assumed he was. Right, Buckner. Like she's wrong. Keep kidding yourself.

"No," she was saying. "I live in Zephyr Cove."

He looked blank.

"It's on Lake Tahoe," she explained with a laugh that said she was used to that reaction. "Just north of South Lake Tahoe. I have a small house there. I only came here because Paul wanted me to open the club for him."

The flight from Reno, he thought. "You sing there?"

"Sometimes. In the winter, in some of the smaller places. I can handle small crowds. And I don't ski, so it keeps me from going stir-crazy."

"It's almost winter now."

She laughed. "Guess they'll have to struggle through without me."

"What do you do in the summer?"

"Goof off, mostly." She grinned. "Providing I make enough money during the winter, of course." She shrugged. "I sell some of my songs. It keeps me in firewood."

"How long have you lived there?"

He saw her look change, and realized he was sounding a little too much like a cop questioning someone. Watch it, he warned himself. But she answered easily enough.

"Full-time? Almost five years. But I've always spent a lot of time there. The house I live in was my father's. He left it to me."

"Then you must not have seen much of your brother," he said tentatively.

"No," she said regretfully. "He left home when he was sixteen, and I didn't see him often after that. I hadn't seen him at all since I moved. I'm glad he came back to California. At least we're in the same state. There's only the two of us now."

She hadn't been anywhere near Miami. God, maybe she didn't know. Maybe she really didn't know her dear brother was neck deep in slime. He never doubted the truth of what she was telling him. If she was lying, he'd hang up his badge.

"—here?"

He fought off the swamping relief to catch only the end of her question. "I . . . what?"

"I asked if you work around here."

He nodded, alarm bells ringing in his head.

"Doing what?"

He owed her this, he thought, but he hoped she would stay clear of questions he couldn't answer.

"Paperwork, mostly." That, at least, was true, he thought dryly. "For a local company. I monitor ship-

ments, keep track of some people, that kind of thing."
Nebulous but accurate.

"Have you always lived here?"

"No. I was born in Iowa, but my folks came here when I was just a baby."

"Are they still here?"

"No. They moved back a few years ago. Said this place was too crazy for them."

"Were you really the last?"

It took him a minute. "Yeah," he said with a laugh. "I guess after me they decided one was enough."

"Waiting for grandchildren now, I suppose," she teased.

He went pale, as if she'd hit him. Then he yanked his gaze downward, swallowing heavily as he stared at the cup on the table.

"Chance?"

Only the sound of her saying his name so tentatively in that silken voice got through the sudden, unexpected fog of pain. And he found himself answering, telling her the thing he never spoke of.

"They had one. Almost. He died before he was born. Along with his mother."

"Oh, God," she whispered. "I'm sorry."

He took a deep breath. "No. I am. It's been a long time, and I don't usually react like that. I guess you caught me off guard."

"Things like that are never really a long time ago." Her voice was soft with an empathy that washed over him like a warm tide.

"No. They're not." He let out the long breath slowly, back in control. "But after four years it's not usually so . . . close."

After that, the conversation was purposely light, full of such things as likes and dislikes, tastes in everything from music to books to movies, and a few childhood escapades recounted with almost sheepish pride.

When she spoke again of her brother, he had to force himself to remember who she was talking about.

"He used to seem so angry, before he left. I know he resented his father being killed when he was so young. But when he came back the first time, for my father's funeral, he was different. Like he'd grown up while he'd been gone.''

Probably made his first deal, Chance thought sourly. But now that that vivid image had been shattered, he was able to keep his mouth shut.

"He told Mom that he was the man in the family now. That he'd always take care of us, that he'd see we never needed anything. And he did.''

Could she? he wondered as he made some appropriate reply. Could she really be so calm about it, sounding almost proud of the brother who had no doubt sent them money, if she'd known where it came from?

I don't believe it, he thought, knowing even as the words formed in his mind that they stemmed more from his own unwillingness to believe it than from any firm conviction. You just don't want to believe you can be fooled so easily, he told himself sourly.

Aware she was looking at him rather curiously, he quickly asked her about the small, prestigious college she'd told him she'd attended. Had de Cortez paid for that, too? Had the man who sold death on the streets lovingly sent his little sister to school?

He couldn't think about it, not now. She was sharp. Sooner or later she was going to realize that he was asking a lot of questions and not answering many of her own. He had to take it on faith for now and analyze it later, or he was going to press her too hard and lose the contact altogether.

Later, keeping it carefully vague, he found himself telling her about Quisto and his family, guessing that it would seem as chaotic to her as it did to him. She laughed at their antics and smiled warmly when he told her of how the matriarch of the clan kept treating him like another son.

"She sounds like my mother," Shea said softly. "She was Cuban, too, and was always taking in the 'lost ones,' she called them. The ones who were far from their own family, or had none of their own.''

"That's Mama Romero, all right. Quisto says he wasn't sure until he was ten how many brothers and sisters he really had."

She laughed. "Quisto... I remember most of my Spanish, but what does that mean?"

He grinned back. "It means his first nephew couldn't pronounce his family nickname. It came out 'quisto,' and it stuck."

"Nickname?"

His grin widened. "Conquistador."

"Oh, Lord." She laughed, a light silvery sound that made him want to echo it. "I was going to ask what his name really is, but nothing could top that."

"He never uses it, anyway."

"Conquistador," she repeated, shaking her head. "Does it fit?"

"Oh, yes. And he's got the little black book to prove it."

She laughed again, and he thought he would give a great deal to hear that sound for a long time to come. The thought alarmed him a little, but he was enjoying himself too much, for the first time in longer than he could remember, to worry about it.

Before he was even aware of it, the sun was clearing the horizon and painting the street in pale morning light. When he realized it and glanced at his watch, he was startled. He stared at her, shaken by how swiftly the time had passed. She saw his look, glanced instinctively at the watch that banded her own slim wrist and looked up at him with an expression that mirrored his own.

"I'd say we've gone past late to early."

"And I've kept you up all night. I'm sorry, Shea." He'd thought it would feel odd, saying her name, but it was so soft, so lovely, like her, it felt good coming off his tongue.

"I didn't notice," she said with a touch of shyness that summoned up an answering warmth in him. "But I guess I am a little tired."

He got to his feet. "We could both use some sleep," he agreed. "I'll walk you to your car. Where did you park it?"

"I don't have one."

"What?" Then it hit him. Why would she need a car when her brother had a fleet of limousines no doubt at her disposal?

"I usually walk."

"Walk?" The huge house de Cortez had bought was miles away, in the hills looking down on the Pacific.

"Yes," she said, looking amused at his confusion. "I didn't see the point of buying or renting a car for such a short time, especially when I can walk."

He knew there were people who didn't share the typical Californian's aversion to walking anywhere farther than two blocks away, but he wasn't sure he'd ever met one before.

"Can I give you a ride? My car's down at the marina."

She seemed to hesitate, then changed her mind. "Yes. I'd like to see the marina anyway. I haven't had time yet."

As they walked the short distance, the conversation began again, with a carefree ease that was unlike anything Chance had known. He talked to Quisto the most, and occasionally to other people on the department, but never with the effortlessness she seemed to call forth.

As they walked around the marina, he caught himself wanting to point out the boat they used, and the building where Quisto lived. He wished fervently that he didn't have to be so damned careful. He'd had so much locked inside for so long, and had thought never again to find the key. But she held it, this slim, lovely woman with the incredible voice and those shimmering gray eyes, and she had opened him up with such gentle care that it was hardly painful at all.

She looked at him rather oddly when she saw the car. "Paperwork must be paying well these days," she said with a raised brow as he held the door for her.

"It has its moments," he said. He didn't dare tell her anything more. He'd already taken far too many chances.

He had started the car and was about to pull out of the parking lot when a sudden chill swept him. He had been about to drive off without a word, heading right for the big house on the hill. Great move, Buckner, just how would you have explained that? Get your head back in the game, mister, or you're going to earn every rotten thing Eaton has to say about you.

"Where to?" He thought it came out just casual enough.

"That way." He barely managed to keep himself from gaping at her as she gestured in the direction exactly opposite of what he'd expected. "I'm staying over on Pacific Street."

"Pacific?" he asked as he made the turn. "That's all businesses."

"I know. I'm living over one of them." She sighed ruefully. "The bakery, as a matter of fact. It's truly lethal in the morning. Have you ever tried to sleep through the smell of donuts and fresh bread baking?"

He smiled. "No. Not since my... wife died." He looked a little stunned that he'd said it. "She used to bake bread every Sunday."

"I'm sorry, Chance," she said, immediately contrite. "I didn't mean to bring back painful memories."

"No," he said, a note of wonder in his voice, "that was one of the good ones. One of the ones I'd... forgotten."

"I know it's hard," she said softly. "The painful ones are so much more powerful, at first. But nothing can take away the good ones, and after a while, they become so strong you can let go of the pain."

He stared at her as they pulled up at a stoplight. "I didn't think so. Until now."

He meant it, and it made him very, very nervous. She was doing something to him, something he didn't understand and wasn't at all sure he wanted. He tore his eyes away from her when a faint beep from the car behind them told him the light had changed.

Because the bakery was crowded with morning regulars for coffee and donuts, he had to park a half a block away. The tempting aroma drifted far outside the open doors, luring in the idle passerby, and he remembered her words with a grin.

"I see what you mean."

"It's horrible. Sometimes I think I could gain five pounds just breathing."

"Don't. Perfection shouldn't be tampered with."

She blushed, and Chance wondered at himself. He'd meant it as nothing more than an acknowledgment of a fact, but it had come out sounding like the kind of thing Quisto would say—a glib, toss-away compliment. Yet she had accepted it and colored as if she received such compliments rarely. That, he thought, was impossible.

"Thank you," she said, again with that touch of shyness, as she stopped at the base of the stairs that led up the side of the building. She'd have a view of the water from the front windows, but not the expansive view her brother's house had.

"You're not staying with your brother?" He tried to make it sound only mildly curious.

"No," she laughed. "Paul's life-style is a little too extravagant for my taste. And there are always too many people coming and going."

I'll bet. But he only said, "Your privacy."

"Yes," she admitted. "I like to decide who invades it."

"Where do I apply?" The words were teasing, but his eyes were serious.

"I think you already have."

She leaned forward suddenly, gave him a swift, impulsive kiss on the cheek, then whirled and ran up the stairs. Chance stood at the bottom for a long time, staring after her, trying to regain control over a heart that had suddenly begun to slam in his chest.

Cheeks flaming, Shea leaned back against the door she had hastily shut. What on earth had possessed her to do that?

As if you didn't know, she told herself chidingly. But just because he happened to be sinfully gorgeous, with that sun-bleached hair and those incredible blue eyes, just because he was tall and lean and solid and had a backside that made her fingers curl, just because he had caused a glow of feminine pleasure simply by admitting he'd been jealous when he thought Paul was her lover instead of her brother, that was no reason to throw herself at him.

She walked across the small living room to look out the window. She could see the ocean, glittering under a bright, distant winter sun. It had snowed in Tahoe yesterday, she'd heard on the news, and she closed her eyes to envision the pure white coat covering the place she loved. Yet this place was appealing, as well, with the sun, the ocean, the smell of clean salt air.

And with one Chance Buckner, who had dropped into her life from out of nowhere and made her more aware than she'd ever been of any man. Would he be there tonight? she wondered a little anxiously. He'd never said, and she'd been too embarrassed to ask.

She'd never cared before, and she didn't quite know how to deal with it. It made her feel even more self-conscious about performing. She'd sung in front of friends before, even in front of a boyfriend or two when she'd been in college, but never had she felt this tight little knot of anticipation. He'd responded to her songs in the way she'd meant them to be felt. She knew it, she'd seen it in his eyes that first night.

She'd felt as stunned as he'd looked. She hadn't thought she'd ever see him again after the encounter on the street. She hadn't been able to understand the odd sense of loss she had felt, the odd sense of longing, the feeling that something important had happened to her and she hadn't realized it until it was too late.

What was it about him? He'd managed to make her feel more fierce emotions in the short space of time that she'd known him than she'd ever thought possible. She'd been amused at their first encounter on the street, finding to her surprise that she'd enjoyed the banter between them. She'd been a little amazed the first night at the club, both at his unexpected presence and the strength of his reaction to her music.

The white rose, standing out among the scores of red ones, had both touched and intrigued her, just as his comments about Paul had angered her. She'd wanted to slap him when he'd continued to harp on her brother, but she'd wanted to giggle when she'd realized why.

She'd felt delightfully relaxed after that, talking to him in a way so totally unlike her that it amazed her. And most disturbing of all, when he'd told her of his wife and child, she'd wanted to hold him close, to soothe away the tortured look in his eyes, the lines of pain on his face.

How had it happened? she wondered. So young…it had been four years, he'd said, and he was only thirty. An accident, she supposed. She knew so well that tearing, horrible pain, although she guessed one never *really* knew the pain the loss of a child, even one unborn, caused unless they'd undergone it. She prayed that test would never be asked of her.

She went through the motions of washing her face, getting ready to go to bed, but she found herself haunted by a small glowing image. A child, a blue-eyed, sandy-haired imp with a ready laugh and his father's crooked grin.

Mechanically she switched on the fan that drowned out the noise of the street below, and slid beneath the covers. She wiped at the sudden dampness of her eyes, never once thinking it odd that she was crying for the loss suffered by a man she barely knew. In the last moments before sleep claimed her, she hazily, rather confusedly thought that it was because she'd known he existed for a long, long time before she'd finally found him.

"Nothing. Absolutely nothing." Lieutenant Morgan slapped the surveillance logs down in disgust. "If this was all we had to go on, we'd have to say de Cortez is a model citizen."

"He's building up to something big," Eaton said in dramatic tones. "I can feel it."

"Right."

Quisto's sarcasm was thinly veiled; Chance said nothing. That seemed to irritate Eaton even more, and he stopped his heavy-footed pacing in front of the spot where Chance half sat on the edge of the table in the conference room, adjusting the Velcro fastener of his ankle holster.

"Did you get anything out of the broad yet? She's got to know what he's up to, and no woman on earth can keep her mouth shut…."

He trailed off. Chance hadn't said a word, but when his gaze lifted to the man's face, it was pure ice. Eaton shivered without knowing why, and backed up a step. Chance lowered his foot to the floor with quiet care and picked up a pencil from the table. It was the movement of a man who needed something to do with his hands so that he didn't do something else.

"Well, he should have something by now." Eaton whined, pointing at Chance. "My boys say he met de Cortez's slut last night—"

A small snap echoed in the room as the pencil gave way under the pressure of Chance's grip. He was aware of Quisto looking at him curiously, but Chance's eyes were fastened on Eaton with deadly intent.

"She's his sister."

"What?" The flat, muddy eyes looked blank.

"If you bumble heads had done your damned jobs, you would have known that. But your background stops with Esteban Mendez getting killed in a deal gone bad. You tracked Paolo Mendez, but never bothered to go any further with his mother after she relocated here. You never bothered to find out that Mendez's widow remarried, and had another child."

"You're certain of this?" Lieutenant Morgan asked.

Chance nodded as he handed him a piece of paper with some notes and dates scrawled across it. He'd never doubted what Shea had told him, but he knew his boss was going to need more than his gut feeling.

"I checked it out with the county recorder this morning. They're sending copies of what they have—birth certificate, marriage license, all that. That's why I was late."

Eaton had recovered now. "That's even more proof. If she's his sister, she must know what he's up to."

"She hasn't seen him in years. And she never set foot in Miami."

"But he brought her here now—"

"She doesn't even live with him. She's staying downtown, a few blocks from the club."

"And you expect me to believe she's here working for him and knows nothing about what he is, what he's doing?"

"I don't much care what you believe."

"I should have known you'd fall for some crazy story from her. She put out for you, Buckner? Is that really why you were late?"

Chance's lean body uncoiled from the table with frightening speed. Only Quisto's swift intervention of his own wiry body halted Chance's movement, giving him a moment to regain control.

"Shut your mouth, Eaton, or I'll shut it for you." Quisto's voice was cold.

"That's enough." Lieutenant Morgan's voice cut through the tension. "Agent Eaton, you are out of line. If you wish to continue to be privy to these meetings, you will cease these personal attacks."

"You can't—"

"We'll continue this in my office."

Morgan literally herded the agent out of the room. Chance sank back down on the edge of the table, wondering why he'd let the man get to him again. Quisto wandered over to the window, looked out for a minute or two, then glanced back at Chance.

"You all right?"

Chance nodded.

"Don't let him do it to you, man. It's not worth it."

"I know."

Quisto waited again for a moment before he said tentatively, "Rough night?"

Chance's head came up sharply. "What's that supposed to mean?"

"Hey, take it easy, partner. This is me, remember?"

Chance let out a breath. "Sorry."

"I saw Hagan's Ferrari at the marina last night. And this morning."

"I couldn't sleep."

"So I guessed." Chance's eyes narrowed. "I just meant you look a little frayed around the edges."

"Thanks."

Quisto grinned. "You did see her, right? The guys in the van were pretty sure it was you."

"Not intentionally. I . . . ran into her."

"She really got to you, didn't she?"

"No."

The denial was weakened by the turmoil in his face, but Quisto let it slide.

"So tell me, why haven't we seen this lady in the music stores? Or in concert, or on TV? She's good enough."

"She doesn't want any of that. She just wants to write the songs, not do them live." His mouth quirked as he thought of the vivid, vibrant performer she was. "She says she's basically shy."

Quisto chuckled. "Shy? The way she makes every guy in the place shift into overdrive? If that's—" He broke off, staring at Chance.

"What?"

"Austin," Quisto breathed.

Chance looked at him quizzically. "So?"

"Shea de Cortez Austin?"

"Yeah. Her mother—"

"Damn."

"What?" Chance asked emphatically.

"S.D.C. Austin."

Chance rolled his eyes in frustration. "Will you please tell me—"

"S.D.C. Austin. The songwriter. Wrote 'Prisoner' for Lisa Beaulow last year. Knocked the new Rolling Stones single right out of number one. Got nominated for a Grammy."

Chance gaped at his partner.

"She's done stuff for everybody from Willie Nelson to whatever that heavy metal group is with the spiderwebs."

"I . . . she never said."

"Modest as well as shy, huh?" Quisto teased.

"Yeah," Chance muttered. Then he looked at Quisto intently. "Look, keep this quiet, will you? Eaton would just love to get hold of this. All he'd see is headlines."

"He'd be frothing at the mouth," Quisto agreed. "You've got it, partner. I doubt if he'll figure it out on his own. He doesn't seem the type to listen to music. Muzak, maybe."

"Thanks."

"No problem." Quisto looked at him consideringly. "She just up and told you all that stuff, about de Cortez being her brother?"

"Sort of."

"Sort of?"

"After she figured out what I thought he was."

Quisto's dark eyes widened in understanding. "I see." There was world of speculation in the two words.

"Oh? And I suppose you think I was late for the same reason Eaton did?" Chance said sourly.

"If I did," Quisto answered softly, "I'd be cheering."

Chance stared at him, then looked away. "She's part of the job." His voice was a little too sharp.

"I know. I also know that she's the first woman that's gotten a real reaction out of you since I've known you. You've been in zombie-land too long, partner."

"Thanks." Chance looked harassed. "Anybody ever tell you you're a nag, partner?"

"Not me." Quisto grinned. "But I've got to say, when you finally get around to it, you've got great taste. I'd be jealous if I wasn't so glad to see you acting like a normal, red-blooded male for a change. She's hot stuff."

"Damn it, Quisto—"

"I know, I know, not on a case. But when this is over, if you're right about her not being involved, who knows?"

"*If* I'm right." The whispered words were full of all his fears of being wrong, and the pain he'd feel if he'd misjudged her.

"Sometimes you've just got to go with your gut, man."

"Yeah." And mine's in knots.

"You know we're set to go back to the club tonight."

Chance nodded.

"Then you'd better get some sleep. Unless your lady is into bloodshot eyes."

"She's not my lady."

"Yet."

"Your mother's right," Chance said sourly. "You're incorrigible."

"That's me," Quisto said, unperturbed. He got up, jerking his thumb at Chance as he headed for the door.

"Go get some sleep. I'll swing by and pick you up to-night."

Chance got up to follow him, but stopped dead when Quisto went rigidly still in front of him. He turned his head to follow his partner's gaze, and went stiff himself when he saw Eaton loitering in the doorway, blatantly listening. The muddy eyes gleamed with conjecture, and they were fas-tened on Chance.

"Out of the principal's office so soon?" Chance asked, wondering how long the man had been there and how much he'd heard. He had to just hope it hadn't been long enough to hear Quisto's revelation about Shea.

"You'll step in it someday, hotshot. And I'm going to be there when you do."

They walked past the glaring agent, ignoring his gibe. They could both sense his beady gaze on them as they went down the hall, and both had to stifle the urge to hasten their steps.

Chance glanced back when they reached the end of the hall, in time to see Eaton scuttle back into the conference room and reach for the phone. Even at this distance he could read the profanity on the man's lips, and see the venom with which he punched out the number. *The man flat makes me nervous*, Chance thought, a little angry at himself for letting the fumbling agent get to him even that much. With a smothered imprecation, he turned back and followed Quisto outside.

Chapter 5

This is ridiculous, Shea told herself firmly, trying to chivy herself out of the silly mood she seemed to be in. She thought she had done it, until she found herself taking such extreme care getting ready that she was in danger of being late for the first set.

You're acting like a teenager on her first date, she told her reflection as she toned down the makeup that was much more than she ever wore offstage. You don't even know if he'll be here.

Involuntarily her eyes strayed to the small crystal vase that sat to one side of the lighted mirror. It held a perfect white rose just beginning to unfurl. She lifted one hand, reaching out to gently touch one of the satiny white petals with a slender finger.

"Shea! You're cuttin' it close!" The voice of Eric Carlow, the lead guitarist of the band, came through the door, jolting her out of her reverie.

"In five," she called back, shaking her head once more at her wandering mind.

She gave her makeup a last check, then got up and went to the rack of clothes that stood against the wall. She hadn't brought many, sticking to her favorite red and white pieces for more versatility. She'd planned on wearing a simple white dress with her red leather jacket, but when she stood before the rack she found her hand stretching past the hanger she'd meant to reach for.

The dress she held up was demure in cut, with long sleeves that came down to a point past her wrists and a high turtleneck collar. It was a shimmering, luminous sweep of bright, gleaming red, shot through with a metallic thread that caught the light and sent it flying in crimson sparks. The lines that were so simple on the hanger became incredibly sensuous when she put it on, the soft material flowing over her body, clinging to every curve.

She wasn't even sure why she'd brought it on this trip. She rarely wore it, knowing she had to be in a certain kind of mood to carry it off. Was she in that mood tonight?

What you should be trying to figure out, she told herself wryly, is whether you're in that mood because of Chance Buckner. Who might not even show up tonight. Resolutely she hung the dress back on the rack. Uncertainty was not the mood it took to wear that dress.

Quickly she slipped on the white dress, a scoop-necked tank of a soft knit, and smoothed the slim skirt down to the hem that ended a few inches above her knees. Then came the short red leather tuxedo-cut jacket. She ran back to the mirror to clip on a pair of red-and-white triangular earrings, and fastened a strand of hand-carved red-and-white beads around her neck.

She gave a last shake to the dramatic mane of hair that was so different from her normal style, slipped on the red high-heeled pumps that had been ready beside the stool at the makeup table, and stood up just as a rap came on the door.

"Shea! Let's hit it!"

"On my way."

She pulled open the door, smiling at Eric as the shaggy-haired guitarist gave an appreciative whistle.

"Lookin' good, mama."

Then he turned and headed down the hall, leaving Shea to follow with the two ever-present bodyguards. The bookends, she thought, stifling a grin. Lord, Paul had been angry when he'd realized they'd let her slip out the back door last night. She was going to have to have a talk with him about that. She was tired of being shadowed everywhere she went. And there was no significance to the fact that it hadn't really bothered her until Chance had come along. No significance at all.

It took every bit of her will not to search the room for him. And then, as she made her way down the path between the tables, she knew she wouldn't have to search. He was there. She didn't know how she knew, but she did. And when she reached the last set of tables before the steps to the stage, there he was.

When he turned those amazing blue eyes on her, she felt as if the rest of the room had slipped away. He was smiling softly, warmly, and she felt a sudden weakness in her knees. Then one of the bookends nudged her, and she snapped back to reality before going onstage.

Midway through the first song she knew it was going to be a good night. They were with her, the people in the crowded club, and it energized her even though there was only one person she was really aware of. She could feel his gaze on her as she moved around the stage, and for a moment she wished she'd worn the red dress. It made her feel sexy and attractive, just the way he made her feel when he looked at her with those blue, blue eyes—

She broke off her own thoughts determinedly, a little astonished at herself. She was not in the habit of fantasizing, especially about a man she'd just met. She was letting her imagination run much too fast, and it was time to slow it down.

But that, she discovered, was easier said than done. Even the songs she'd chosen for this set reflected her confusion, songs of tentative hope, and fear of disappointment. The words of the last song seemed to hover in the air as she took her bows to the enthusiastic crowd.

"Your head knows better
But you keep on tryin'
What your mind's tryin' to sell
Your heart ain't buyin'"

She usually went back to her dressing room between sets, but she knew the moment she saw Chance standing beside his table that she wasn't going to this time. She came to a halt before him, the other band members eyeing him curiously as they went past. When Chance spoke, his words were simple. And irresistible.

"Will you stay?"

She nodded, earning a cough of disapproval from one of the bookends. Chance started to speak, but at the look that flickered in her eyes, he lapsed into silence to let her handle it. The flash of thanks that lit the gray depths was more than payment enough.

"You just run along, boys. I won't get lost."

"But Mr. de Cortez—"

"I'll handle my brother." She smiled sweetly at them. "And I promise not to slip out without telling you and getting you in trouble."

Chance smothered a grin at the carefully worded promise. He had no doubt that she meant she would indeed slip out—but she would tell them first.

"You know the boss's rules, Ms. Austin. No fraternizing with the customers."

So nothing could slip out of an unwary mouth? Chance wondered, eyeing the matched pair with a little more interest.

"I'm going to sit down now, boys. The only way you can stop me is physically, and I don't think my brother would like a scene in front of all his guests." Her voice dropped a little, and a note of tenacious determination came into it. "And I guarantee you, if you try it, a scene is what you'll get."

Chance was cheering inwardly, trying not to let it show. She might be all soft beauty and spun silk on the surface, but the core was rapier steel. She hadn't wasted any time with arguing, but had gone directly to the one weapon they couldn't fight.

The bookends hesitated a moment after she sat down in the chair Chance had pulled out for her.

"Pete won't like this," they warned, then scurried off in tandem. To report her indiscretion, no doubt, Chance thought. So Pete Escobar was in charge tonight. *I wonder where the loving brother is, and what he's up to?*

"—glad you're here."

Her soft words jerked him out of his contemplation. Damn, he hated thinking about de Cortez when she was around. He hated thinking about what he was, that brother she loved. He hated thinking about why he himself was here, and what she would think if she knew. But most of all he hated wondering if she really didn't know about her brother's dealings, or was just an incredibly good actress.

"Sorry," he said, having missed most of her statement. "I was watching the bookends. What did you say?"

She smiled at his name for her shadows, then lowered her eyes as she said shyly, "I wasn't sure if you'd be here tonight."

"I couldn't miss my favorite songbird." He glanced around at the busy room before adding wryly, "Neither could a host of others, it seems."

"They like the club," she said lightly, disclaiming credit for the continued good business.

"They like the entertainment. Particularly the beautiful lady with the voice."

Even in the dim light he could see her blush, and he marveled at it. How could someone who did this for a living, even if it was only once in a while, be so unpretentious? She was on a stage, in the spotlight, and had to know that men were watching her eagerly, some as much for that slender, curved body as for her dynamic voice and talent.

And he wanted to kill them all, he thought in a sudden rush of protectiveness. He didn't want them ogling her, lusting after her. He glared around the room as if to pick them out for that harsh retribution.

"Maybe your brother's not so wrong," he muttered. "There's too damn many people watching, realizing you sat down here. They might think you're setting a precedent here."

In her new determination to go slowly, Shea refused to acknowledge the pleasure his unconsciously possessive tone gave her, but she couldn't seem to stop the words.

"I prefer to think of it as making an exception."

His gaze snapped back to her face. Her color was still high, but she met his look steadily. She had, he thought, the craziest way of making him melt inside. Instead of the usual things he heard from women about his hair or eyes or body, things that left him coolly unmoved, she tossed out a few words that subtly complimented all of him. She made him feel as if she saw him as a whole, not a collection of parts that by chance happened to be attractive to the opposite sex.

"Thank you."

She smiled and shifted her eyes to the vase that held the customary three red roses. Then she looked back at him.

"I never did thank you for the rose."

He grinned suddenly, and Shea felt her heart take an odd little tumble in her chest.

"Sure you did. You sent me a Band-Aid."

She couldn't help grinning back. "It seemed like the least I could do. I didn't mean to stab you."

"I was . . . out of line."

But it had worked, he thought. It had gotten her attention. Again he smothered the knowledge that it had been a device to do just that, for the sake of the case. She was silent, seeming to sense his unease, and in his haste to fill the gap he reached for the first words that came to mind.

"But I really thought he was . . . that you . . . that he . . ." He stopped, floundering.

"That he 'owned' me, I believe you said?" Her tone was mocking, but her eyes were aglow with a teasing light.

"Yeah. And I didn't much like the idea." And that, he thought, was the absolute truth.

"Paul is a little . . . protective. I think he feels guilty for all the time he was gone, that I didn't see him at all."

Paul de Cortez never felt guilty about anything in his life, Chance thought. But she believed it. He knew she did. She couldn't know. Right, Buckner, keep trying to convince yourself. I thought you gave up the rose-colored glasses years ago. Ask the questions, Buckner. He did, but he had to work at keeping the bitter undertone out of his voice.

"But you heard from him, didn't you?"

"My mother did. More, after my father died." She smiled, a soft, affectionate smile. "He took care of us."

"He did, huh?" He heard the sour note in his voice and hastened to cover it. "Did you ever wonder—"

"Well, well. Turn my back for a minute, and look what happens."

Quisto grinned at both of them as he pulled out the chair he'd deserted for a cruise of the room several minutes ago. Before he sat down, he reached for Shea's hand, bent over it and kissed it with a grand flourish.

"Ms. Austin, my pleasure."

"And you," she said, looking him up and down, "must be Quisto." Her voice was dry but her eyes were dancing.

He looked a little surprised that she knew. He sat down, his eyes flicking to Chance, who glowered at him.

"Yes, *señorita*. Quisto Romero, always at the service of a lady so lovely. *Y talentoso, tambien.*"

"Talented, too? Such praise. *Gracias*, Señor Romero."

Quisto's brow shot up, and he rattled off something in Spanish. Shea answered him as quickly, and a wide grin split Quisto's face as he sat down.

Chance watched them rather glumly. Since he'd known the young Cuban, and during trips to Quisto's family home, he'd picked up a smattering of the language, but this rapid exchange was beyond him.

"Hey, my friend," Quisto said with a devilish grin, "no wonder you can't resist her. Not only is she gorgeous, and talented, she's half Cuban, as well. Why didn't you tell me?"

Chance's mouth twisted in wry embarrassment. "It must have slipped my mind." Right, Buckner. Not one word she's said to you has slipped your mind.

"Sure." Quisto turned back to Shea. "I presume from your name that it's your father who had the misfortune of not being a *Cubano?*"

She laughed. "Yes. He left me his name, and his eyes."

"An inheritance to be proud of, songbird."

At his quiet words, Shea looked back to Chance. The implied intimacy of the nickname he'd given her seemed to please rather than embarrass her.

"Yes," she said softly. "And I am proud."

Chance had always looked on Quisto's machinations—usually successful—with the ladies with an aloof amusement. Tonight, however, as he watched his partner turn that charm on full bore, he found himself anything but amused. He was irritated, heading rapidly for angry, and only the fact that it just seemed to make Shea laugh kept him from issuing the scathing warning that was hovering on his lips.

When he realized what was happening, that he was nursing a full-blown mad against his own partner, he sank back in his chair in stunned disbelief. It had been so long since he'd felt anything for women but a weary wish that they'd stay away, since he'd considered them anything except a perhaps attractive nuisance that seemed painfully bent on upsetting his hard-won equilibrium, that he didn't recognize at first what he was feeling.

My God, he was jealous. And of Quisto and his easy charm. Shaken, he slid a sideways glance at Shea, who was laughing at something Quisto had said. He watched the sparkle in her eyes, and the dimple that appeared in her cheek as her mirth deepened. Then he looked away.

He couldn't do it. He couldn't look at her and see just a job. Not when those wide, thickly lashed eyes made his stomach knot, not when just hearing her laugh made him feel a warmth he'd never felt, not when that slim yet ripely curved figure made his body respond with a suddenness and a fierceness that left him breathless.

Bail out, Buckner, he told himself. Leave it to Quisto. He's a hell of a lot better at it than you are, anyway. It was a fine line to walk in the first place, and you've lost track of it now. You've committed the cardinal sin in police work—you've lost your impartiality. You're already so far gone that it'll rip you apart if she's dirty; if you go any further it will destroy you. You're out of it.

The decision brought him a sense of relief. He'd walk away, turn the connection with her over to Quisto, who would never in his life let a woman get to him. That, just weeks ago, the same would have been said of him, did not even occur to him. He was too busy wondering at the magnitude of the release he felt. It told him he'd made the right choice, and barely in time.

And then he made a fatal mistake. He lifted his head and looked at Shea.

"Mmph."

The muffled exclamation broke from Chance when Quisto's elbow dug not very subtly into his ribs. His eyes snapped open, and only then did he realize he had nearly dozed off.

"—continue monitoring the wiretaps," Lieutenant Morgan was saying, "but the chief has advised me if nothing breaks in the next few days, we'll be turning the bulk of the investigation back to the feds. We have other cases to handle."

Chance sat up, awake now. "But it's our city, our case."

"And we'll continue to watch him. But the chief can't justify to the city council the expenditure this is taking when we're not turning up anything."

"What happened to sticking with it, whatever it took?"

"It collided with the realities of city finance," Quisto said dryly.

"Yes," Lieutenant Morgan agreed, "but you have to admit, if this—" he gestured at the now voluminous surveillance log "—is all we have to go on after three weeks, it's going to take more time and manpower than we can handle alone." He shrugged.

"He's dirty," Quisto said positively. "He's just building a good front."

Jim Morgan looked at Quisto for a moment, then switched his gaze to Chance, raising an eyebrow in query. Chance nodded.

"He is. He's got all the moves. He's just waiting."

"For what?"

Chance shrugged. "I don't know. I just know that that's one leopard that can't change his spots."

After a moment, Morgan nodded. "I'll stall them for as long as I can. Keep on it. If nothing turns up, maybe we'll have to get a little more active."

They got up to go, but turned back when Morgan called to Chance.

"The county recorder's office sent this over for you yesterday."

Chance took the manila envelope but didn't open it until he and Quisto were back in their own cubbyhole of an office. It was small and cramped, but they preferred it to the alternative of the open, chaotic room that housed the rest of the detective division of the department.

Chance slid the contents of the envelope onto his desk and picked up the top sheet of paper. It was a copy of a birth certificate, documenting the arrival in Los Angeles County of one baby girl, Shea de Cortez Austin, on June 29th, twenty-six years ago. Small, he thought, a smile creasing his face unaware as he looked at the tiny footprint. Six pounds, four ounces. Eighteen and a half inches long. Probably all legs even then, he mused, his smile widening.

He let out a long, weary breath, rubbing at his eyes as the print on the page blurred. He leaned back in his chair, swinging his feet up to the desk. The past few days had been exhausting. From the moment he'd decided that he wasn't turning the contact with Shea over to Quisto or anyone else, which had been the instant he'd looked at her again, he'd been running nonstop.

He was at the club every night, where even the bookends had come to accept him, although it was with the disgusted look of men forced to endure a mosquito they would just as soon swat. After her last set, he took Shea out for a late dinner, ever conscious of that fine line between business and pleasure, although sometimes not sure which side of it he was on. Then they would go for a walk, and just talk for hours, until the dawn broke, sending its lovely pink light flooding down from the mountains toward the Pacific.

It was then that the line blurred the most. He found himself talking in a way he'd never done before, about anything and everything, although always conscious of having to take care in certain critical areas.

And he laughed with her. It had felt so strange, the first few times, as if he'd taken some long-stored-away tool out of a dark cupboard and found that, although rusty, it still worked. The line almost disappeared then, until something would remind him, and it would suddenly leap into sharp focus, hitting him like a lethal kick in the gut.

Then he was off to take his shift on the surveillance team, relying on cup after cup of coffee—so strong it ate at the foam cup—to keep him going. The potent liquid did nothing to ease the guilt he felt when he dropped Shea off at the bakery and she wished him a good day at work. And nothing seemed to be able to stop the warmth that spread through him when those gray eyes went soft with concern that he wasn't getting enough rest.

"You look so tired," she'd said this morning. "You can't keep staying up all night with me and working all day."

"You let me worry about that," he'd said gruffly.

They would have let him off the surveillance because he was, as they phrased it, "working" her, but Chance wasn't about to give Eaton any more ammunition. So he put in his time and then went home to grab a couple of hours of desperately needed sleep before getting up to go back to the club.

He knew he couldn't keep it up forever, but he felt driven in a way he'd never known before. He'd been as obsessed before, in the days after Sarah's—and his unborn son's—awful deaths, but he'd never gone at anything quite this way. Somewhere along the line it had become more important to him to prove Shea's innocence than her brother's guilt, and it was a new twist for him.

"Chance?"

"Mmm."

"Did you know her mother committed suicide?"

Chance's feet hit the floor abruptly. "No."

"Yeah. It's here on the death certificate."

Chance took the piece of paper Quisto held out. He stared at it for a moment, then reached for the phone.

"This is Detective Buckner. I need some cases tracked down and copies pulled. Yes, I've got the numbers." Quisto watched him stare at the certificate as he waited. "The first one's a coroner's report from January." He read off the number. "I need the autopsy report, too. And a copy of case number—" he squinted at the scrawled number and read it off, too "—as soon as you can. I know you're busy. So am I."

He covered the mouthpiece for a moment, reaching out to shuffle through the rest of the papers that had been in the envelope.

"And pull anything you can find on a Sean—" his voice wavered for a moment when he read the next name "—O'Shea Austin. It may only be a death report from about twelve years ago." He rolled his eyes at the answer issuing from the receiver. "Yes, I know that's a long time ago. If you can't find anything locally, try county-wide. And thanks."

He held the receiver away from his ear, and Quisto laughed at the pungent suggestion the records clerk had for Chance before he hung up.

"I don't think she's happy with you."

Chance shrugged. "It's a lot of work. And I don't mind. It's better than being treated with kid gloves."

Quisto knew what he meant. After the death of his family, Chance had been viewed as such a tragic figure around the department that no one would even question him, let alone snap at him. The women in the department especially seemed to take it upon themselves to treat him like a wounded child; the men who lived with the knowledge that it could just as easily have been one of them, couldn't deal with it and avoided him all together, increasing his isolation.

It had gone on for two long years, until Quisto had become his partner and had refused to treat him like a fragile shell. The rest of the department had gradually followed suit and had at least seemed to forget. For that, among other things, he was intensely grateful to his boisterous partner. Someday, he thought, maybe when they were both maudlinly drunk, he would tell him so.

Chance smothered a yawn and swung his feet back up on to the desk as he scanned the last of the papers. It was a marriage certificate, with the original application attached—nice work, he thought, appreciating the extra step taken by the county employee—issued to Elena de Cortez y Mendez, widow and housewife, and Sean O'Shea Austin, divorced and a contractor. He studied it, trying to ignore the qualm of guilt he felt about prying into her personal life without her knowledge.

Again the words seemed to blur and slip, and he rubbed at his eyes as another yawn broke through. Quisto got up suddenly, reached out and gathered up the papers from Chance's desk, stuffed them back into the envelope and stepped back.

"Come on."

Chance looked startled.

"You're dead on your—" Quisto glanced at his position in the chair "—butt. You go home and get to sleep. I'll handle the rest of today, and you can take the club gig tonight."

"I'm fine."

"Right. Red, white and blue eyes are in. Come on." He grinned. "You'd probably rather be on your own tonight anyway."

"We've got too much to do—"

"It's almost two. If you go now, you can get at least five hours and still make it to the club in time."

Quisto gripped his arm and pulled. Suddenly the thought of those precious hours of sleep were too tempting and he gave in. He fell asleep in the car, and was barely aware of stumbling up the stairs and into bed.

"What I do on my own time is my business," Shea said, looking at the slim, elegantly dressed man across the room from her.

"This is *my* place," he said, smoothing his pencil-thin mustache with one gold-ringed finger, "and *I* decide how the people who work here will act."

Shea got up from the stool and glared at him. "This was your idea, remember? You know I don't care for performing. I came as a favor to you."

Paul de Cortez looked unmoved by her anger. His dark hair, slicked back with some type of gel, glistened. His skin was beautifully olive, his face handsome, but somehow his eyes detracted from his looks, as if the barely perceptible tightness around them and the hint of coolness in them truly reflected his soul.

"That does not mean you can socialize with the customers. You are my sister, not some hired floozy."

Incongruously, Shea wanted to laugh at the outdated term. It enabled her to get a grip on her slipping temper.

"Yes. And you are my brother. But that doesn't mean you can run my life."

"Oh?"

"No. And if I want to see him, I will."

"You will not. You don't even know who this man is."

As quickly as her anger had ebbed, it flared again. "I'm beginning to think I don't know who you are." Something odd flickered in the narrow dark eyes, but she didn't stop. "I don't see hide nor hair of you for years, but now you think you can run my life?"

"I've always taken care of you. Or have you forgotten?"

His tone of voice stiffened her spine.

"No. I've never forgotten that you took care of me, and of mother. But we never asked for it, and that doesn't give you the right to tell me what to do." Chance's words came back to her. "You don't own me."

"No?"

Shea stared at her brother, wondering if she had really seen the dark, ominous shadow that seemed to slide over his face. For a split second, it was as if she were looking at a stranger, and one that somehow frightened her. Then it was gone, and she told herself she was imagining things.

You're just disappointed, she told herself, because Chance wasn't here tonight. You're unhappy, and you're taking it out on Paul.

"I'm sorry, Paul. I'm just... wound up, I guess. I love you, and I know how much I owe you."

Paul de Cortez nodded, pleased, as if something that had unexpectedly popped out of line had settled obediently back into place.

"And I'm just a brother who's worried about his little sister," he said smoothly.

"He's really nice," she began, but stopped when Paul's expression darkened again.

"We'll discuss this again later," he said, glancing at the expensive thin gold watch on his wrist. "It's almost time for the last set."

The conversation was still nagging at her when she took the stage, but her concern fled on joyous wings when, at the table he'd been the first night, she spotted Chance. The smile he gave her sent little darts of warmth shooting through her in all directions, and she smiled back without bothering to hide any of her delight at seeing him there.

When she came back out of her dressing room, it was to thread her way through a milling crowd of departing patrons. Many thanked her for the show and praised her songs and her voice, still others had suggestions for the rest of her evening that ranged from innocent to lurid. One was so obscene she stared at the man in shock; in seconds Chance was there, and his powerful, forbidding presence made the rest of the group melt away like butter from a hot knife.

"Thank you," she said a little breathlessly as he guided her back the way she'd come.

"We'll use the back door," he said briefly, painfully conscious of using the crush to his advantage, so he could check out the rest of the hallway. He already knew exactly where the door exited to, but he wanted a glimpse up the inner stairs, to see if there was anything there except the room being used as an office.

There wasn't, just the solitary door at the top of the steps. He got no chance to look further; one of the bookends was there, watching him suspiciously, as he had been all night.

"Where's the other half of the set?" he asked Shea.

"Oh, Paul needed him for something. A run to the bank, I think, although why he needs to make four deposits a day, I don't know. Hey, it's raining!" she exclaimed in surprise as they stepped outside. Chance nodded.

"It has been all evening. I think that's why I was...late."

"You were late because it was raining?"

His mouth twisted in a sheepish grin. "I fell asleep. I sleep like a log when it's raining."

A pleased smile curved her mouth. She told herself it was because she was glad he'd at last gotten some rest, not because it answered the question of where he'd been.

"I'm glad, then," she said softly.

She shook her head, raising her face to the fine mist as they came out of the narrow alley into the parking lot.

"Whew," she said, savoring the brisk, clean, rain-scented air. "They were a little rowdy tonight."

"What did that guy say to you? You looked rather alarmed."

She gave an embarrassed laugh. "He had a rather crude suggestion for my evening's activities."

Rage, hot, potent and instantaneous, boiled up inside him. "Damned son of a—"

He broke off as she lifted a slender finger to his mouth. The heat of anger became heat of another kind at the feel of her touch on his lips.

"It's all right. I'm...not used to it, but I know how people are." She shrugged. "It's why I don't perform much."

"But you do in Tahoe?"

"I do, if I need to."

"Need to?" He had to ask, he thought, or he'd give away that he already knew.

"It gives me a chance to try out new material. Songs that I've written during the winter. That way I can work on any problems before they're sold to somebody."

"But...they're you. You should sing them." He meant it. He'd thought it ever since Quisto had told him how successful other people were with her music.

A smile he'd never seen before crept across her face, and he knew that his instinctive words had pleased her immensely.

"Thank you," she said softly.

They walked to where he'd parked. He'd brought the Lamborghini this time, giving the Jeep an apologetic smile as he left. I promise, he'd said, feeling a little silly talking to a car, one of these days I'll have the time to fix that tire.

He didn't think he was consciously trying to impress her by bringing the even more expensive car, but as she stared at it when he came to a stop beside it, he wondered. When she lifted her gaze to his face, there was something in the wide gray eyes that told him if he had been trying to make an impression, the one he'd made hadn't been the one he'd wanted.

"It's not mine," he said hastily. "The . . . Ferrari broke down."

"So naturally you got this as a loaner?"

"Sort of. I . . . borrowed it."

God, he hated lying to her. To cover his discomfiture, he quickly unlocked the door for her. He paused for a split second as he walked back to the driver's side, feeling an odd prickling at the back of his neck. He looked around, yet saw nothing but people heading innocently for their own cars, some casting sideways glances at the sports car he was about to enter. After a moment he shrugged it off and got in.

The swish of tires on wet pavement seemed to soothe them both. The talk was comfortable but inconsequential during the quick meal they ate at the diner he'd first taken her to, and when they were done and walking back out to the car, she looked up at him.

"It's a little wet for a walk," she said, referring to their usual habit after eating.

"I know."

"I . . . would you . . ." She ducked her head. He looked at her and heard her take a quick breath before she looked back. "I have a fresh bottle of Amaretto if you'd like to come up."

Chance found it suddenly hard to breathe. It was the first time since that hasty, unexpected kiss that she had made any kind of overture to him. They'd touched, of necessity on occasion, and he had even once or twice dared a quick brush of his lips against her hair or her cheek, but never again had she made a move toward him.

He wondered, as he stood in the small apartment over the bakery, if he'd made another big mistake. The place was just too warm, too welcoming. He'd expected an impersonal furnished place, knowing it was only temporary for her. And it was, he supposed, beneath the wealth of personal touches she'd added. A handmade afghan over the sofa, a collection of luxuriant plants, and bright, framed prints on the walls. The centerpiece was a stunning, expansive photograph of Lake Tahoe in winter, the pristine white of fresh snow meeting incredibly clear water sparkling under a winter sun.

"It's beautiful," he said, nodding at the picture when she handed him small glass of the sweet but potent almond-flavored liqueur. She'd introduced him to it over one of their late dinners, and he'd found he liked the taste. They sat on the sofa, looking across at the dramatic picture.

"Yes," she said. "It's my homesick pill."

The thought that she was longing for her home made him feel oddly disturbed.

"If you go up to the end of my road, the view is almost the same as that." She sighed. "It's so beautiful like that, after a fresh snow. But it's beautiful in spring, and summer, and fall, too."

Chance shook his head. "All the time I've lived here, and I've never made it up there."

"You should." Her voice was eager. "It's so wonderful. Maybe someday—"

She stopped, and the sudden color in her cheeks told him what she'd been about to say.

"I'd like that," he said softly, as if she'd finished the invitation. "Would you . . . show me around?"

"Yes." The single syllable sounded a little breathless, and she turned her head to stare at the photo again.

Several long, silent moments passed, the easy conversation they enjoyed outside lost somehow in the intimacy of this small, cozy room. At last, having drained the last of the warming liqueur, he leaned forward to set the glass on the long, narrow table in front of the couch. At the same moment, Shea shifted to move her legs, which had been curled beneath her on the sofa. They came up short, bare inches away from each other.

Eyes locked, their arms moved in slow, concerted motion, mirror images as the empty glasses were set down. Shea swallowed, her lips parting as she tried to draw in a breath. She didn't realize that she had moved, that she had tilted her head back as she looked at him. He didn't touch her, but she felt as if he had, as if he were pulling her toward him. It was an odd, magnetic tug, unlike anything she'd ever felt.

She knew in the instant before he moved that he was going to kiss her. She knew it, and her heart leaped in shivery anticipation. She expected a more intense form of the warmth that flared in her whenever he casually touched her, or when he flashed that crooked grin, or when she looked at the thick sweep of his lowered lashes below the sandy brows and the tousled, blond-streaked hair.

What she got was a sudden, fiery eruption, a burst of heat and sensation that raced along tingling nerves the way wildfire raced down a mountain. She melted before its raging force, going slack beneath the feel of his mouth on hers. She heard him make a sound, a low, husky growl from deep in his throat, then his hands came up to cup her face.

His tongue darted out to flick over her lips. She heard a tiny whimper of pleasure, not even realizing at first that it had come from her. As her lips parted for its escape, his tongue probed past them, seeking the sweet warmth of her mouth.

She felt the thick tangled silk of his hair and knew that somehow she had lifted her arms to encircle his neck. She threaded slender fingers through the heavy strands, loving the feel of it as it slipped over her skin.

He was engulfing her with his heat, pressing her back on the couch, only the taut muscles in his arms holding some of his weight off her. His mouth was devouring her, and she was reveling in it. She opened for him, urging his tongue deeper as her hands slid from the back of his head to his shoulders, pulling him even closer.

The solid wall of his chest was too tempting to resist, and she arched involuntarily, pressing her breasts against the muscled expanse. A hoarse groan broke from him, and he lowered his body to hers as his kiss became fiercer, deeper.

Shea's fingers dug into his shoulders, and she fairly rippled beneath him. She felt an odd undulation take her, ending in an upward thrust of her hips against his. She heard him gasp, felt the rigid column of aroused male flesh against her stomach, and a tiny moan rose from her throat. She felt his arms tighten around her.

His hand slid downward, stroking, caressing, sending little darts of fire through her. He paused for a moment, and she could feel the muscles of his arm tense, as if he were fighting his desire to move further. Then, on a sharply released breath, he did move, his hand gently cupping and lifting her breast as his thumb brushed over the tingling peak.

"Oh!"

She couldn't help her startled gasp at the heat that crackled through her at the touch. She felt the response of the tender flesh, felt it tauten and rise as if asking for more, then felt it even more when he touched her again, as if she could feel the tightness, the change just as he did.

Suddenly, with a choking sound that echoed with pain, he was gone. Shea whimpered at the sudden loss of the sweet warmth, at the instant protest of her body to the removal of his. Slowly her heavy lids lifted.

He sat looking down at her, something shadowy and incomprehensible to her in his eyes. A shudder rippled through him even as she looked. He shook his head, slow and dazedly, like an animal too much in shock to know how hurt it was. And then, without a word, he was on his feet and gone, leaving her staring at her closing door in cold, unrelenting silence.

Chapter 6

Quisto took one look at the bleary-eyed pale face of his partner and quickly stepped back, holding the door open to let him in. Without a word, Chance walked past him, waiting until he heard the door close before turning around. Only then did he seem to see Quisto's tousled hair, unshaven jaw, and the crease in his perfect olive skin that indicated he'd been facedown in a pillow.

"I..." Chance stopped, shoving his hands into his pockets and staring down at the floor. "I'm sorry. I guess I didn't think about how late it is."

"You don't look up to thinking, period, my friend."

Chance appeared to be a man who had suddenly decided he'd made a wrong move. He started toward the door. "Sorry," he muttered again. "Go back to bed."

With that spry quickness of his, Quisto blocked his partner's way. "What's wrong?"

"Nothing. I—" his eyes flicked to the door of the bedroom "—didn't mean to...interrupt you."

Quisto assumed an air of exaggerated woe. "Alas, not tonight, *amigo*. Even I must, on occasion, strike out." Then the kidding mien was dropped, and he looked at Chance steadily. "Sit down. I'll get you a drink."

"No, I—"

"Sit down. Or shall I sit you down?"

Chance looked at him for a moment before a wry smile tugged at one corner of his mouth. Quisto might be a couple of inches shorter and a few pounds lighter, but Chance knew his quick, wiry strength too well to take the threat, even made in jest, lightly.

"Yes," the young Cuban said, as if he'd read his thoughts, "it would be an interesting fight, wouldn't it? Are you going to make it necessary?"

Chance's weary body made the decision his mind was too confused to make: he sat. A minute later Quisto was pressing a glass into his hand. He took it, tossed the contents back in a quick but awkward movement, gasping a little at the jolting impact of the potent liquid.

"Easy, *amigo.* You and Jack Daniel's are only passing acquaintances, remember. That's Tennessee sour mash, not water."

Chance blinked to clear his eyes, the whiskey's effect fading a little, but his voice was still a little unsteady. "You out of tequila or something?"

"Almost. Only enough left to keep the worm wet. Didn't think you'd want that."

Chance's stomach churned at the thought. "No. Thanks."

Quisto leaned back in the lushly upholstered chair that was opposite the twin that Chance sat in. He studied his partner for a moment before he said softly, "What is it?"

Chance made a low, negative sound.

"Come on, buddy, something hit you like a ton of bricks tonight."

"No."

"Right. That's why you're at my door at four in the morning, looking like you've been hit by a truck, and downing two ounces of straight whiskey like it was milk. You, the invincible, unflappable Chance Buckner."

Chance laughed shortly, bitterly. "Is that what you think?"

"Isn't that what you want everybody to think? Isn't that the image you work so damned hard at? Hard as nails, self-sufficient, doesn't need anybody?"

Chance stared.

"You think I don't understand?" Quisto asked gently. "What better way to keep the world at arm's length? Especially when you've got such a good excuse. Who's going to argue with you? Pretty selfish, *amigo.*"

"Selfish?" The word seemed to surprise him even more than Quisto's unexpected perceptiveness.

"Sure. Don't let anybody get close so you don't get hurt. Pretty one-sided, pal."

Chance gave him a sour look. "Taking up armchair psychology?"

"Did I make you mad? Good. At least you don't look like death warmed over anymore."

Chance looked startled, then rueful as he sat back in the chair. "I've been had," he grumbled.

"Nothing but the truth, man. If the shoe pinches, it's not my fault." He grinned at the pained look Chance gave him for the mangled axiom. Then, before Chance had time to throw his protective walls back up, Quisto asked quietly, "It's Shea, isn't it?"

Chance wanted to deny it, meant to, but the protest seemed to drain out of him. He studied the empty glass for a long moment. He'd never opened himself up to anyone before, not like he wanted to with Shea. But he couldn't, didn't dare, and everything he'd been holding in for so long was beginning to fester. Just when Quisto thought Chance wasn't going to speak at all, his voice came, low and hoarse and tight.

"I'm out of control, Quisto. I . . . can't deal with it anymore." His head came up; the look in his eyes matched the ragged sound of his voice. "You were right. She got to me." He laughed harshly. "I didn't think there was anything left in me to get to, but she found it." His fingers tightened around the glass. "And I have to sit there and lie to her, every day, and it makes me sick!"

Quisto leaned forward, intent. "Listen, Chance. If she knows, if she's involved with her brother's dealings, then it won't matter. It'll hurt, but at least you'll know it never would have worked. And if you're right about her, if she's innocent, maybe she'll understand.''

"Understand? What, that I used her to put her own brother away?''

"That you had to do it.''

"But he's her brother, Quisto. And he's made damned sure she thinks he's lily-white. She'll never believe it. And she'll hate me for it.''

"That's what's really bothering you, isn't it?''

Chance let out a shuddering sigh. "Great, huh? Eight years as a cop, and I do the stupidest thing possible. I get myself tied up in knots over a prime suspect in a major investigation.''

"You do pick your moments,'' Quisto agreed dryly. "I've watched women throw themselves at you for two years now, and get nothing but bruised egos. This one rips your thumb open and you turn to mush.''

Instinctively Chance looked at the now grubby bandage that still wrapped his thumb. He'd thought of taking it off, knowing it was probably healed enough, but he'd been reluctant to for reasons he hadn't wanted to delve into. Pretty dumb, Buckner, hanging on to a stupid adhesive bandage. His mouth twisted in rueful self-deprecation.

"Okay, partner,'' Quisto said softly. "I'll take the club for a while. Give you a chance to... regroup. Maybe something will break soon, and it'll be all over.''

He felt like a coward, but Chance nodded in relief. "Thanks.''

"Sure.'' Quisto got to his feet, took Chance's glass and went to refill it. "Sure you don't want the worm?'' he called out over his shoulder.

Chance grimaced, Quisto laughed, and Chance felt a little less like a cringing, frightened fool.

"Whew! Hot stuff, baby!''

Shea smiled at Eric's appreciative whistle; she needed every bit of moral support she could muster right now. She felt her smile wobble.

"You all right, Shea?''

Eric's eyes were warm with sympathy as he looked at her, and she had to look away.

"I'm fine. Let's go."

"We've got a couple of minutes yet." The shaggy-haired guitarist leaned forward and touched the dying white rose. "You have a fight with him?"

"I don't know."

Equally shaggy eyebrows quirked. "You don't know?"

She sighed. "I didn't think we did."

"But he hasn't been around for three or four days."

"Five," she said glumly.

"Why don't you just call him?"

She made a face. "I did. But he's got an answering machine on at home, and he never called back."

"So maybe the machine's broken. Try him at work."

"All I have is a pager number."

Eric frowned. "A beeper?"

She nodded. "He said he's always out of the office and that was the only way to reach him."

Unaware she was frowning herself, she remembered the day he'd given her the numbers. He'd been open and straightforward about his home number but oddly restrained about the other. She'd only pressed because it was beginning to bother her, this vagueness about his job. She'd even tried the number once, hoping they would answer with a company name, but had been met with a computerized voice that told her to punch in the number she wanted him to call. She'd hung up without doing it.

"Don't you think that's a little…odd?" Eric's voice was carefully tentative.

"Only when he's not around," she admitted ruefully.

Eric grinned suddenly. "Don't tell me the ice maiden's melting!"

"Give me a break, Carlow," she said with mock sarcasm. "Any woman who doesn't tumble for your charms immediately is an ice maiden to you!"

"Can I help it if I'm irresistible?" He gave her a look of mock anguish. "Except to you, the one woman who is immune to my charisma!"

For the first time in five days, Shea laughed. Eric had tried, during the first few days she'd been here, to get her to succumb to his not inconsiderable appeal. She had at last taken him aside, told him that yes, he was talented, gorgeous and otherwise tempting, but she was not in the market. He had been not at all wounded, and had soon become a good friend. A good enough friend to resist pointing out that for someone not in the market, she had fallen hard and fast for Chance Buckner.

Impulsively she gave him a swift kiss on the cheek. Eric looked at her in surprise.

"Let's go, Mr. Charisma. We're on."

He laughed and followed her, never guessing how much it was costing her to put on that cheerful face when inside she was dreading going out there to face another crowd that did not contain the tall, blue-eyed man with thick blond-streaked hair. If she found anybody when she scanned the crowd, it would be Quisto, and she didn't want to confront him again. She had, that first night, wanting to know if he knew what had happened to Chance. But the young Cuban had only said that he was busy, he didn't know where.

She'd tried to hide her hurt, but knew it had flared in her eyes before she could control it.

"You make it hard for me, *querida*. I don't want anyone to get hurt, but Chance is my friend."

She had left the table hastily, afraid she looked as wounded as she felt, and wondered why there had seemed to be a hint of warning in those last words. The days had gone on with no sign of Chance, and she avoided Quisto whenever she saw him, although she wondered why he kept coming around when Chance was so thoroughly and obviously avoiding her. But when she saw the sideways glances he garnered from the female club-goers, she guessed she had an answer to that.

She had tried to bury the turbulent feelings, but the conversation with Eric had brought them all bubbling back to the surface. Her emotions added a poignant note to her voice as she sang that night. She wavered between remembering those hot, luscious moments of pleasure and remembering the chill that had swept her when she had looked up into a pair of blue eyes that had looked nothing less than tortured.

At first she'd thought herself a fool, that she'd let too much of what she'd grown to feel for him show and had driven him away. But then she remembered that he'd begun that passionate kiss, remembered that he'd been just as caught up in it as she had. She had the memory of urgently aroused flesh pressing against her to prove it.

Heat suffused her at that particularly intimate memory, and her voice caught in her throat. Fortunately, it was in the chorus of a quiet, lonely ballad, and it only made the song sound more heartfelt. She was grateful when Eric stepped up to sing lead on the next number, allowing her to retreat out of the spotlight and try to gather herself.

She didn't understand herself, didn't understand her reaction. She'd fended off enough amorous men, especially when she was singing, which somehow seemed to make her public property in their eyes. None of them had made her feel this way. None of them had ripped her composure to shreds, had driven all thought of resistance from her mind with the first touch of their lips on hers.

She paced the darkened area at the rear of the stage, aware that Richie, the group's drummer, was looking at her a little oddly. She reached for the pitcher of water kept on a table there, as if that's what she was after.

Why? She'd asked herself the question countless times over the past five days, since he had dropped out of her life as abruptly as he had appeared. Why had he looked at her like that, as if he were fighting some horrible, painful battle and losing?

Or perhaps he'd won.

She set down the glass she'd filled, feeling suddenly as cold as the ice water it held. Perhaps the battle she'd seen in his face was against his own urges, and rejecting her had been his victory.

She wrapped her arms around herself, shivering as a row of mental dominoes toppled one after the other. All the vagueness, the odd, obscure answers he gave her, his expression when she caught him looking at her unguardedly, the fact that although he'd told her about his past, he'd never really told her anything tangible about his present, not even where he lived....

All the pieces toppled, leaving standing only one explanation that she could see, glaring in the bleakness of her mind. He was shutting her out, and had been all along. He wanted her, at least he had that night, but not enough. He wanted her, but he didn't want to want her. Or he wanted her physically, but nothing more, none of the emotional involvement she now was certain she'd made obvious she already felt.

"Shea!"

The hiss of her name from the drummer whirled her around. She recognized the music and realized she was going to blow the next song if she didn't snap out of it. She barely made it up front by the end of the intro, and plunged into the song with Eric's eyes on her in sympathetic understanding. It only abraded an already raw wound, and she turned away.

She supposed in some part of her mind functioning separately from the part that directed her body to move and her mouth to form the words of the song, that she should be grateful. He could have just gone ahead and then disappeared. She wouldn't have stopped him.

She suppressed a shudder. She, who had always been so careful, selective enough to be called picky by her friends, would have tumbled into bed with a man she barely knew, had only met weeks ago. Yet when he touched her, it didn't seem to matter, just as it didn't matter that she knew so little about him. All she knew was that no one had ever made her feel like he did.

She forced herself to concentrate on the music, shutting all thoughts of him out of her mind. She was just congratulating herself on how well she'd done when a tall figure, made shadowy by the glare of the footlights, moved in a way that made her heart leap.

Stop it! she ordered herself, whirling away to devote the rest of the song to the other side of the room. Only two more numbers, she thought wearily, and the set—and the long, long night—would be over. Tomorrow was the one night she got off per week, and she was looking gratefully forward to it. She needed time to hole up and lick her wounds, she thought, like the deer she had sheltered last spring. She should be thankful it wasn't worse, she told herself sternly. Somehow it didn't help.

She accepted the applause of the audience with a silent apology. They had not had her best and she knew it. Although performing live was not her favorite thing to do, she tried to give it an honest effort. She had failed miserably tonight. Her mood was dark and obvious. Even the bookends kept their distance, sensing that when she told them to leave her alone, they'd better listen or find out if she had her brother's fiery temper.

They'd tell Paul, but she couldn't seem to care. When at last she walked outside into the rain that had lingered halfheartedly all week, her slender shoulders were slumped wearily and her steps a little shaky. As soon as she cleared the canopy that sheltered the front door of the club, the rain began in earnest. Figures, she thought sourly. She'd be soaked by the time she got home.

She turned up the collar of her jacket and huddled into it as she headed down the wet sidewalk. When a dark, broad figure loomed suddenly out of the shadows, she jumped back with a startled little cry. Strong arms shot out to catch her, steady her, and she knew instantly.

"Chance." It took the last of her breath, and she could only stare at him. Then memory flooded back, and she tried to pull away.

"I know," he said softly, "but please, don't. Let me take you home."

"No, thank you." Her voice was flat, impeccably polite. Chance winced.

"Shea—"

"I didn't care for what happened last time, thank you."

"I want to talk about that, but if we just stand here you'll freeze."

"I never get frozen twice in one week," she said, her flippancy not hiding the pain behind it. The reference to the night he'd left her made him want to cringe, but he held his ground, knowing he deserved it, from her viewpoint.

"At least come sit in the car for a minute. I'll turn on the heater and you can get warm."

"Before the freeze?"

"Shea, listen. I know you're upset, and you have every right to be, but will you at least listen to me?"

"Give Chance a chance?" Her voice broke, robbing the quip of any humor.

"Please?"

She found herself, much to her dismay, unable to resist the quiet plea. She chastised herself as she let him lead her through the parking lot. When he stopped before an elegant Jaguar sedan, she barely smothered a groan.

"Another loaner?"

There was a touch of bitterness in her tone that made him look at her intently. "Sort of."

"Sort of. What is that, the standard Buckner answer to any question he doesn't want to answer?"

"Just get in," he said, a little gruffly. "I brought it because it's got more room and a better heater."

"How thoughtful."

"Shea, please." He held the passenger door for her. "Just listen to me for a minute. Then, if it's what you want, I'll leave."

Rather woodenly she got in. He hurried around the car, as if afraid she were going to jump out. Not a bad idea, she thought. When the driver's door opened and he didn't get in, she glanced that way. He seemed to be staring into the darkness behind them, although at what she couldn't guess. After a moment he rubbed the back of his neck in an odd little movement and got into the car.

He turned to look at her, lifting a hand to slick back his wet hair. She knew her own was nearly as wet, could feel it clinging to her neck. She ignored it.

Now that he'd gotten her here, he seemed to have forgotten why. He just stared at her, something akin to pain or resignation in his eyes, not quite either one but a combination of both.

"I tried to stay away," he whispered finally.

To have it confirmed that he had truly done it intentionally lacerated her already raw nerves. "Perhaps you should have," she said coolly.

He drew back. "Do you...mean that?"

"I think I do."

Pain flashed in his eyes, and she stared at him in amazement. It had been he who had bolted from her, who had avoided her for days, wasn't this what he wanted?

"Because of...the other night?"

His voice was taut, hoarse, and she felt an incongruous, unwelcome need to ease his distress. She smothered it adamantly.

"Partly."

"I know it was rotten, but I..."

"You what? Came to your senses? Regained your better judgment? I'd rather not hear it, if you don't mind. I've been a big enough fool already."

He stared at her. "You've been a fool?"

She smiled, a wintry smile that didn't reach her gray eyes. "I've made some big mistakes in my life, but falling for you would seem to be the topper."

He gaped at her then. "I...Falling for me?"

She looked away in irritation, staring at the rich wood of the dash. "Were you under the impression that I react that way with any man who happens to kiss me?"

"No, but—"

"Look," she said, her voice suddenly fierce. "I may not have much experience in these things, but I do have a little pride, and I'd like to salvage what's left. I think I'd better go."

"Shea, wait. Listen, I—"

"Listen? To what? You never tell me anything that isn't ancient history. Anytime I ask about what you do, you just avoid answering, or give me some glib remark...."

She stopped, running her fingers over the smooth wood of the dash as if she found comfort in its polished surface. She felt something give beneath her fingers, and gave a startled jump as a glove compartment she hadn't even known was there fell open in front of her. She stared for a long moment before a muffled, protesting moan broke from her.

"Oh, God."

"Shea—"

"I knew it. Deep down I knew it." Her eyes, glistening with tears of disillusionment, were fastened on his face. "This just proves it."

"Shea," he began again, reaching for her.

"No!"

She scrambled out of the car, leaving the door open as she dashed through the parking lot.

"Shea!"

With startling speed he grabbed the gun she'd found and started after her, stuffing it into his waistband at the small of his back. He left the door of the Jaguar open, not caring, as he tried to catch up to her.

"Shea, wait, damn it!"

He saw her through the heavy rain, a few yards ahead. She was running in high heels, and the sidewalk was so slick he expected to see her go down any second. The thought lent speed to his feet, and he caught up with her just as she reached the corner.

"Stop it, you crazy little fool!" he shouted, his heart slamming with terror when he realized she had nearly stepped out in front of the dark sedan that had come up behind them from the direction of the club. "Are you trying to get yourself killed?"

"Leave me alone," she cried, hammering his chest with small, clenched fists.

"Shea, stop—"

"Go away!" A choking, wrenching sob broke from her. "Go and have a good laugh at the stupid, naive woman who was too blind to see what was in front of her nose!"

"Damn it, will you calm down—"

"I hate you! I hate you and what you do! You don't care who you hurt, who you destroy, as long as you have your fancy cars and your women. Well, I'm not one of them! I won't ever be, so just leave me alone!"

Chance grabbed her shoulders, exerting more force than he'd expected to have to. She was stronger than she looked.

She was also on the verge of hysteria, and he put every ounce of stern calm he could manage into his voice.

"Exactly what is it," he said slowly, "that you think I do?"

"I may be slow," she choked out, "but I'm not a complete idiot. The fancy cars, the beeper, all the vague answers about your work...and a gun to...to protect your 'interests,' I suppose? No wonder you knew what that guy was on at the café! Did you sell it to him? Or did someone you sold it to sell it to him? Or maybe you sell it to innocent little kids, huh? Where exactly do you stand on that trail of misery?"

The pain and disappointment in her eyes was almost tangible. Chance stared at her, stunned.

"You think...I'm a dealer?"

"Just let me go, please."

"Answer me! Is that what you think?"

"Yes! And it disgusts me!" She twisted from his grasp, her voice coming out as a tortured moan. "God, I wish I didn't love you. I'd go to the nearest phone and turn you in so fast—"

She broke off with a gasp of pain as his fingers dug into her shoulders. He stared at her, his eyes so intent they seemed to burn into her.

"You wish what?"

She shook her head.

"Say it, damn it! Say it again!"

"All right! I love you! Is that what you wanted? Are you satisfied? Will you let me go now?"

"Oh, God, Shea." He pulled her into his arms. She fought him, pushing at his chest. "Shh," he soothed. "Stop it, songbird, it's all right."

"No," she moaned, shaking her head.

"Yes."

He pressed her head to his chest, smoothing back her wet hair with a gentle hand. He knew as surely as he'd ever known anything that she was as innocent as he'd wanted to paint her. And if he was wrong, it wouldn't matter, because he would walk out onto some lonely beach somewhere and follow Marty into hell.

"I'm going to tell you something, Shea, and I want you to listen. I want you to listen and believe, because it's the truth. It's not all of the truth, but it's as much as I can tell you."

She choked back a sob as his hands went once more to her shoulders. He held her away from him and looked steadily into her eyes.

"I don't," he said firmly, quietly, "sell drugs. Not to children, not to anyone. I never have, and I don't help anyone who does."

She stared up at him, her cheeks wet with tears and rain.

"I know how it must look to you. And I wish I could explain it all. But I can't. Not now. I can only ask you to trust me."

"But if you're not—"

He put a finger to her lips and shook his head. "I can't. If you can't accept that, I understand. I'll take you home, and get out of your life. Just say so."

Her mind was whirling, and for a moment it seemed the world was, too, much too quickly. She swayed on her feet, and before she could steady herself he had swept her up into his arms. He carried her back to the waiting car, only dimly aware that another dark sedan was making its way slowly along the wet street. Or maybe the same one, afraid that he might have hit her after all. Or just wanting another look at the wet, bedraggled but still gorgeous woman.

He set her in the car with exquisite care, then knelt beside her to fasten the seat belt. She looked at the luxurious interior rather numbly, then murmured, "All these cars..."

"They aren't mine. They belong to a CEO with a fetish for distinctive transportation. He lets me drive them." He smiled at her. "My car happens to be a very undistinctive Jeep, and happens to be very un-leakproof."

"He sounds generous."

"He is. But I do a favor for him now and then in return."

Speculation glowed in the gray eyes, supplanting some of the strain. "Like security?"

"Occasionally," he said with complete honesty. Good, he thought. If she thinks I work for some private company, all the better.

"What is he CEO of?"

"About three different electronics and computer development companies. Generally known as PLH, Incorporated."

More of the strain faded, and he knew it was because he had, for once, given her a straight, unequivocal answer. It was worth the risk, he thought, to have her look at him without doubt in her eyes.

"He also," he said tentatively, "rents me the apartment over his garage."

"That," she said, a little of the sparkle returning to her eyes, "must be the size of most houses."

He smiled, but it was a little shaky because of the enormity of the relief that had flooded him. "Would you like to...see it?"

Her eyes widened. Never had he even suggested that she come to his place. He wasn't shutting her out anymore. "Yes," she said, a little startled at her lack of hesitation. "Yes, I'd like to."

His smile widened and steadied. He got to his feet and walked around to climb into the driver's side. He reached for the key but then stopped. He turned sideways to look at her.

"You believe me?"

Slowly she nodded. "If I didn't, I wouldn't be here."

"I know I'm asking you to take an awful lot on faith."

"I find I have more faith than I realized."

Chance felt a sudden pressure in his chest and a stinging behind his eyelids. He hadn't shed a single tear since he'd seen Sarah's heavy casket lowered into the ground, but he was perilously close now, and from a few simple words.

"Thank you," he said hoarsely, and started the car.

Her eyes widened as they pulled through the tall, elaborate iron gates. She stared in wonder at the main house and commented wryly on the size of the garage, but she was utterly charmed by the pool. He had left the waterfall on, and in the rain it looked for all the world like some tiny jewel of a mountain lake caught in an early winter storm.

"Remind you of home?" he asked softly.

"Yes," she admitted, her eyes shining with pleasure.

She nearly jumped at the loud squeak emitted, even in the rain, by the two noisy steps.

"Sort of a makeshift burglar alarm," he said. If she noticed a slight undertone in his voice, she didn't comment.

"This is really nice," she exclaimed when he flipped on the lights. "And it *is* huge!"

"*Your* place is nice, " he said as he hung up their dripping jackets, "this is . . . a place to sleep. Want some coffee?" He looked back over his shoulder from the kitchen alcove. "Or some hot chocolate?"

"Chocolate sounds wonderful." She kicked her high heels off her chilled feet and promised her toes they'd be warm again sometime.

"Hot chocolate it is."

"This is beautiful." She looked around at the carpeting of pale blue, and the furnishings and drapes of a matching blue patterned with gray and a soft mauve shade. "It must have been decorated professionally."

"That's what I mean. There's not a touch of personality in the place."

"Not even yours?"

He shrugged. "I'm just renting it. I didn't mess with anything."

Sitting on the pillowed couch, they sipped at the chocolate, Shea silent as she tried to formulate the difficult words in her mind. At last she just settled on the simplest.

"I'm sorry I thought what I did."

Chance gave her a soft, understanding smile. "I can't blame you, under the circumstances."

"I should have trusted you."

"How could you, when I didn't trust you enough to at least tell you what I could? Which isn't," he added wryly, "much."

"It's all right. As long as you're not..." She lowered her eyes. "I hated the thought that you were one of them."

"I don't care for them much myself."

"Chance?"

"Mmm?" It was all he could manage as he swallowed the last of the chocolate.

"Why did you stay away?"

He'd been dreading that question, knowing it would take truths he'd barely admitted to himself to answer it. But with everything else he had to hold back from her, she deserved to know.

"I said there were things I can't tell you yet, and some of them are why I didn't want to...get involved. But mostly it was..."

"Was what?"

"I was scared," he said simply.

The gray eyes rounded in surprise. Her lashes were still damp, clinging together in thick little spikes, and she looked wide-eyed and innocent. She *was* innocent, he thought exultantly, and it was all he could do not to reach for her right now. He wanted to taste her sweet mouth again, feel those slender curves beneath him—

"Scared? Of what?"

"You." He shifted on the couch, trying to ease the discomfort of his sudden arousal.

"Me?" She gaped at him.

"You...made me feel things I didn't ever want to feel again, because it hurts too damned much when you lose them. And then you made me feel things I'd never felt at all, and that scared me even more. And on top of everything else, I felt guilty."

"Guilty?"

"Because I was feeling anything at all. Because I was here to feel it. Because of..."

"Because of your wife?"

He nodded, his eyes fixed on a swirl of color on the sofa. "I know she wouldn't want it that way, but I still felt like I was...betraying her somehow."

"By being with me?"

"At first. And then it was...I never felt like this with her. It was good, but it was never...I mean, it was just a kiss, but it was...cataclysmic."

"Oh, Chance." He lifted his head at the soft note that had come into her voice. "I never really loved anyone before, so I don't have anything to compare it to. I just know no one has ever made me feel the way you do."

He let out a long sigh, grateful that she so easily accepted, didn't try to deny what he had once felt for Sarah. It was followed rapidly by an expanding pleasure at what she had implied—not only that she loved him, but that what she was feeling was as new to her as what he felt was to him.

"I loved Sarah," he said softly, "but by comparison, I must be absolutely nuts about you."

Suddenly, without either of them being certain who had moved, she was in his arms. She was hugging him fiercely, burying her face in the soft thickness of his sweater. He just held her for a long time, smoothing the strands of her hair as it dried into a dark, silken cloud.

She shifted her weight, one thigh pressing against the part of him that he couldn't stop from responding to her closeness. He smothered a groan, but it escaped when he felt her hand slip up under his sweater to caress his bare skin. He lowered his head to press his lips to her forehead, then forgot what he'd meant to do when her searching fingers flicked over the sensitive flesh of his nipple. He sucked in a low, harsh breath.

"Shea?"

"What?" Her hand continued its explorations, finding his other nipple and sending another jolt through him.

"Did you mean...what I think you meant by coming here?"

"If I didn't then, I do now."

He groaned, low and deep in his throat. "You're sure?"

Her hand slid down his chest to his belly, to linger at the snap at his waistband. "If you are."

He covered her hand with his, and slid it down to the aching thrust that strained at the denim of his jeans. He pressed her palm against himself, unable to restrain a convulsive little jerk of his hips.

"Do you think I'm sure?"

"I think," she said silkily as her fingers traced the full length of the hardened column of flesh and he gasped with pleasure, "that you missed me almost as much as I missed you."

Chapter 7

Chance didn't care anymore about the risk he was running. He didn't care about anything except the feel of Shea in his arms, and the fact that she was driving him crazy with her hands and her mouth, and had been since he'd set her down on his bed.

He fumbled with the annoying number of buttons on the red silk blouse she wore, his fingers made clumsy by the fact that she had already tugged off his sweater and was running her hands over him. When she leaned forward and pressed her lips to the center of his chest, he very nearly gave up on the buttons and ripped away the soft fabric.

At last, as her slender fingers tangled in the sparse scattering of hair over his breastbone, he freed the last button and the blouse floated down into a scarlet puddle. The matching skirt, still damp at the hem, soon followed, leaving her in the one-piece bra slip she wore beneath it. He reached for the fastener, but had to stop when she leaned forward again and brushed her tongue over the flat disk of his nipple.

"Lord, Shea!"

Shea looked up at him, her eyes wide with wonder at the way he trembled at that slightest flick of her tongue. He was so solid, so strong, yet she could do this. Such a heavy, drugging pleasure filled her at the thought that she could feel her muscles go slack. She swayed against him, trying to brace herself with her palms against his chest.

With a growl of impatience he stripped away the silky slip, the clinging panty hose, but then stopped with a look that bordered on reverence as she stood naked and trembling before him.

"Oh, Shea," he murmured tautly, his eyes going over her with a hunger he couldn't, didn't even try to, conceal.

Her color was high, but she didn't back away when he reached for her. He pulled her to him, and a little gasp escaped her as her breasts were crushed against his chest.

She felt as if she'd been waiting all her life for the feel of his naked skin against hers. She twisted sinuously, rubbing her breasts against him.

Chance groaned as she moved, her taut nipples two points of fire as they slid over him. He moved his hands down from her shoulders, knowing he had to touch that pebbled hardness centered in the abundant swell of her breasts. He cupped the feminine curves, lifting and savoring the soft weight.

Shea moaned, her head lolling back as she arched herself to him. When his fingers crept up to stroke her already tingling nipples, she gasped with startled pleasure.

That tiny sound ripped through his control as if it had been a saber. He picked her up with barely restrained haste, then laid her down with a slow care that made the muscles in his arms and chest stand out with the strain.

He went down beside her, his hands eagerly caressing every inch of silken skin. He traced the delicate line of cheek and jaw, down the long curve of her throat and over the fragile line of her collarbone. He once more lifted the ripe curves of her breasts, feeling a shiver of pleasure take him as she arched upward to give him their full weight. His hands slid down to the indentation of her waist, and over the jut of her hipbones. He trailed his fingertips through the dark curls between her thighs, thinking of himself nestled between them, thinking of them parting for him.

The thought sent him rocketing to full arousal, his body surging to such a sudden hardness it made him groan at the aching pressure of it. He wanted to reach for the snap of his jeans, had to get out of the unbearably tight confines of the cloth. He started to do it, but couldn't bear to take his hands off her when she lay there, open to him.

Shea had smothered a little cry of dismay as his hands left her, but it changed to a sigh of pleasure when they came back, to stroke and caress the tender flesh of her stomach. It took a few seconds for the meaning of his aborted movement to penetrate her pleasure-drugged mind. When it did, and the resultant images formed vividly in her mind, she was swamped with the sudden, urgent need to see him, touch him.

With an eagerness she couldn't conceal, her fingers shot out to undo the snap he'd tried to reach. He raised his head suddenly, and he seemed to stop breathing.

"Chance?" She was suddenly doubtful.

"Yes." It came out on a long, harsh breath as he shifted himself to give her greater access. "Please."

She tugged at the zipper, her fingers trembling. After a moment it gave in a rush, the swollen, straining bulge beneath giving it impetus. She tugged at the heavy cloth, and at the cotton of his briefs beneath, until suddenly his rigid flesh sprang free into her hands.

He threw his head back, a throttled groan tearing from his throat as she clasped him between her palms. His hips jerked forward convulsively, and he groaned again as her fingers measured his length, moving from the blunt tip to the thatch of sandy curls at the base. The hot, boiling tide rose, fierce in its suddenness, and he had to grab for her hands.

"Shea, stop. You've got to stop."

"You don't . . . want me to touch you?"

"I want it more than anything. But I can't . . . if you keep doing that, I'm going to be the most humiliated guy in this state."

She blushed as his meaning came home to her. "I didn't know . . ."

He smoothed her damp hair back from her forehead. "It's been—" He broke off, shaking his head. "I was going to say it's been a long time. But I think it's been forever."

"Oh, Chance," she murmured, reaching for him.

He kicked free of the tangled clothing and moved over her. He retraced every path his hands had taken with his mouth, tasting her smoothness, kissing each curve and hollow, flicking his tongue over every sensitive place. He was relentless, never stopping until her every breath was a gasping little moan of pleasure.

Shea heard the tiny sounds but was only vaguely aware that they came from her. He was everywhere, hands, mouth, setting blaze after blaze, causing a tidal wave of heat that rolled around inside her as if trying to burst free, the pressure building until it was almost more than she could bear. She was being engulfed, inundated with more sensations than her nerves had ever had to carry, and she was quivering helplessly under the onslaught.

He moved back to draw the taut crest of one breast into his mouth again, suckling first gently, then fiercely, and she cried out at the sudden rush of an even more intense heat. She clutched at him, her nails digging into his shoulders as she lifted herself to him.

She'd never felt so hot, so swollen, so utterly ready, and when she felt the huge, throbbing heat of him against her thigh, she knew she had to have him now. She wanted him inside her, moving, wanted him to be part of her, so deeply the boundaries between them were lost.

"Please," she gasped, "now, please, Chance."

He lifted himself over her, his earlier fantasy coming true as she eagerly parted her thighs so he could slip between them. He took her mouth in a crushing kiss, plunging his tongue into her mouth as his thick, pulsing flesh probed for entry to her body.

At the last second, with a shuddering effort, he paused, lifting his head to look at her.

"Are we all right?" he asked thickly.

All right? Lord, Shea thought dazedly, she'd never felt more all right in her life. Why was he waiting? Why wasn't he giving her what she needed, had to have? Why wasn't he filling this horrible emptiness with that wonderful gift of himself? And then the real meaning of his question struck her.

"Oh, no," she moaned. "I don't...I didn't...there was no reason..."

He groaned, a low, gravelly sound of pure, heartfelt frustration, but he pulled away from her.

"Maybe it will be all right," she urged, thinking she would die if he stopped now.

"Maybe's not good enough," he said hoarsely, trying to convince a body that was screaming for her soft heat. "I'm not taking any chances. Not with you."

"Chance, no—"

"Don't put any pressure on my nobility here," Chance growled, "it's on shaky ground to begin with."

"Oh, Chance, I'm sorry."

"So am I." He fought to control his rapid breathing as he looked down at her with a face still drawn taut with passion and need. "Later, I might tell you how good it makes me feel to know that there wasn't any reason before now. But right now I think I'll just curl up and die."

Shea smothered another little moan. "At least I know you didn't plan this."

"No," he agreed wryly, "or I would have been prepared. I guess there hasn't been much reason for me, either. If I—"

"What?" she asked as he broke off, looking at the nightstand beside the bed. Shea hadn't noticed it before, but she stared at it now.

"Quisto gave it to me," he explained at her look. "As a joke. At least, I think it was a joke."

In spite of her aching body, she smothered a laugh. It was a crate turned on end, a drawer added at the top. It was clearly labeled "Ammunition" on one side, and "80 mm shells" on the other.

"Eighty millimeters?"

He grimaced. "I think he kept the 100 millimeters for himself."

She tried to smile as Chance muttered "I wonder," and reached for the drawer of the whimsical piece. He opened it, and came up with a small flat, square package and a grin.

"Quisto said it came fully equipped. I should have realized that for him, that included these."

"Always prepared, huh?" She tried to cover her self-consciousness with a light tone, but she blushed as she eyed what he held. "Is he a Boy Scout gone bad?"

"Maybe in a past life. Now he's just the one who's always telling me I've been alone too long."

"You don't think so?"

He let his gaze skim over her slender body, then come to rest with tenderness on her flushed face. "I didn't. Until now."

She lowered her eyes shyly. "I'm glad," she whispered. Then her gaze came up to fasten on the small packet he held. "And I'm glad you found that."

"So am I," he agreed fervently, then his mouth twitched wryly. "You're not the only new experience waiting for me, it seems."

Her brows shot up. "You mean you've never...?"

He shook his head. "Just happened that way, I guess. Hope I can figure the thing out."

"Let me try," she said softly, taking the packet from him.

The heat that had merely ebbed a little at the interruption flared to life again at the thought of her hands on him. He knelt on the bed, then sat back on his heels as if offering himself to her. She felt the throbbing pulse begin in her again as she reached for him.

She took her time sheathing him, and somehow made it the most erotic thing that had ever been done to him. She paused between each minute movement for a stroking, teasing caress, until he had to lean back with his hands propped behind him to keep from grabbing her and driving into her right now.

"You're beautiful," she whispered, cupping him in her palm when she was done. His body arched forward like a bow at the tender, intimate caress, his hips thrusting against her hand. Then he came up off his hands and engulfed her with his heat and strength, driving into her with one fierce thrust, a hoarse cry breaking from deep in his chest as his name tumbled hotly from her lips.

The shock of having the aching emptiness filled so completely, so swiftly, wrenched gasps of stunned pleasure from her. Fired by the sounds, he withdrew and drove deep again, and she cried out once more. She was careening out of control on some crazy ride over tumbling rapids, each rise and fall bringing a sensation she knew she couldn't bear, and each successive one showing her she had only begun to know what her body could do under his touch.

"Oh, Shea," he gasped out as he pushed into her again, "you're so tight...it's so good..."

She couldn't speak, couldn't find words, only knew she wanted more, and more, and then more. Her hands slid down his back to grasp his hips and add what strength she had left to his pounding thrusts. She raised her legs to wrap around him, as if she feared he would leave her, and found to her joy it let him drive even deeper. The tumbling current she was riding became a boiling, reckless cascade, plunging, surging wildly.

"Chance! Please, I can't!"

"Yes," he gasped, "you can, with me, now."

She knew he wanted her to let go and go tumbling over the cataract that awaited her. She couldn't; it would be the end of her, she knew it. And then he drove into her one last time and she knew she didn't care. All thoughts of holding back were seared away by the driving heat of his body in hers, and instead of hanging on she released her grip on reality and threw herself over the drop, his name echoing from her throat as she went.

A harsh, gasping shout blended with her cry. "Yes...oh, Shea, I can feel...you squeezing me...I can't—"

The rest of his words were an unintelligible ragged sound as his body arched against hers and his head went back, every corded muscle in his body standing out in sharp relief as the last fragment of his control shattered and he erupted into her hot, sweet depths.

He jerked convulsively, grinding his body into hers as the pulsing waves of release took him; she received gladly, eagerly, once more thinking him so incredibly beautiful as she looked up at him through the lingering mist of her own pleasure. And when he collapsed atop her, she took his weight with joy, her arms locking around him as her legs had earlier, to hold him close and keep him with her.

He was gasping for breath, his face buried in the curve of her neck and shoulder. She felt the inner muscles of her body clench around him once more as another tiny echo of that soaring pleasure rippled through her; a hoarse croak of sound came from him as his hips jerked sharply in response.

She felt his muscles tense, then go slack, as he tried to move and couldn't. She ran her hands up his back, then down to cup the tight curve of his buttocks, savoring the expanse of sleek, smooth skin stretched over lean, fit muscle. A little shiver rippled through him at the sliding caress.

She made a small sound of protest when he tried to move again. "Don't."

A low, husky chuckle rumbled up from him. "You like holding up two hundred pounds of dead weight?"

"Every ounce."

The chuckle became a long, shaky sigh. He locked his arms around her and slid to one side, taking her with him, slipping one muscled thigh between hers to hold her. He moved his leg upward until it pressed against the soft warmth that had welcomed him, like a safe harbor only dreamed of on a long, hard journey.

For a few minutes he just held her tight against him, staring up at the ceiling as he had so many nights before. The rain pattered on the roof, rain that before had seemed cold and isolating but now added a sense of cozy privacy. Everything was so different now.

"You don't know how many times I've lain here, thinking about you," he whispered. "Even after that first day on the street, when all I knew was you had the greatest pair of legs I'd ever seen. After I heard you sing, heard you tearing me apart with your words, I was thinking about you here, like this, until I was so hot and hard I couldn't stand it.'' He gave a rueful little laugh. "I've been taking a lot of late night swims these past few days. But I had to shut off the pool heater. Damn thing wasn't cold enough.''

She giggled, a pleased, feminine little sound that sent a feathery wave of delight down his spine.

"Easy for you to laugh," he said gruffly. "I was the one who woke up in the same damned condition because when I finally did get to sleep all I did was dream about you.''

"You think I haven't done my share of dreaming? I knew I was in trouble the first night at the club, when I saw that you were hearing, really hearing my music. Then when you showed up with that white rose, I was really a goner.''

Chance nearly quivered with satisfaction. Not one old, tired word about his hair, his eyes or his shoulders. Or his derriere, although her hand was resting rather intimately on that particular part of him, as if she liked it. And she'd certainly seemed to find it to her liking a few minutes ago....

The memory had potent results, and when Shea felt the sudden resurgence against her thigh, she looked at him with a spark of devilry lighting eager gray eyes.

"Chance?"

"Yes?"

"I think you got the wrong nightstand."

He laughed, deep and easy, an unfettered sound she'd never heard from him, free of the awkwardness, the restraint, she'd always sensed before. And when he began to touch her, she knew that that wasn't the only restraint that had slipped.

Much later, in the early hours of morning, Shea awoke from a hotly erotic dream in which Chance was somehow managing to caress both her breasts and that newly awakened, throbbing place between her thighs all at the same time. She blinked to clear away the heated fog of the dream, but it wouldn't go, and she realized with a little shock it hadn't been a dream at all.

He had propped himself up on one elbow, and was using that hand to tease the begging peak nearest it. His mouth was laving the other, tugging with his lips and flicking the responsive flesh with his tongue. His free hand was cupping the dark curls, his fingers stroking the soft, feminine folds, then returning to a slow, circular caress of the tiny bud of flesh he'd aroused.

It was a startling feeling, to realize he had aroused her so thoroughly as she slept. She felt the muscles of her abdomen ripple before the continuous waves of heat and sensation, and she knew by the way his fingers slid so easily over her flesh that she was ready, more than ready for him.

And then he stopped. Suddenly, abruptly, painfully. Her eyes fluttered open, a tiny whimper rising from her.

"Chance?"

"I just wanted you to know what it was like to wake up like that," he teased gruffly, "like I have for days now."

"Oh." She squirmed restlessly. "Okay, okay, I feel sorry for you." He laughed and leaned down to give her a soft, gentle kiss. "Does this mean I have to go swimming?" she asked plaintively.

He laughed again; it was becoming almost easy now. "Only if you want to."

"The only thing I want is you."

"Then take me," he said, his voice suddenly thick and hoarse. She did.

A sharp, rapping noise pushed its way into his consciousness, but he ignored it. It couldn't be someone at his door. Nobody could get past the gates without the combination known by only a handful of people, none of whom would be here at this hour.

He fought waking up, not wanting to surrender the delight of this dream. She seemed more real than ever, cuddled close against his side, and he knew that if he surrendered and opened his eyes he'd have the bleak emptiness of this room and the aching tightness of a frustrated body to deal with.

Then, as a soft murmur tickled his ear, reality flooded back with a joyous rush, hardening his body with a fierceness that made those other awakenings a pale shadow. He looked down at the slender hand that was curled so trustingly in his, remembering with heat how that hand had been curled around him as she had awakened him in the dawn hour the same way he had awakened her before. The same way he wanted to again, right now.

The rapping came again, and he shook his head in annoyance. A quick glance at the clock brought him abruptly awake; it also gave him the identity of the persistent knocker at his door. Quisto. One of that handful of people.

With exquisite care and tearing regret, he extricated himself from the tangle of sheets and long, silken legs, hoping she wouldn't wake up. He pulled the sheet over that too-tempting body, then looked for something to put on that wouldn't strangle his urgently demanding body. He glanced down at himself, at the part of him that had much more pleasant ideas about what it should be doing, and decided there wasn't an article of clothing in the world that wouldn't cause the swollen flesh pain. He settled for grabbing a bath towel and knotting it around his hips as he went to open the door.

"Hey, partner, you get drunk and pass out or something?"

Quisto's cheer was as bright as the sun that had dawned after the rain, but a little less welcome.

"No," Chance said gruffly.

"Well, you sure don't look like a guy ready to go out and take on the evil forces of the world here, buddy."

"I'm not."

Quisto's brows rose at his tone as he held out a thick manila envelope. "Here's your stuff from Records."

Chance took it and tossed it onto the desk in the corner as if it were junk mail instead of something he'd been waiting for for nearly a week.

"Hey, you sick or something? I mean, I know you've been pretty grim lately— Uh-oh."

Quisto's quick eyes had spotted an irregular splash of color on the pale blue carpet. Chance followed his gaze to see the pair of bright red high heels Shea had taken off last night. Chance saw the dark eyes flick to his closed bedroom door, and he let out a tight, compressed breath as he closed his eyes to avoid the look of discovery, the look of censure he was sure would be in his partner's face.

"I hope you know what you're doing, my friend."

Chance opened his eyes to find only understanding and compassion there. "I don't. I only know I couldn't do anything else."

"Then congratulations."

Chance looked startled.

"Welcome back to the world, *amigo.*"

"Kicking and screaming," he muttered under his breath.

"But back, nevertheless." A grin creased Quisto's face. "Never thought I'd get to say this to you instead of the other way around, but I'll cover for you, partner."

"Thanks."

"See you later, then."

Chance nodded as Quisto turned to go. Then, as a vivid memory came to him, he spoke again. "Hey, partner."

Quisto looked back over his shoulder, eyebrows lifted, and at last, Chance matched his friend's grin. "Thanks for the nightstand."

There was a second's pause, then a delighted chuckle. "Came in handy, did it?"

"Saved my life." It was light but heartfelt. Quisto laughed.

"That good, huh?"

"I only hope you find out for yourself someday."

"Oh, no, not me. I leave the fireworks and trumpets to the serious guys like you. I believe in pure recreation."

"And I didn't believe in fireworks and trumpets."

Quisto paused. "You wouldn't lie to your partner, now would you? It's really . . . like that?"

Chance's expression gave him his answer.

"Oh, boy," he breathed. "I hope I don't find one like that for another twenty years or so."

"I don't think you have much say in the timing," Chance said wryly. "I sure as hell didn't."

When Quisto had gone, Chance stood for a long moment in front of the desk, staring at the brown envelope as if it had a life of its own, and a malevolent intent to destroy his. He heard a noise from the bedroom, and hastily shoved it into the desk drawer that already held the documents from the recorder's office and the copies of all the local and federal files he'd brought home. He'd intended to read them, to force his mind back into professional channels, but instead had wound up staring into space, hearing a song, seeing a pair of gray eyes.

"Chance?"

Her voice was soft, husky with sleep, and so incredibly sexy his body snapped to attention as if she'd touched him. He looked toward the bedroom door, and that crazy, consuming fire kindled inside him, pouring downward to add its heat and pressure to already hardening flesh. She had done as he had, wrapping herself in a towel, and it left her long, golden legs bare and beckoning.

Memories of them wrapped around his waist, of them hugging his hips as she straddled him, riding him with wild abandon, surged through him, and he found it a little hard to walk as he crossed the room to take her in his arms.

"Sorry, songbird. I had to shoo away a pesky Cuban."

"Quisto?" Her fingers came up to her lips. "Oh! Are you supposed to be working? What time is it? Are you late?"

"Yes, yes, almost eight, and not now, because Quisto's going to cover for me." He lowered his head to take her mouth in a gentle kiss of greeting. "Good morning," he said softly.

"Yes," she answered, lifting her hands to cup the sides of his face, "it is, isn't it?"

He nodded slowly. "Are you hungry?"

"Yes."

In that one syllable she managed to make it quite clear that food was the absolute last thing on her mind. Chance laughed, tugged away the towel that encased her, then sent his own flying after it. He picked her up and strode back into the bedroom.

"I was hungrier than I thought," Shea said as she fed Chance another forkful of the massive batch of scrambled eggs they'd made when their protesting stomachs had driven them into the kitchen.

"Mmm."

He caught a yellow fleck with his tongue as it fell from the fork, wondering why being fed by hand, an act that was so humiliating when it was necessary, could become so erotic when it was voluntary. With the right person.

She watched the flick of his tongue, a swirling heat rising in her as she remembered what that tongue had done to her last night. Chance glanced up at her as he reached for the glass of milk that sat on the tray. His hand fell back to the bed.

"God, Shea, don't look at me like that."

She blushed. "I can't help it."

"Damn," he said hoarsely. "It's like I'm always on the edge around you."

"I didn't know...it's so..." She lowered her eyes. "It almost frightens me, it happens so fast."

He suppressed a shiver. "I know." He tried to get himself under control, making his tone light. "Do I need to buy a shotgun? I'm not poaching on some Tahoe mountain man's territory, am I?"

She blushed again. "No."

"Why?"

"I moved there because I love it, and for the privacy to work away from the phoniness of Hollywood, not to go looking for a man."

"Are they all deaf and blind, or what?"

"No. A few...tried. I wasn't interested." She met his eyes steadily. "I guess I was waiting for you."

He couldn't control the rippling response to her words this time. "Lord, songbird, you are good for a guy's ego."

"You don't hurt a lady's, either."

"Thanks." He grinned at her, and popped a slice of orange from the tray into her mouth.

"Mmm. I'm glad I don't have to sing tonight."

"Me, too." His grin spread. "Unless you want to sing for me, of course."

"I thought I had been."

Her cheeks flamed even as she said it, and Chance burst into a delighted laugh. He set aside the tray and reached for her, pulling her into his arms as he propped himself up on the pillows against the headboard of his bed. He felt the stirring of the desire that was never far from the surface around her, but he tried to ignore it.

"Tell me about your place in Tahoe."

She sighed. "It's so beautiful! It's about halfway up a mountain, with hundreds of trees, and a view of part of the lake. My father built it years ago, before they put all the restrictions on development." A flicker of pain crossed her face. "He wanted to retire there."

Chance hugged her close. "I'm sorry, Shea."

"God, it was such a stupid thing to happen."

"Was it an accident?"

She made a choking little sound, and a shudder went through her. He tightened his arms around her.

"No," she said at last. "It was a horrible case of being in the wrong place at the wrong time. He got a call that there were some people trespassing on one of his construction sites." She smiled briefly. "Dad was very...accountable. He always took things like that very seriously."

"So he went there."

She nodded. "And walked in on a drug deal."

Chance went utterly still. Shea shuddered again at the appalling memories.

"They shot him," she whispered. "Over and over. The police said they kept on even after...it didn't matter anymore."

"Baby, I'm so sorry."

If he'd needed any further proof that she knew nothing about her brother's activities, he had it now. He held her while she shook against him.

"It's been twelve years, but sometimes..."

"It seems like yesterday. I know, songbird."

She seemed to go taut in his grasp, and then she lifted troubled eyes to his. "Oh, God, I'm sorry, Chance. You do know, don't you? I didn't mean to make you remember."

"It's all right." He didn't want to talk about himself, he wanted to ease the pain in her eyes. "Did they ever find them?"

"Two of them. Charlie Hill and Mickey Lopez." She said the names as if they were etched in acid in her mind. "They never caught the one who did the actual shooting."

"The two they got wouldn't roll?"

She looked at him quizzically. "That's the word the investigators kept saying, that they wouldn't roll over."

Oops, Chance thought. Watch it, Buckner. But she went on as if she'd dismissed his slip.

"They were just kids, they should have been scared enough to, but they wouldn't talk."

"Kids?"

"They were only seventeen."

And more scared of the shooter than the cops, Chance mused. He'd have to pull the report—no, it was probably already in that envelope he'd shoved into the desk drawer.

And suddenly it was there again, the line he'd crossed—leaped over joyously—last night. The job had loomed up between them once more, and he was seized with a desperate need to tell her everything, to end the deception, to give her the honesty she deserved, the honesty she'd given him.

"I was almost surprised," she was saying quietly, "when Paul came home for Dad's funeral. He'd been gone more than seven years, and he and Dad had never really gotten along well, anyway."

She'd done it herself, he thought numbly. She'd brought up the subject he'd always been probing at, digging for any crumb she might drop. She'd brought it up, and now he didn't want to hear it. But he couldn't just ignore her, not when she was opening herself up to him like this.

It was ripping at him, the knowledge that he should take this opportunity and milk it for all it was worth, and the realization that the thought of using her like that made him sick. He wanted to tell her to stop, that he didn't want to hear a damned word about Paul de Cortez.

And then what? The feds weren't going to give this up. Eventually they were going to nail de Cortez. And there was no way Chance would be able to conceal his part in it from her. And there wasn't a hope in hell that she'd believe he hadn't been using her, hadn't been lying about everything.

She would hate him, and at the moment he wasn't sure it wasn't exactly what he deserved.

"Chance?"

"Sorry." He took a breath and made himself ask. "Why didn't they get along?"

"Dad didn't like some of the kids he was hanging out with. He was always on him about it. He said that's why he left, but..."

"But?" He hated this, knowing he was listening to every innocent, open confidence for any clue that might help them break Paul de Cortez.

"I don't think he ever forgave my mother for getting married again. I guess she was supposed to stay in mourning for his father forever. And he resented that she wanted to put that part of her life behind her. She didn't want to be reminded of any of it. I don't know much about that time, but I don't think she was very happy."

"But he didn't...take it out on you?"

"No." She wrinkled her nose. "I love my brother, don't get me wrong, but he's awfully...old school. I don't think he considers women important enough to expend much energy on."

He couldn't do it anymore. He had to stop this. The choice he'd made last night was irrevocable. She was no longer a source of information, she'd become so much more. He'd find another way. And when it was over he would pray that she would believe, that he hadn't destroyed a bond that was incredibly strong yet so very, very fragile.

"I can't think of anything better to expend energy on than a woman. The right woman."

She caught her breath at the look in his eyes. "I'm glad you decided I'm the right woman," she whispered.

"I had no choice." He swallowed heavily. "I think it was decided for me the first time I saw you."

"Oh, Chance," she murmured, slipping her arms around his neck. "I feel like I've been waiting all my life for you."

"I gave up hoping for this a long time ago," he answered softly. "I didn't think it was possible. Especially for me."

"I love you."

It sent a little ripple of pleasure down his spine, and set up a tiny knot of fear in his stomach.

"I love you, too, Shea."

He said it with a fierceness that startled her, but then he was kissing her and she couldn't think of anything but the joy building in her again.

Chapter 8

Chance tightened the last lug nut, then let the Jeep down on its newly repaired tire. He wondered if it would even start, it had been neglected for so long, but it turned over at the first twist of the key.

That chore done, he double-checked to make certain he had all the papers he'd taken from the desk, and pulled out of the garage and down the driveway. It was a brisk winter day, but he'd left the soft top off the Jeep anyway, and enjoyed the fresh chill in the air as it blew over him, tangling his hair.

He'd taken Shea home in the Jag, reluctantly parting from her so she could get to a morning rehearsal she had scheduled with the band. They'd spent the last day and night together, sharing feelings and intimacies that left them both breathless. He told her things he'd not talked of for years, even about Sarah when she asked.

"I did love her, Shea."

"I know that. You always will."

He hugged her for her understanding.

"How did she die, Chance? She must have been so young."

"She was...in my car," he said carefully, hoping she would assume it was a traffic accident even as he hated himself for being so devious. He knew he couldn't tell her the whole truth without opening up a line of questions he couldn't answer. "She was only twenty-four. She was...so happy. About the baby." He shuddered, unable to go on.

Her quiet sympathy was somehow more soothing than any of the platitudes that had been poured over him since Sarah's death. He clung to these precious hours with her, shoving the hovering cloud out of sight at least for a while. And when at last he'd had to surrender her back to the world this morning, he'd done it so grudgingly she'd laughed. Then he'd gone back home and spent the afternoon poring over the stack of papers from the desk.

He couldn't shake the feeling that there was something here, some clue that would give them the break they needed. In his more sour moments, when he was missing Shea the most, he told himself he was just grabbing at straws, desperate to find something that would save him from having to use her any longer.

He laughed, a bitter, ironic sound. Here he was searching for some way to wind up this case so he could come clean with her, all the time knowing that if he found it, it would no doubt mean the end of whatever trust she had in him.

When he'd been holding her, it had been easy to convince himself that they would work it out somehow. But now, in this empty place that had never really been a home to him until she had warmed it with her presence, the truth ate at him. He would be the man who put away her brother, the man who had used her to do it. She wouldn't care that he hadn't wanted to, that the moment he realized how deeply he felt about her, he had stopped, she would only know she'd been used in the worst way, and she would hate him for it.

He was two miles from the station when the thing that had been flitting around the edges of his consciousness finally worked its way through his preoccupation. A series of images played back in his mind one after the other, the tiny scenes in his rearview mirror for the past several minutes.

His eyes flicked to the reflecting square once more. The edges changed, trees, buildings, all sliding past in a constant flow of motion, but the center remained the same, now and in all the images that unreeled in his mind. He made a quick, unsignaled right turn, his eyes flicking back to the mirror the second the maneuver was finished. When the long, dark fender of the sedan plowed into sight, tires letting out a protesting squeal as they took the strain of the hasty turn, he knew he'd been right.

"Figures," he muttered, giving voice to his first instinctive thought. I had to pick today to leave the horsepower at home.

Possibilities raced through his mind, the who, the why, but he shoved them aside. What mattered now was losing the extra appendage he'd acquired. Instincts honed by intensive training kicked in, and he began to plan. He'd been a street cop long before he'd been assigned to detectives, and he knew this town down to every twist and turn. And in seconds he knew where he was going.

He upped the speed of the Jeep a little; the sedan clung like a burr. He slowed and made a few made more turns, obligingly signaling each time. As he'd hoped, the sedan dropped back a little.

Spotting a busy convenience store with one empty parking spot, he pulled in, leaving the tail stranded on the busy street. He grinned to himself when he heard the blare of horns on the street, guessing that the sedan was wreaking havoc trying not to lose sight of him.

He went through it in his head as he went inside, calculating the time it would take for the car to circle the block. Of course he could be wrong, the guy might be smarter than he thought, he mused, but if he was, he would never have spotted him in the first place.

Of course, you've been out in the ozone for so long, Buckner, he could have been dogging you for days and you never would have noticed. Something tickled at the recesses of his mind, but he didn't have time to think about it now. He grabbed a couple of items, paid for them and headed for the door.

He sauntered casually back out to the Jeep, a soda in one hand and a bag of potato chips in the other. He took a long swallow of the cold drink, then climbed leisurely into the Jeep as if he had all the time in the world.

Just as he started the engine, the sedan came into view down the street. Chance nodded to himself, the mental equivalent of a check mark. He hadn't doubted the sedan was truly following him, he'd only wanted to see how inventive the driver was.

Not very, he thought. Had it been him, he would have pulled into the next driveway, which happened to be a fast-food restaurant, with a drive-through that would have let him keep a visual on both the Jeep and the back door of the convenience store. Instead, the blue car had circled the block, leaving Chance more than enough time to be gone by the time he came back around.

"Okay, mister," Chance muttered as he started the Jeep, "let's start the party."

He began decorously enough, driving at the standard five miles over the speed limit. The sedan's driver seemed sure of him now, apparently convinced that he hadn't been burned after all. He kept a careful two car-lengths back. When Chance reached the intersection he'd been looking for, he pulled into the left-turn lane and waited for the light to change.

A glance in the mirror told him the sedan was holding back, inching along, not wanting to make the obvious move of pulling into the left-turn pocket right behind him. Chance yawned widely, raising his arms for an exaggerated stretch, knowing that in the open Jeep his movements would be clearly visible.

For a moment, just one, sweet second in time, he let the memory of the past two days—and nights—slip into his mind. The memory of Shea, innocent and stunned by the extent of what they'd found together, and later confident, abandoned, and eager for more. God, he loved her—

The green arrow flipped on, piercing the bubble of reverie. For one crazy second Chance was tempted to just sit there. What would the guy do, honk at him? Chuckling inwardly at his follower's imagined dilemma, he made the turn. As he went, he slipped one hand into his jacket pocket and fingered through the keys there. He went past the key to the office, his locker key, and the small key to his file cabinet. Then came the distinctively shaped key that unlocked his terminal of the department computer system, which told him that the one he wanted was next. He isolated it and moved it to his left hand.

Two blocks up, after a careful check of traffic to gauge the space and timing, he changed to the number two lane, leaving his signal on for a right turn. The instant he saw the sedan creep out from behind a small station wagon, committed to a duplicate lane change, he wrenched the wheel left and dived across the road into a narrow side street. He sent the Jeep flying up the hill, and at the top darted into a driveway and ducked between two long, narrow buildings, each a row of small businesses.

The Jeep slid to a halt at the end of the left-hand building. Chance leaped out, knowing he had only seconds. The key slid neatly into the control of the door opener on the outside wall, and the metal roll-up door began to open. He raced back to the still-running Jeep. He was inside, with the door rumbling back into place, in less than twenty seconds.

He looked around the cavernous room, lit only by a shaft of winter sunlight from a skylight. The name on the lease for the place was an innocuous "Frank Jones," but in reality the huge garage was used by the police department for searching and investigating vehicles impounded for criminal reasons. It was empty now.

He went back to the door, to a panel that consisted of several glowing lights and a numbered keypad. He quickly punched in a number, and one of the lights blinked out. He ran back to the Jeep, swung into it and then up on top of the roll bar. Balancing carefully, he gathered himself and jumped.

His hands locked around the metal cross beam of one rafter. He pulled himself up in one smooth movement, and in less than a minute was through the skylight and onto the roof.

He ran the length of the building until he reached the point where his height would make him visible from the street, then crouched down and worked his way to the edge. He was just in time to see the dark blue sedan cruise slowly down the hill back toward the main street. It made a U-turn at the bottom, came back, reached the dead end and turned again. This time, as it went by, the driver slammed the wheel with his fist in frustration. Chance grinned.

At last the car pulled away, tires barking out the driver's anger. Chance waited awhile to make sure he'd really gone, then made his way back to the garage and his Jeep.

As he drove, he kept the questions that were spinning in his mind on a back burner, letting them percolate for a while. When he got to the station, he closeted himself with the department computer and the stack of files and papers he'd brought. He ran the plate of the blue sedan first, somehow not surprised when it came back not in the Department of Motor Vehicles files.

He switched back to the department system. After a half hour of inquiries, cross-references and old case numbers, he shut it down, staring at the blank screen for a few seconds. Then he reached for the phone and made a couple of calls, cashing in on some long-owed favors. He wasn't sure what he was looking for, or whether it would do any good, but something was nagging at him so insistently that he couldn't stop himself.

"Well, well, the stranger's here. I didn't think you were going to make it."

Chance glanced up to see Quisto leaning against the doorjamb, his quick, dark eyes bright with curiosity.

"I had some things I needed to check out."

"So where's the lady?"

"She had a rehearsal this morning."

Quisto came in, pulling the door of the small office closed after him. He tossed his jacket onto the back of his chair and raised one leg to sit on the edge of his desk. For a long moment, he just looked at his partner.

"I sprout horns or something?"

Quisto grinned suddenly. "Wings, maybe. You're flyin', partner."

Yeah, Chance thought. Good word. But he shifted uneasily, not comfortable yet with this new feeling. "What? No lecture on professional ethics?"

Quisto shrugged. "Nothing you don't already know about that, I'd guess." His expression was suddenly serious. "And if you ask me, bending the rules a little is a small price."

"Price? For what?"

"For getting that damned look out of your eyes."

Chance sat back in his chair, staring at his partner. "What look?"

"Like your heart gave up a long time ago and was just waiting for the rest of you to follow."

Chance was shaken by the surprisingly evocative words. He stared at the young Cuban as if he'd never really seen him before.

"Don't look in the mirror much, do you?" Quisto said softly.

Chance felt as if he were waiting, but he didn't know what for. Then he realized it was for the shutting down of his emotions, which had become a habit whenever anyone probed into that sensitive area of his psyche. It didn't come. At last a small, reluctant smile curved his mouth.

"Not until this morning," he said wryly, "and I didn't recognize who I saw."

Quisto grinned. "I'll bet." Then, serious again, "It's not going to be easy, man."

"I know."

"Just remember...if it all breaks down at the crunch, I'm here, partner."

Chance had to swallow before he could speak. "Thanks."

"Anything I can do?"

"No." He shook his head. "Yeah. You still got that little honey from the airline on a string?"

"Me? Keep a lady on a string?"

"You spread yourself any thinner," Chance said dryly, "and you'll be transparent."

"I told you, I leave that one-man, one-woman stuff to the guys who can handle it. So what do you need?"

"Just your charm, buddy, just your charm. For one tiny little bit of information."

Quisto's brow furrowed when Chance told him what he needed. "Flight records for when?" He wrote it down. "You looking for someone in particular?"

Chance shrugged. "Someone familiar."

"You think it's— Never mind, I know, if you didn't think it was important, you wouldn't ask. I'll see what I can do."

"And quick, huh?"

"Of course."

"I mean it. Somewhere I've rattled a cage. Somebody's been tailing me. Plates on the car aren't in the file."

Quisto sat up, his eyes narrowing. "You get a look at him?"

"Yeah. He looked like every third guy on the street." A ghost of a smile flickered across his face. "With a temper."

"I gather you lost him?"

"Yeah." He sighed. "But I don't know how long he's been on me. I didn't spot him until this morning, but—"

"What?" Quisto asked when he broke off, brows furrowing.

"I think he's been on me for days." The pictures had flipped through his mind rapidly—the times he'd felt the odd sensation of a presence near the club, and the car that had been hovering the night he'd gone after Shea. "I just didn't realize what was bothering me." He snorted in disgust. "Stupid idiot."

"You've been . . . preoccupied."

"Yeah. And if he'd had different orders, I'd have been dead."

"You think it's de Cortez?"

"Who else?"

"Seems a little extreme."

"I gather he's got some rather archaic ideas about the treatment of women."

"Ah, the old machismo, huh? Women in their place, behaving properly and all that?"

"Something like that."

"So you figure he's checking up on little sister's new boyfriend?"

Chance winced a little at the word, not sure he liked the casual connotation it held. "Maybe. Or maybe he just wants to be sure I'm not going to be a problem for him."

Quisto paused, considering. "He can't have made you yet. He would have been down on you like a sea gull on a fish head."

"Thanks for the analogy," Chance said dryly. "I don't recall ever being compared to a fish head before."

A teasing, bantering light appeared in Quisto's eyes. "But I'll bet you've been compared to a lot of other things in the last couple of days."

To his amazement, Chance blushed. Quisto saw heat flare in the depths of the blue eyes, saw him swallow tightly, and thanked the Lord that he, Quisto, was immune. It must be frightening for a woman to have so much power over you.

"Well, you'd better stay clear of here unless you're sure you've lost him. If he burns you, the whole house of cards could collapse on us."

Chance went cold inside. That's what he was living in, a dream world, a house of cards, liable to crumble at the slightest breeze. And when it happened, he would lose Shea as completely, as permanently as he had lost Sarah.

"I'm sorry, buddy," Quisto said. "I didn't think."

"Not your fault," he said gruffly. "I'm the one who lost sight of the line, I'm the one who's got to live with it."

Quisto started to speak, then stopped; there wasn't really anything to say. He glanced at his watch. "You ready for our weekly dose of Eaton salts?"

"No. But I don't have much choice, do I?"

Tuning out the drone of the federal agent, Chance went through the files again. He leaned forward and picked up the surveillance log, now a two-inch-thick sheaf of detailed entries, every call made to and from the club, every person in and out.

He read them, then read them again, unable to get rid of the same feeling that there was something here, something he wasn't seeing. Sighing, he flipped back to page one. He was halfway down the worn sheet of paper when something Eaton was saying got through to him. His head snapped up.

"—soon as we get approval."

"What?" Chance fixed the man with a narrow stare.

"Oh, decided to join us, did you?"

Chance ignored the sarcasm. "What did you say?"

"If you'd been bothering to pay attention—"

"So I wasn't. Say it again."

"I said, I'm tired of waiting. We're going to make a move."

A chill rippled down Chance's spine. "Being in a hurry," he said carefully, "is what blew you out of the water in Miami."

An odd, almost malevolent gleam came into Eaton's small eyes. "If you're worried about your jurisdiction, don't be." His voice was a shade too casual. "In the, ah, spirit of interagency cooperation, we're more than happy to let you handle the inside work. Especially since you have developed such an excellent...contact." The word dripped with sarcasm. "All you have to do is use her to get in to see her brother."

Use her. A wave of nausea, so sudden and fierce it made his head start to spin, swept Chance. He knew in that moment, when he heard the words he'd thought himself so often, spoken in that oily, repugnant voice, just how hopeless it was. She would see it this way, as a cold, calculating decision made by cold, calculating men, a decision reducing her to a mere pawn in an ugly game. And she would never believe that wasn't exactly what he was.

Chance's expression didn't change, but Quisto had been looking at a pair of dead blue eyes for two years now, and he didn't miss the flicker of anguish that dimmed the renewed life in them.

"And you've cleared this with your brass?" Quisto responded quickly.

Eaton hesitated then shrugged. "Not yet. But that's only a formality." His pudgy face set into stubborn lines. "I'm going ahead with this."

"And just how," Quisto said sarcastically, "do you propose we approach a man who is, to all appearances, a law-abiding and upstanding local businessman with your 'offer'? Shall we just stroll up and say, 'Nice place you've got here, got any coke stashed in the back room?'"

"You'll just say someone in Miami sent you to see him—"

"You think he won't check that? That he'll just take our word for it?"

"I've thought of that," Eaton said smugly. "If he does call, one of my men in Miami will intercept it. He'll tell him what he wants to hear."

Quisto laughed. "He made all your people in Miami, remember? That's why you came crawling to us."

"Listen, you little—"

"You listen, *pendejo!*"

Quisto's voice was icy as he cut Eaton off with the insult. Chance had asked him once what it meant and gotten Quisto's patented grin. "No Anglo meaning, *compadre.* But 'bastard' comes close." And it was clear Quisto's tone had told Eaton all he needed to know about the meaning of the word; Eaton's face reddened as the young Cuban faced him down.

"You," Quisto spat out, "and your crew of idiots do nothing without us."

"We'll do what we damned well please! And I guarantee you that we'll take down that bitch just as hard as her brother. And you'd better watch your mouth, punk. Your lieutenant isn't here to save your butt now."

"No, he's not here, is he?"

Chance's voice was soft yet somehow deadly in its very flatness. Eaton's nostrils flared with unease, and his face wore the expression of a man who had disdainfully kicked a wolf he'd thought safely dead, only to have it lunge for his throat.

"He's not here," Chance repeated. He shifted his gaze to the two other agents who had accompanied Eaton— brought, Chance was certain, to give the man some borrowed feeling of authority. His eyes flicked to the door, then back to the men. They took the cue, and without a backward glance at their boss, they scrambled out.

Eaton started to squeak an angry protest at the desertion, but it subsided when Chance got to his feet and closed in on him. Chance glanced at Quisto, silently offering him the same out, and got a sour look in return as his partner made his intentions clear by taking a seat on the edge of the table. Chance nodded in acceptance and understanding.

"It's just you and us now, Eaton. So I'll tell you exactly what will happen if you take one tiny step without clearing it through us. I'm going to send de Cortez an autographed picture of you, and I'll make damned sure it's nice and clear so his muscle will recognize you when he sends them after you."

"You wouldn't do that," Eaton blustered, but the unease in his eyes shifted to fear.

"Wouldn't I?"

"You're a cop. You want de Cortez."

"When he's done with you, I'll have plenty of time."

Eaton tried to muster his bravado. "I'll have your badge for this, Buckner! You're out of law enforcement for good!"

"For what?" Quisto said innocently. "I didn't hear anything."

"And I didn't say anything." Chance stared him down until, with a muttered oath, the man waddled out as fast as he could manage.

"All right!" Quisto crowed. "Nice move, partner! Put that little weasel right in line."

"Yeah."

Quisto turned toward him. "You don't look very happy about it."

"I know."

Chance gathered up the papers he had spread on the desk. He left the conference room without another word, still struggling to deal with the realization that had hit him during Eaton's threatening tirade. Faced with a choice between Shea and this man who was supposedly one of his own, he hadn't the slightest doubt of what choice he would make.

* * *

Chance drummed his fingers restlessly on the table, waiting. He'd spoken to Shea on the phone this afternoon but hadn't seen her since he'd taken her home, and if he hadn't been so anxious he would have been ruefully amazed at how much he missed her.

His entire afternoon had been a running battle with all the myriad possibilities for disaster that were whirling in his mind. And with a conscience that was sitting none too easily. If de Cortez had put the tail on him, why? To check him out, or to protect his sister? He grudgingly admitted the man seemed capable at least of that much concern for her.

If it hadn't been de Cortez...

No, it had to be. Nothing else made sense. And, he tried to reassure himself, Quisto was right. If the tail had made him for a cop, he would have known by now. Paul de Cortez would have made some kind of a move.

Some kind of a move. Eaton's plans nagged at him. He knew that if nothing broke, they were going to have to do something. Even Jim Morgan had mentioned having to do a little prodding eventually. He didn't want it to happen that way. He knew it was cowardly, but he didn't want to have to be the catalyst. It would be bad enough just picking up the pieces if de Cortez made a mistake big enough to nail him for, but to go in and force it, especially knowing that to do it he'd have to lie to her again, a huge, horrendous lie...

Quit kidding yourself, Buckner. There are no degrees in this. She'll hate you just as much. Sure, de Cortez is dirty, but it isn't going to make any difference in the long run. He's still her brother. She believed you when you told her you didn't deal or deal with dealers, but if you have to go in as just that, there's not a chance in hell she'll ever believe you again.

Unless you tell her you're a cop. She'd believe it then, if you showed her the evidence. She'd believe, when it was there in front of her... and hate you anyway. For how you did it, for using her. And she'd think everything else you told her was a lie, too. Especially about loving her. She'd think it was just part of the game. And you couldn't think of anything more cruel, more capable of destruction.

He had to stall. He had to have more time. Every minute with her was one more minute of faith-building between them. One more tiny bit of armor against the chaos to come. One more fragile little hope that, when it was over and the pain had eased a little, she might remember, might believe.

The lights came up on the stage, and the chatter in the room stopped. She might not like to perform, he thought, but she had this place in the palm of her hand before she even stepped onstage. The crowd seemed bigger each night, with faces he'd seen frequently mixed among the others in the rapt audience. Some of those regulars cast sideways glances at him, recognizing the man she sat with between shows, the only person in the place she made the exception for.

The music began, a slow, pulsing beat that was new to him, the chords from the guitar an oddly delicate counterpoint. His eyes searched the stage for her. Was this what they'd rehearsed this morning? It was intriguing, whatever it was. But where was she? The spotlight was on center stage, but it was empty.

He noticed people leaning forward as the beat subtly altered, quickened, building anticipation on a level that was almost imperceptible. Eric's fingers flew over the strings, dancing, sending waves of sensuous melody through the air. Chance felt his heart pounding, and himself on the edge of his seat.

A brilliant red flame rose from behind the stage, an incredible vision that shimmered as it moved, as it seemed to float toward the spotlight. The sweep of red grew brighter as it approached, glittering with each step, until the spotlight caught it and sent red sparks flying.

Chance couldn't stop the gut-level gasp of pleasure that escaped him at the sight of her, but it didn't matter—the rest of the room seemed to have done the same. She looked radiant, transported, and she took his breath away. And when she began to sing, her voice was a husky, sexy sound that made him groan as he remembered the last time he'd heard her sound like that, when she'd cried out his name as he drove deep inside her.

> "Never believed the dreamers
> When they told me how it could be
> Never believed the cryers
> When they told me how it was
> Got no choice now,
> Don't know what's come over me
> My head don't understand
> But my crazy heart does
> It must be love."

Chance felt something shift, then break inside him. Some last, hardened part of his heart, numbed from too many blows, from too many bitter memories, unknotted and let go at last. The determination he'd lost when she'd been out of his sight came flooding back. There had to be a way. He would find it, somehow.

A relentless, throbbing ache settled deep inside him, hardening his body to an urgent thrust as he watched the slim figure in the incredible dress move around the stage. The fabric seemed shot with light itself, sending crimson sparks out in a shower that seemed to linger even after she had moved sinuously away. It clung to her, the glitter painting her every curve. Dancing, sparkling ruby earrings, strands of red spots of light, dangled from her ears. Her hair was a wild mane, thick and tousled, looking as it had this morning, tangled from his hands.

His hands drew up tightly into fists as he tried to fight down the tide of insistent, urgent need. He wanted to grab her and run to the first private place he could find, strip that tantalizing dress off her and drive his aching flesh into the slick, wet softness that had welcomed him like a long-missed part of herself.

It was some cruel joke, he thought. After years of numbness, to find the one woman who aroused him to the point of pain, the one woman to whom he would hand over his heart and soul without a second thought, and it had to be like this. He felt like a wild animal caught in the jaws of a vicious trap, with the only hope of survival the gnawing off of a part of his own body.

No, damn it. He wasn't going to let it happen. Not again. Losing Sarah and their unborn child had nearly killed him; he wasn't going to give up Shea without a fight.

When the set was over and the vision in red began to move toward him, the ache became an agonizing need he wasn't at all sure he could control. When she paused by the table, he didn't dare stand up; only the draping of the white cloth hid his problem from the world. She didn't even speak, just nodded slightly toward the door of her dressing room and kept going.

After a moment of the fiercest effort he'd ever had to make in his life, he was able to rise and follow her. He was met at the entry to the hallway by one of the bookends. The other was nowhere in sight.

"Where's your clone?" Chance asked sweetly when the bulky man, clad in the customary tuxedo, moved to block his way. A snarl was his only answer. "Go ahead, pal," Chance coaxed. "I'm feeling just about mean enough to pull your tongue out through your ear."

A long, tense moment spun out between them before at last Chance's eagerness to see Shea won out and he shouldered his way past the tuxedoed wall.

She was in his arms the moment he closed the door.

"God, I missed you," he breathed.

"Good," she said simply.

A pure, joyous laughter bubbled up inside him as the impossibility of it all slipped away in her intoxicating presence.

"I love that sound," she whispered, her arms sliding around his waist beneath his jacket. "It sounds so much better now."

He bent his head to press his lips against her hair. "I... hadn't used it for a long time."

"I know." She looked up at him shyly. "Did you like the new song?"

"You know I did. Is that what you were working on this morning?"

She nodded. "I've had the music in my head for a long time. I just couldn't find the words. I guess the time wasn't right before."

He let out a sighing breath. "Oh, Shea," he murmured.

She moved closer, and he knew in a minute she was going to realize exactly what kind of effect the song had on him. He took a step back, holding her shoulders as he let his eyes sweep over her.

"You got a license for that dress, lady?"

She smiled shyly. "I don't wear it very often. It takes more nerve than I usually have."

His eyes went soft, glinting deep blue in the soft light of the room. "But you had the nerve to do it today?"

She lifted her head to meet his warm gaze. "Today," she said softly, "I could have done anything."

He hadn't meant to kiss her. He'd thought he didn't dare; he was too close to the edge already. If he kissed her, he wouldn't want to stop until they were both hot, panting and naked, crying out for each other with desperate need. But when she said those quiet words, then stretched up to press her mouth to his, his resolution vanished in the flaring heat.

He jerked her tight against him, not caring anymore if she knew what she'd done to him. She gasped as she came in contact with his hardened body, then went soft and warm in his arms, arching to press her hips harder against him. Her tongue flicked over his lips, then past them, to find and stroke his own. He groaned, catching the tip of the sweet, welcome probe and sucking gently.

Shea's arms tightened around him, then loosened as her hands slid down from his waist. She could feel the tautly muscled body beneath the heavy linen of his slacks, and a sigh of pleasure slipped from her lips when her fingers curled around the swell of his buttocks.

And then the kiss wasn't deep enough, hot enough, or hard enough, and she raised her arms to encircle his neck. Her fingers tangled in his hair, then tightened, pressing his head down to her even harder.

Chance let his hands slide down her back, over the sparkling fabric of the dress, to the gentle swell of her buttocks. In a convulsive motion he cupped her, pressing her tight against him, his breath escaping in a rush against her lips as his hips jerked involuntarily forward.

He tried to stop, tried to pull away, but she made a breathless little sound of protest that sent a rocket of heat through him. And then her hands were up under his sweater, stroking his bare skin, making every muscle quiver beneath her fingers. He shuddered, then gasped when her caressing fingers reached his nipples and rubbed them lovingly. He wrenched his mouth from hers.

"Shea," he growled warningly against her ear.

"Please." It was a soft breath of sound. She moved, arching her back, rubbing the swollen heaviness of her breasts against his chest.

"God!" It burst from him. "Shea, stop. If you don't, I'm going to take you right here against the damned wall."

"Yes," she moaned, "please."

A harsh, ragged sound came from deep in his chest. "God, don't say that."

"Now," she said, her gray eyes smoky and begging beneath the thick fringe of lashes. "Right now. It's been so long."

He forgot everything he'd learned about control. He barely had the presence of mind to reach back and lock the door. Even as he did, Shea's hands were busy, tugging at the buckle of his belt, then his zipper. Her eagerness stunned him in the seconds before a firestorm flared inside him at the first touch of her hands on him as she freed him from his clothes. He shuddered violently as she clasped him in her hands. Then he erupted into motion.

He tugged at the red dress, pushing it up out of the way, its glistening length only a nuisance now. His hands found the silken flesh of her legs and slid up her slender thighs. He was hanging on by a thread of control; only the fear that he might hurt her if she wasn't ready for him slowed him.

His fingers encountered a brief triangle of silk at the top of her thighs, and when he tugged at it and heard the fabric rend, he realized that thread of control had dwindled to a mere fiber. He shuddered again at the heat that radiated from her body when she was free of the interfering cloth.

When his seeking fingers found her, hot and wet and waiting, he groaned her name harshly.

She was raining sweet, blazing kisses over his mouth, his face, his jaw, his throat, all the while her hands were caressing his swollen flesh urgently, almost demandingly. He truly meant to at least carry her to the couch, but when her fingers squeezed and coaxed the blunt tip of that male flesh his only thought was that he would die if he didn't get inside her now. Right now.

His hands cupped her buttocks, kneading them, then lifting. She locked one arm around his neck, the other lowering as she reached to guide him home. He groaned as her wet, hot flesh closed around him, yielding even as it gripped him, stroked him.

"Oh, Chance," she moaned, "I—"

She broke off with a sharp cry as he lowered her fully onto him. He turned slightly, pressing her back against the wall of the dressing room, and thrust his hips forward, pushing himself inside her to the hilt. She gasped, shuddering.

"Hold on, songbird," he said hoarsely, and she fastened her arms around his neck. He slid his hands down her legs until she locked them around him, then put his palms flat against the wall on each side of her lolling head. Braced, he began to move, thrusting fiercely, savoring the tiny cries of pleasure she made as much as the incredible waves of sensation that swept him as she took him so hot and fast and deep.

It was strange, and oddly erotic, touching her nowhere but in that most intimate place. His fingers curled against the wall, but he didn't dare sacrifice the support. She clung to him desperately, arms and legs enfolding him, her legs tightening with each thrust to urge him deeper.

His entire world narrowed to those inches of flesh buried deep in her body. The only place he touched her was all the meaning he needed in his life, that it was Shea, and that she was giving herself to him so freely.

"Shea," he said raggedly, "Shea...I can't...wait."

"Don't," she whispered hotly in his ear. "Now. With me."

Shea thought the thick, guttural sound he made the most beautiful thing in the world. And then, as she felt him swell and burst inside her and her own soaring flight began, she knew she'd only touched the tip of the beauty he would show her now. With a breathy little cry of his name, she went soaring after him.

Chapter 9

Chance didn't know which had awakened him, the smell rising from below or the growling response of his stomach to the delectable odor. He yawned, opened his eyes and snapped to full alertness when absolutely nothing looked familiar.

Then Shea stirred beside him, making a sleepy sound as she snuggled against his shoulder. The night came rushing back to him then, the two remaining shows at the club that had had him in perpetual heat when he thought of what had taken place in her dressing room. Afterward they had gone to dinner as usual, but the memory of their own hunger of a different kind was there to read every time gray eyes met blue.

He'd been hesitant when she had shyly invited him to stay at her place, the unpleasant recollection of a dark blue sedan intruding. But he decided if he left his car at the club and they walked, taking a back way he knew, cutting through quiet alleys and between commercial buildings, it would be safe enough.

They'd made love again, in the lovely, carved carriage bed that unexpectedly graced her small bedroom. But he hadn't really looked at the room then. He'd been too intent on showing her that slow, sweet, drawn-out love could make her fly as high as the frenzied coupling in her dressing room. But he looked now, noticing that she had brought the same charm and warmth to this part of her temporary home as she had to the living room.

The colors were bright, the plants were healthy and flourishing, and the room was neat but not obsessively so. What he liked the most, he realized with a little stab of surprise, was the organized clutter of feminine trappings on the small dresser. A couple of bottles of perfume—one, he guessed, the spicy scent she wore that drove him nuts—a hairbrush with a beautifully carved wooden back, a loose lipstick and a pair of gold hoop earrings. It tugged at him in a way he didn't quite understand, a way that made his life without her seem more empty than he had ever realized.

He lay there for a long time, just enjoying the way she cuddled against him. If somewhere buried in his subconscious was the motivation that someday memories of this might be all he had of her, he refused to acknowledge it.

When dawn passed to the full light of morning, he gently slid out of the bed, grabbing his watch off the nightstand. A much more traditional nightstand, he thought with a grin, a grin that was followed by a rush of pleasure at the memory of Shea so embarrassedly trying to tell him that the precautions they'd been using weren't necessary anymore, that she'd stolen some time to go to a doctor.

"You didn't have to do that, songbird," he'd said, touched.

"It's a good thing I did, though," she said, a mischievous grin curving her full mouth delightfully despite her blush. He knew she meant neither one of them had stopped to think about it in her dressing room. "Besides," she'd added in a whisper, "I don't like...anything between us."

It had been at that point, his body rising to the flash point faster than he'd ever thought possible, that he had been introduced to the ornate antique bed she slept in. He looked back at that bed now, at the slender shape still huddled in the tangle of covers, at the silken tangle of dark hair spread more over his pillow than hers.

He felt the familiar tightening of his body at the sight, but the lump that threatened to close off his throat and the stinging of his eyes overpowered even that fierce response. She was so sweet and warm and open, she made him feel alive again, as if there were some point to his existence beyond just surviving from day to day.

He tugged on his clothes and quietly let himself out. He went down the stairs and turned right, letting his nose lead him to the open bakery door. He didn't know what she liked, so he asked for one of just about everything, then waited as the delighted clerk started to fill a large white bag.

He yawned and ran a hand through his tousled hair, thinking that maybe he wouldn't get a haircut after all. Shea said she liked running her fingers through the hair that brushed the top of his shoulders, and the little shivers that activity sent rippling down his spine weren't something he wanted to give up.

He locked his laced fingers behind his head and stretched, wondering at how lazily content he felt. It was a feeling he'd never known before, and he was loving every minute of it. When he went back, he thought, he'd wake her up slowly, planting a row of kisses from the graceful arch of her feet to the graceful arch of her brow, and he'd take at least an hour to do it. He'd kiss every—

He almost heard the thud as reality kicked down the door of his fantasy house of cards. Out of the corner of his eye, he saw, sitting a half a block past the bakery, a dark blue sedan, the mirrors angled so that the car's occupant could watch the front door of the bakery. And the stairway that led to Shea's door.

The sinking sensation in his chest was followed by a surge of anger. He hated being followed. And he hated it even more because, as a cop who'd spent his share of time doing just what that man was doing, he knew that some lurid speculation about what he and Shea were doing was no doubt uppermost in the driver's mind. The beautiful, private moments they shared were being sullied, and he had had enough. After yesterday, they had to know he knew they were tailing him, so he had nothing to lose.

"That's four seventy-nine, sir."

Chance turned back to the clerk and handed her a ten. "The change is yours if there's a back door out of this place."

She looked at him oddly, but apparently decided that a man who had time to stop and buy donuts wasn't a real hazard, and gestured down a narrow hallway.

It took him a few minutes to work his way down the narrow alley. When he peered around the corner, he saw the man in the car slumped down in the front seat, yawning as he kept a careful eye on the outside mirror. Chance reached into the bag he carried, then crept forward soundlessly.

"Mornin'," he drawled as he casually leaned against the driver's door of the car. The man leaped up, banging his knee sharply against the steering wheel. "You look hungry. And tired." He held out a donut generously frosted with chocolate. "Why don't you eat this and go home and go to sleep? Just leave me a number, and I'll call and tell you where I'm going. It'll save us both a lot of aggravation."

"You really are crazy," the man muttered, reaching for the ignition.

"Me?" Chance raised his eyebrows in mock innocence. "I'm just trying to help out a fellow being, that's all. I—Oops."

He smothered a grin at the man's roar of outrage as the dropped donut smeared its way down his shirt to his lap.

"Gosh, I'm sorry. You be sure and send me the bill, okay?"

"I'll send you more than that, hotshot!" The man was still fuming as Chance stepped aside with an elaborate bow, and ushered the car back into the street. He was still grinning as he started back up the stairs to Shea. He might not have accomplished much, but he sure felt better.

Shea was huddled on the sofa, her lower lip caught between her teeth, when he opened the door. For one brief second he saw pain and naked vulnerability there before joy leaped into her eyes even as she sprang to her feet.

"What is it, songbird? What's wrong?"

"I thought . . . you'd gone."

He dropped the bag onto the table and pulled her into his arms. "Without even saying goodbye?"

"I didn't know...I thought..." She shivered slightly. "I don't have much experience at this."

He hugged her fiercely. "Neither do I, love. I should have waited, or left you a note or something. I'm sorry. I guess I've been alone too damned long."

She lifted her head to look at him. "Then I guess we'll just have to keep practicing, won't we?"

He smiled at her tremulous tone. "I guess we will. But I warn you, it may take a long time to get it right."

"Oh, I hope so," she whispered, turning her head to press a soft kiss in the hollow of his throat.

"You keep that up, and you'll miss out on breakfast," he warned.

"Breakfast?"

Resolutely he broke away from her to pick up the bag. "I couldn't resist," he said sheepishly. "I don't know how you sleep through that smell in the mornings."

"Easy, once you get used to it," she said, laughing softly as he spread out on the napkins every possible kind of pastry she could imagine, "although I have had some strange dreams about singing to an audience of apple fritters."

He echoed her laugh. "A shrink could have a field day with that one, songbird."

She grinned as she reached for one of the mentioned fritters. "Not anymore. My dreams have definitely improved lately. Much more...exciting."

"Oh?"

The one syllable came in a husky tone that made her want to forget all about breakfast and see if she could lure him right back to bed with her.

"Yes. And now when I wake up, I find out they're not just dreams anymore."

She didn't finish the apple fritter until much, much later.

They arrived back at the club, for Shea to go inside and for him to pick up the car—he had the BMW, needing the radio in it to keep in touch now that he had to be careful about going to the station—and found Pete Escobar leaning on the fender.

"Nice welcoming committee," Chance muttered as they crossed the parking lot. "All it needs is the dynamic duo."

Shea laughed. "They're off running errands, I imagine. Paul keeps them pretty busy. Seems like one or the other of them is always running to the bank or somewhere." She wrinkled her nose in a way that made something warm and comfortable begin to glow inside him. "The other one is always glued to me, it seems."

"Not always," Chance said with an exaggerated leer.

"Hush," she said with a stifled giggle. "I meant in the club and you know it."

They arrived at the car, and Chance looked pointedly at the fender Escobar was leaning on.

"You scratch it, you paint it."

Escobar glared at him but straightened up. Then he zeroed in on Shea.

"Your brother is not a happy man," he said sternly.

"*Buenos días,* Pedro," she said sweetly.

"Pete!" Escobar snapped, then spoke sharply in Spanish, the words too rapid for Chance to understand.

"I have told my brother," Shea answered coolly in English, "that he'd better back off. And that goes for you, too, old friend or not."

Escobar spat out a curse Chance had heard before, the last time Quisto had slammed his finger in a file cabinet drawer.

"Testy in the morning, isn't he?" Chance observed mildly to no one in particular. Shea giggled.

Escobar whirled on him, fury flashing in chocolate brown eyes. The book on him was accurate, then, Chance thought. It didn't take much to set off his volatile temper. More words came, low and hissing. Then the angry man turned back to Shea.

"Your brother is waiting for you. Go inside."

Shea drew herself up, sudden anger radiating from her. "I don't take orders from you, or my brother, Pedro. And I will not stand here and listen to your foul mouth any longer. I didn't like it when you were a teenager, and I like it even less now that you're supposedly man enough to control your temper."

Her gibe hit home, and Escobar straightened up stiffly. "If you please," he said with icy formality, "your brother would like to see you in his office."

"Much better. Please tell him I'll be there in just a minute."

Without a word Escobar turned on his heel and stalked off, rage evident in every step. Shea turned to look up at Chance.

"I'm sorry. He's known my brother since they were children, and sometimes he gets this way."

Chance only smiled. "Remind me not to ever get on your bad side."

"You couldn't," she said earnestly.

Chance felt the trap clamp shut tighter, tearing at already lacerated emotions. *Oh, I could, songbird. I will. I just hope to God you love me enough to forgive me.*

"Besides," she was saying, her expression a blend of shyness and teasing that he found irresistible, "I seem to remember you saying last night that I didn't have a bad side."

"Yes, I did, didn't I?"

He lifted his hands to cup her face, tilting it back for his kiss. It was warm and sweet and gentle, with nothing of passion and all of the love he'd come to feel for this woman who sang his soul. When at last he lifted his head and looked into her eyes, he knew that she had understood. The gray depths were full of an answering love and more than a touch of wonder.

"What did you mean, you told your brother to back off?" he asked after a long moment. "Has he been giving you a hard time?"

"No, not really."

Color tinged her cheeks, and he wondered why on earth he had ever thought her capable of lying about anything.

"You're a lousy fibber, songbird," he said softly. "He's been on you about me, hasn't he?"

"Like I told you, Paul just gets...too protective sometimes."

"And he wants to protect you from me," Chance said. It wasn't a question.

"He just worries, that's all. It's not you, personally."

It should be, Chance thought bitterly. God, it should be. He'd known in the moment he'd seen the pain in her eyes when she'd thought he'd left without a word that he had the power to hurt her terribly. And if he did his job, that's exactly what he'd end up doing. But if he didn't do his job, if he pulled out, the operation would still go on, with Eaton in charge and out for her blood, as well as de Cortez's. She'd be left in the middle, without him to at least try to keep her safe. And he'd have to disappear from her life, or tell her what he was, and the result would be the same anyway. The jaws of the trap were relentless, crushing, and the more he thrashed around trying to find the way out, the more damage it did.

"Chance, what is it? My God, what's wrong? You look ill."

"I . . . I'm fine. Too many donuts, I guess."

"Do you want to come in—"

"No. Really. I'm okay. I'll see you tonight, okay?"

There was no sign of a tail, but Chance took a round-about route anyway. He looked for anything, knowing that since they knew he'd made them, if they were going to stay on him they would at least change cars. At last, satisfied that if they were still tailing him they were using a multiple car tail so complex he wouldn't be able to spot it anyway, he parked the BMW in the lot of a small restaurant a few blocks from the station.

He sat there for a while, sipping a cup of coffee, looking once more through the files that were always with him except when he was with Shea. Thank God she had absolutely no snooping tendencies, he thought. If she found this pile in his apartment, it would all be over.

He was sick of reading it. He'd read it so many times he was sure not much of it penetrated anymore. He could practically quote each line of the surveillance log line for line. It soured his stomach, which didn't help the coffee any. Not to mention that he really had gotten carried away with those damned donuts.

But it had been worth it, he thought, especially when Shea had insisted on licking his sticky fingers. He, of course, then had to return the favor, but he hadn't stopped at her fingers. He hadn't stopped until she was crying out in shocked pleasure, her hips bucking in his hands as she lifted herself for his mouth.

"Whatever you're thinking, man, judging from that smile, it's rated for adults only."

Quisto slid into the booth across from him, grinning widely.

"You're late," Chance said, ignoring the gibe.

"Hey, I just got your message." He chuckled. "One of those fine ladies from the Del Mar Club was introducing me to the intricacies of chess last night."

"Chess?"

"A new version. Each captured piece has a . . . special meaning. And the penalty for losing is—" he rolled his eyes expressively "—amazing."

"So that's why your mind's in the gutter this morning."

Quisto grinned, undaunted. "Nope. That's why I recognized where your mind was. Aren't you eating?"

Chance's stomach gave a warning lurch. "No."

"Well, I'm starved."

When the waitress had taken his huge breakfast order, Quisto glanced out the window to where the BMW was parked.

"Any sign of your caboose today?"

"No." A smiled tugged at the corners of his mouth. "At least, not anymore."

"Anymore?"

Chance told him of this morning's encounter. Quisto laughed uproariously.

"I'll bet he about went through the roof when you snuck up on him!"

"I think he was more upset about the chocolate."

"Damn, I would have loved to have seen his face! Speaking of which, I suppose it was no one you knew."

"No . . ."

"No, what?"

"Nothing. Nothing I can hang a name on, anyway."

"Come on, give. I know that clever little mind of yours is working on something."

Chance shrugged. "He just didn't strike me as the kind of guy de Cortez would have working for him. He was too..." He shrugged again, unable to find a word that fit. "Told you it was nothing concrete. Just a feeling, a gut-level reaction."

"Long before I became your partner, my friend, I heard about your gut-level reactions. Don't shine it on."

"Maybe."

His breakfast arrived, and Quisto pulled some folded papers out of his pocket as he began to eat.

"Here are those reports you ordered. And I should have those names from the flight records you wanted by the end of the week. I hope you appreciate the sacrifice I'm going to have to make to pay for them."

"Some sacrifice. As I recall, she's tall, blond, built and just silly enough to believe all those lines you throw around."

"I'm wounded, my friend." Quisto's try at an expression of hurt failed completely. "Anyway, this came for you, too." He handed over a small stack of papers. "Pretty rotten, about her father. But at least they got two of them."

"But not the triggerman."

Quisto shrugged. "Sometimes that's the way it goes. She's had it rough, hasn't she? First her father murdered, then her mother committing suicide. That report's in there, too, by the way. Take a look at the note. It's kind of odd."

Chance dug out the report, forcing himself to put out of his mind that this cold, factual report was about the woman who had been Shea's mother. They'd found her, it said, in the bedroom of the house where she'd lived with Shea's father. A neighbor, coming over to chat, had become concerned when she found the door open but no sign of Elena Austin.

There was a final line that indicated that next of kin, daughter Shea Austin of Zephyr Cove, Nevada, had been notified by local authorities. He wondered with a qualm how it had been done. He'd always hated death notifications and knew that he'd probably been a less-than-kind bearer of bad news on occasion. He hoped that whoever had told Shea had had more compassion than the average cop sent on a distasteful assignment.

He flipped the page and found a copy of the note Quisto had referred to. It *was* odd, he thought. The wording was odd, and it appeared to be on a torn scrap of paper.

"Lab report says they figure she wrote it after she took the pills," Quisto said. "That's why it's kind of incoherent and fades out at the end."

Chance nodded, forehead creasing as he studied the note. "I don't get it," he said after a minute. "'I can't bear the guilt. It was my fault, just as the *demonio* is my fault.'" He looked at Quisto.

"It means 'demon.'" He shrugged. "Didn't make any sense to me, either. There's no record that she'd been having any psychiatric problems, hadn't seen a doctor or anything." He looked at Chance curiously. "Shea hasn't said anything?"

"Just that her mother died a few months ago."

"Any more on de Cortez?"

"He tries to order her around. And he didn't get along with her father. They rarely heard from him between the time he left home and her father's death."

Chance's voice had gone flat, expressionless. Quisto's look softened, went warm with sympathy. "I'm sorry, Chance."

"Not your fault."

"I don't envy you, my friend. You've picked a very rough path to follow."

"You don't know the half of it, partner."

"And I hope I never do. This is tearing you apart, buddy."

Chance stared at the papers on the table without seeing them. "I know," he whispered finally.

"You want to bail? I'll take it. I can keep Eaton in line."

"It won't make any difference, not in the long run. I'd rather be there. Just in case."

"You think she might get caught in the cross fire?"

"Eaton still thinks she knows."

"Eaton's an idiot."

Chance's head came up, a new warmth in his eyes. "Thanks."

"Sure. So you're still in?"

Chance nodded.

"Okay. I'll tell the lieutenant."

"He . . . knows?"

"I don't know how much," Quisto said, "but it wouldn't take a genius to figure out something's going on. Especially somebody who's known you before."

Chance hesitated a moment before asking softly, "Have I changed that much?"

"Night and day, partner. I just hope . . ."

"I know. So do I."

Chance sat silently for a while as Quisto finished his meal. Then, with sudden decisiveness, he gathered up his files, added the new items Quisto had brought and slapped them shut. His partner looked at him curiously.

"I think," Chance said, "it's time for me to go face-to-face with the headliner in this little game."

Quisto stared, his last forkful of eggs halfway to his mouth. Slowly he set it down.

"You want to explain that? Didn't we just go high and to the right and threaten Eaton with dire bodily harm over the same thing?"

"Relax. I didn't mean like that."

"How did you mean it?"

"He's been riding Shea pretty hard about me. I'm just going to be legitimately angry about it." Because I am, he thought sourly.

"Why?"

"Because I want to see him close up. Listen to him, see how he moves, see if I can find a clue to what he's up to by how he reacts."

"I meant why has he been on Shea?"

Chance's mouth quirked. "She wouldn't say, but from a little meeting we had with Escobar this morning in which the words 'damned gringo' popped up a couple of times, I would guess it's my sad lack of your noble Latin heritage."

Quisto grinned. "Can't blame him for that."

"So adopt me."

"Not me. Check with my mother. She'd take you in a Cuban minute."

"I know. She told me she'd trade you for me any day."

Quisto took a swipe at him as Chance got up from the table, glanced out the window, then back at his partner.

"Watch my back when I leave, okay?"

Quisto nodded. "I hope they've quit tailing you. I need another cup of coffee, not a chase at this hour."

Chance grinned at him, buoyed by the thought of finally confronting the man who'd been the center of this. When he put the files back in their hiding place beneath the carpet in the trunk of the BMW, he glanced around quickly. Nothing.

When he got to the club, there was a truck making a delivery through one of the side doors, so he followed a tray of bread inside. He smiled when he heard the music; his grin widened when he heard the words in an impatient male voice.

"Jeez, Shea! How many times are we going to do this?"

"Only till it's right," she answered sweetly, to a chorus of groans.

"The way we're going, we'll be here all day. If we—" Eric stopped, looking across the empty room from the stage. "Don't look now, guys, but we may get a break after all."

Puzzled, Shea turned to see what Eric was talking about. When she saw Chance, she blushed furiously.

"What are you doing here?" she asked a little breathlessly when he got there. "You said you had things to do today."

"I do. I just added seeing your brother to the list, that's all."

"Paul? Why?" Distress widened her eyes suddenly. "Oh, no, not because of what I said? Chance, no, really, it hasn't been that bad—"

"Hush, songbird. I just think it's time he and I came to an understanding, that's all. Is he here?"

She tried to protest, but Eric answered helpfully, "He's in the office, down the hall and up the stairs."

"Eric!"

"He's right, Shea. Paul's been on your case something fierce." A glint of admiration shone in eyes half-hidden by a mop of shaggy hair. "And if your man here's got the guts to call him on it, then I'm all for it."

"Thanks," Chance said with a nod. Shea's eyes were on him, still troubled, and he grinned crookedly at her. "Easy, songbird. I'm just going to talk to him, not beat him up. I'll be back in a minute."

He couldn't deny the adrenaline rush that shot through him as he went up the stairs. The man had existed only on paper, only in distant glimpses and the words of his sister for weeks now. At last he was going to see the reality. He stopped at the door at the top of the stairs, schooling himself to the role of angry...angry what? Boyfriend? Suitor? Lover?

All of them, he decided firmly and rapped on the door. The murmur of voices he'd heard but had been unable to make out stopped abruptly. The door swung open, and without waiting for an invitation, Chance took one long step inside.

Immediately, the man who had opened the door and his near twin closed in on him. He recognized the bookends and grinned at them.

"Ah, together again at last, I see."

"You son of a—"

"—wonderfully charming lady who hates it when I bruise people. But if you insist..."

"Leave us. Both of you."

The command snapped from across the room, and was obeyed instantly. One bookend tightened his grip on the briefcase he'd never let go of, and the other led the way. Whatever Paul de Cortez was, he had those two apes under his thumb. Holding the door for the two with exaggerated politeness, Chance bowed them out. Then he closed the door and turned to face the man he'd never met. And found the coldest pair of eyes he'd ever seen.

The impression was gone as quickly as it had registered, replaced by a bland, unreadable mask. But Chance knew he'd seen it, the chill that was as cold as death. Indeed, he'd seen dead eyes with more warmth than had been in that reptilian glance.

"Mr. Buckner, I presume?"

The words were polite, but the voice held a wealth of leashed anger and power.

"Of course," Chance agreed easily. "But then I'm sure you already know that."

Something flickered in the near-black eyes. "Yes. I do. Shall I tell you what else I know?"

"Certainly. I'm ready to be impressed."

Chance felt reasonably secure. When he'd begun undercover work, his connections with the department had been buried so deep it would take a miracle to uncover them. And even with all his power and wealth, Paul de Cortez couldn't order up one of those.

"You are thirty years old. You do occasional work for your landlord, Peter Hagan, of PLH, Incorporated. Beyond that, you do nothing, preferring to live off the healthy insurance money left to you by the death of your wife four years ago."

It was the official line, the slightly distorted facts that had been planted for anyone who bothered to look. Just enough truth to make it believable, just enough left out to protect his cover. Chance had never liked the bit about the insurance, but he knew it worked.

"In short," de Cortez was saying coldly, "hardly the kind of man I would approve of for my sister."

Chance was unmoved by the thinly veiled insult. "Neither your sister nor I need or want your approval," he returned, his voice equally cool. "The only thing I want from you is to get off her back. Whatever choices she makes, whatever she does, has nothing to do with you."

"She is my sister. That means nothing to your kind, but we take our family responsibilities seriously."

"She's her own woman," Chance said, "and the sooner you realize that, the better."

"Are you threatening me?" He was incredulous.

"Let's call it a promise. You have a problem with me, you bring it to me, not her." On a hunch, he decided on a pointed jab. "Unless, of course, you prefer to hide behind a woman."

Ah, Chance thought as de Cortez came up out of his chair, the chink in the armor. That misguided machismo would bring him down, someday. A man with too much pride always made a mistake in the long run, somewhere.

"Get out," de Cortez spat.

"Sure," Chance said equably. "Just one more thing. You say one more thing to her, and I'll have the whole town buzzing about how the great Paul de Cortez yells at his sister because he's afraid to take on a 'damned gringo' man to man. And you sic those two matched hounds of yours on me, and I'll do the same thing. It's either you and me, or nothing." He turned and went to the door. De Cortez was furious, he could see it his face.

"You just let me know," Chance tossed over his shoulder, then closed the door behind him.

Chance half expected a rain of gunfire to splinter the door, but it didn't happen. Then he heard a resounding crash from the office he'd just left, and he couldn't help grinning. He'd prodded the rattler in his cage, giving him one more thing to think about. It might be the one thing too many that made him trip up.

It had gone pretty well, he decided, considering he hadn't really thought it out beforehand. When he hit the bottom of the stairs and again heard Shea's voice, he knew why it had—he'd meant every word of it.

She ran to him when he came out of the hallway, her eyes searching his face.

"Easy," he said, laughing. "What were you expecting? Mayhem?"

"I... He has a horrible temper, you know. I was worried."

"Don't be. I think we understand each other now."

She let out a sigh of relief. "In that case, I'm glad."

He leaned over and kissed the pert tip of her nose. "About what?"

"That you... wanted there to be an understanding."

Shea ducked her head, afraid that he would recognize the feeling behind her words. She knew she was clinging to every precious sign that this was more to him than just a casual affair, every hint that there was a future for them. She was trying desperately not to assume too much, but it was very hard when she was so full of emotions she'd never felt before. She hadn't known it was possible for her to feel this way about someone, was almost frightened at how quickly this complex, sometimes elusive, man had become the most important thing in her life.

"I want there to be a lot more than that," he said softly, tilting her head back with a gentle finger under her chin, and she blushed at how accurately he'd read her.

"I'm glad," she said finally, simply, thinking it the greatest understatement in history. "You'll be here to-night?"

"Of course." He looked suddenly wary. "You're not going to wear that red dress again, are you?"

She laughed. "Why?"

"Because I don't think I can stand it." Then his mouth twisted ruefully. "Hell, I can't stand it anyway."

She giggled. "Then sit."

"Oh, feeling cute, are we? " he growled. "Maybe a little midnight swim is in order."

"Only if you're there." Her eyes were smoky with promise, telling him exactly what kind of swim she had in mind. His body clenched suddenly, fiercely.

"That," he said huskily, "is an idea with great potential."

He was still—somewhat painfully—dwelling on that potential when he arrived home, still sans his erstwhile satellite. He was halfway up the stairs when he remembered the files. He'd wanted to go over what Quisto had brought, in detail.

I wonder, he thought as he spread everything out on a table, if this is what a schizophrenic feels like. Like two different people, each one functioning on his own level, and only running into trouble when the two collided. When he was with Shea, when the case was out of his mind, he was one person, and times like now, when the case was occupying most of his mind—minus the part that seemed permanently labeled with her name—he was another. But when the two overlapped, he wasn't sure who he was anymore. All he knew was that he'd never felt a pain like this tearing, trapped agony, and he didn't know how much longer he could endure it.

He made himself concentrate, reading the surveillance log yet again and the reports forwarded by his friend in Miami. Then the backgrounds compiled by Metro-Dade police, then the documentation on de Cortez's activities there. Last, he once more read the reports on Sean Austin's brutal murder, and Elena Austin's suicide nearly twelve years later. He went over it, over it, and over it again, until his eyes were bleary and his mind screamed in protest.

He finally yielded to the weariness long enough to take a shower and change clothes. Then he fixed a sandwich, popped a soda and sat down again. And began again. Damn, it was here somewhere, he could just feel it. His mind started to drift, back to the scene in de Cortez's office. With a grin he remembered the bookends' hasty departure, one of them clutching that briefcase as if it had held pure gold.

Wearily he yanked his mind back to the matter at hand. They'd spent hundreds of hours, watching and waiting, for nothing. Wouldn't it just be a joke, he thought grimly, if de Cortez had truly decided to go straight? If the big dealer had truly left the business? If the shipment they were expecting, waiting to catch him with, never came? If they kept running around in circles while de Cortez laughed his head off?

Then an image of cold, dead eyes formed in his head, and he knew different. The man hadn't changed. His experience in Miami had just made him more cautious. And why should he rush? In the best estimates of Metro-Dade, he'd left the Sunshine State with over two hundred million dollars, leaving behind that much and more in confiscated property, cash and cocaine that could never be traced to him.

He reached for the log again, even knowing it would tell him nothing new. That was what was the most frustrating—this damned feeling that wouldn't go away, that the answer was staring him right in the face and he couldn't see it.

The jangle of the phone startled him. He went to it quickly, hoping it might be Shea in spite of knowing she would be busy getting ready for the night's shows.

"Chance?"

"Yeah." Definitely not Shea.

"Hey, it's Jeff. Listen, I don't know if it means anything, but we just got something that might be a break."

Chance went very still. "What?"

"I'm not sure, really. Just something…different. On one of the phone taps. I tried to find Romero, but I couldn't track him down. I know you're kind of in limbo, but…do you want to come down and hear it?"

"Ten minutes."

He barely remembered to scoop up the clutter on the table and stuff it into the desk before he raced down the stairs.

Chapter 10

Shea ran her fingers over the keyboard, searching for the right combination of notes. She tried another riff, but she didn't like that, either. She was finding it hard to concentrate.

The others, except for Eric, who sat on the edge of the stage adjusting his guitar, had gone out for an early dinner before the first set. She wasn't the least bit hungry. Still running on donuts, she said to herself with a little laugh.

"He's been good for you, hasn't he?"

She turned to find Eric watching her intently. "Is it so obvious?" she asked with good humor.

"You've changed since you first got here. You were so quiet all the time. Like you were really sad about something."

"I was." She smiled softly. "And you're right. He is good for me."

"I know. You were always beautiful, but now you're ... glowing."

"Why, Eric! Are you trying to flatter me?"

"I save the flattery for people who need it. You don't."

"No." She blushed. "I get enough of it already."

"Good." Eric grinned. "I like a man who's got sense enough to know when he's got a good thing."

"And I like a handsome, talented man who isn't afraid to be a friend."

"Now who's flattering who?"

"No flattery, just truth."

Eric looked embarrassed but pleased. "He's crazy about you, Shea. Anybody can see it."

"I hope so."

She tried not to think about the things she still didn't know about Chance, the secrets he still held inside himself. She felt as if she were out of control, hurtling toward some unknown destiny, a destiny he somehow held in his hands. It was a strange, unsettling feeling, and when it crept in on her like this, it made her more than a little uneasy.

"Sometimes it's scary, it got so strong so fast," she said softly.

"Hey, sounds like a song. 'So strong, so fast,'" he intoned soulfully.

"Just tune the guitar," she said with a laugh, turning back to the keyboard, shaking off the mood.

"All right, all right. Shea?"

She looked back over her shoulder. As if he had sensed her doubts, Eric said softly, "If anything goes wrong, you know you've got a friend, don't you?"

She gave him a warm smile. "Yes. Yes, I do."

And this time, when she turned back to the keyboard, she found the notes she wanted.

"I know it doesn't sound like much—"

"No. You're right. It's out of sync."

"That's what I thought. He's never said anything like that before."

Chance reached for the rewind button on the recorder, hit it, then hit the play button. After a moment, the words came again, in de Cortez's voice.

"Yes, everything is ready, everyone will be here. It will be a very big day. Most profitable for everyone."

That was it, one little variation in one phone call among all the phone calls they'd been listening to for weeks. But it was the first, and so far the only, time de Cortez had ever mentioned money. And this meant, apparently, big money. Chance knew what it would take for de Cortez to consider something "profitable."

"Do we know where the call came in from?"

"Local. I got the number, but I haven't called the phone company to back-trace it yet."

"Don't. One of his pet tricks in Miami was to have plants in the local phone company operations. That's how he knew the feds were onto him there, and he got out before they could pin anything on him."

"Is there anything special coming up at the club that he could be talking about?"

Chance quit staring at the recorder and shifted his gaze to the young detective who had been in the van the first day he'd seen Shea. When he didn't answer right away, the young man shifted uncomfortably.

"Look, I didn't mean anything. I just...that agent keeps talking...and you are working the sister, aren't you? I thought you might know."

It wasn't his fault, Chance told himself. If it was anybody's, it was Eaton's. "It's all right." He took a deep breath. "I don't know of anything. But when you find Detective Romero, make sure he hears this, okay?"

Jeff nodded, relieved.

"And if you happen *not* to see Eaton," he added pointedly, "it wouldn't break my heart."

Jeff grinned. "I'll manage to miss him."

"Thanks."

He left the office and was on his way back to the car when he ran into Lieutenant Morgan.

"No tail today?"

Chance shook his head. "They know I made them. I think they may have given up."

"Keep up the precautions for a while longer anyway."

"Right." He hesitated. "I...saw de Cortez this afternoon."

Morgan's expression told him Quisto had not let anything slip about his confrontation. The lieutenant looked startled but not angry, so Chance quickly gave him an edited version.

"What's your estimation?"

"I'm more sure than ever that he's just biding his time." And that it's in front of my nose if I could only see it, he added in silent frustration. The nagging feeling that there was something obvious he was missing wouldn't go away.

Morgan nodded. "Stay with it." He looked at Chance consideringly. "Are you all right?"

Chance stiffened. "Fine."

"Take it easy. It's your friend asking, not your boss."

"In that case," Chance said dryly, "I'm screwed up."

"Irreversibly?"

"Depends."

"On?"

"Lots of things. Timing. Trust. Faith."

Morgan nodded slowly. "Anything I can do?"

"Yeah. Pull me out."

"I can't, Chance. You know that. You're our best shot at the inside."

"I know. I was kidding. I think."

Chance opened his mouth to tell Morgan about the taped conversation, then shut it again. If he told the lieutenant, the lieutenant would be obligated to tell Eaton, and that was something Chance definitely did not want to happen. Not yet, anyway, not until they determined if it really meant anything. Eaton was too damned ready to go off half-cocked, and this tiny clue might be the last little bit of pressure on the trigger. Eaton was a fool, and Chance wanted him under control as long as possible.

What the hell did it mean? he wondered as he drove to the club. Or did it even mean anything? And what day was he talking about? Shea would have mentioned it if anything special had been on at the club, wouldn't she? He supposed he could ask—

No, damn it! He wasn't going to pump one more bit of information out of her. She wasn't de Cortez's sister anymore, she was his songbird, and he wasn't going to do it.

The doorman, who usually met him with a nod of recognition, tonight met him with a wide-eyed look of awe.

"Something wrong, Danny?"

"No, sir," the man said hastily. His eyes darted warily around, then back to Chance. "I just heard you had it out with the boss," he whispered. "Man, that took guts. He's a little—" he made a descriptive circular motion with a finger pointed at his head "—you know?"

"He tell you not to let me in?"

"Oh, no, nothing like that."

Of course not. He couldn't risk any scrutiny, not with the "big day" coming up. Whatever it was. A shipment? A November snowfall in Marina del Mar? His eyes narrowed suddenly as he looked at the doorman.

"Anything coming up here soon, Danny? I heard somebody talking about something special going on at a new club in town, but I didn't hear where. Here, maybe?"

The man's forehead creased. "No, not that I know about, man. Don't need special things, not with Miss Shea packing them in like this."

Interesting, Chance thought as he found a table up front, though not necessarily conclusive. But after the scene in de Cortez's office, he'd half expected to be persona non grata here. That he wasn't might mean nothing. Or it might mean that de Cortez just had too much on his plate right now to deal with his little sister's lover. It might mean that the one little inconsistent note in the one little conversation was the break they'd been staying up nights for.

He saw Eric and the others take the stage, and then Shea. The sight of her hit him like a kick to the solar plexus. She hadn't worn the red dress, but he was at a point where it didn't matter much anymore. He was convinced if she came out in a gunnysack it would be just the same.

Not, he thought wryly, that what she was wearing could in any way be classified as a gunnysack. It was a clinging knit jumpsuit, her usual red, with a six-inch-wide white band at the neckline that was pulled down off her slender shoulders, leaving them bare and tempting. The contrast of the long sleeves that came from beneath the wide band made her shoulders seem even more naked, and Chance thought he was going to be lucky to make it through the evening without a replay of last night's episode in her dressing room.

Just the thought made his body heat as if struck by a torch. He'd never been so out of control, never been so crazy. He'd taken her standing up, backed against the wall, still completely dressed, for God's sake. And he'd loved it. And from every sign, so had she. Innocent little Shea had loved it.

He heard the usual talk flowing around him in the moments before she started to sing. Envious or admiring comments from the women; appreciative, hungry, even lewd ones from the men. He wanted to throttle them all. She was his, and he didn't want any of them leering at her, thinking about her. He was glad she didn't like this, because for damned sure he didn't. He'd make sure she didn't do it again, ever.

Unless she wanted to, he amended silently. If she really wanted to, or needed to, to try out new material as she'd said, he supposed he could live with it. He just wouldn't like it much.

It didn't hit him until the first sweet, crystal notes of her song began to rise. When it did, it was more of a blow than the first sight of her had been. He'd been speculating about the future as if they had one, together. He'd let himself dream, and decorated his foolish dream with her beautiful presence. He'd let himself fall into the trap of thinking beyond the moment, when he knew that moment was all they really had.

Oh, God, Shea!

For a moment he thought he'd groaned it out loud. He sat there, the soaring sound of her voice washing over him, wanting to scream out his anger and frustration. Why, damn it? Why now? Why did he have to meet her now, like this, why was she related to that slime, why was he a cop? He entertained these and a million other whys that clawed away at his guts like the talons of some merciless bird of prey.

He realized he was shaking, so badly he had to clench his fists in an effort to stop. He felt as if everything were closing in on him, as if he were caught in some lifeless desert gully with a flash flood bearing down on him, carrying boulders big enough to crush him with ease.

It was a feeling so strong he hadn't quite shaken it by the time the last set was over, the accolades of the crowd had rained down on Shea, and he'd met her in the hall.

"You didn't come back between sets," she said, looking at him a little oddly.

"I didn't dare. It would have been a replay of last night in there."

She stopped just inside the door out of the hallway into the narrow alley to the parking lot.

"Would that have been . . . so bad?"

"Damn it, Shea, don't say things like that." He shoved open the door and tugged her outside. "You don't know what it does to me."

"I don't?"

He grabbed her then, pulling her hard against him. His hands slid down her back to her slim hips, pressing her close.

"That's what it does to me," he said harshly, knowing she had to feel him against her stomach. "It makes me want you right here, right now, and to hell with the world."

He didn't wait for an answer, he just took her arm and headed out of the temptingly empty alley.

He wished the BMW wasn't an automatic. He could have used the release of slamming the car through the gears. It was hard to vent your emotions when the car shifted smoothly of its own volition, when it wanted to, when all you wanted was to red-line it before giving it the next gear and jamming it to the floor again.

By the time the iron gates of Hagan's home swung open, Shea knew something was very, very wrong. Chance was tense like a tightly strung wire in the seconds before it snapped. He'd barely spoken on the drive here, just as he'd barely spoken through the light meal they'd had at a small Italian restaurant that invited quiet confidences. After a while she had subsided into silence herself, tired of trying to carry the evening alone.

She wondered what on earth had happened since this morning. Something obviously had. She hadn't seen or talked to him, so it couldn't be anything she'd said or done. At least she kept telling herself that. He was so wound up, it could be anything. When she asked, all she got was a short, sharp "nothing," and a continuation of the silence.

When he opened the door for her, his grip on her elbow as he helped her out of the car was like a vise. She winced and pulled away.

"I think," she said as she rubbed at her arm, "you're the one who needs the midnight swim."

He stared at her, then looked down at the hand that had clamped on her arm, as if he'd never seen it before. Contrition flooded his face.

"God, Shea, I'm sorry. I didn't realize."

"So I gathered. Want to tell me what's bothering you?"

Yes, his mind screamed. Yes, I want to tell you. I want to tell you everything, make you understand, and beg you to forgive me. But I can't, because of my damned job, and because I can't handle what I know I'll see in your eyes.

"Chance," she whispered, staring in shock at the bleakness that had taken over his eyes. "What is it, love?"

That last word, the endearment given so easily, so sweetly, so honestly, in spite of all the things he'd kept from her, broke him. He whirled away from her, stumbling over to one of the chairs that sat beside the pool. He sank down into it, the shaking he thought he'd beaten off returning full force.

Then she was there, kneeling beside the chair, reaching for him. She didn't speak, didn't push for an answer, just held his hands tightly with her own. After a long moment he spoke, his voice so low she had to strain to hear him.

"Did you ever...have to do something...that made you hate yourself?"

She sat back on her heels, shaken by the barely controlled intensity in the harsh words. Twice she tried to answer, but knew the words were wrong, were only trite reassurances. At last she said simply, "No. I've had to do things I've hated, but never anything that made me hate myself."

"No. No, you wouldn't, would you? You'd find another way. Why can't I?"

"Chance?"

She whispered it, frightened by the tremors she felt rippling through him. Then she felt him go rigid, the tendons in his hands standing out beneath her fingers. She could feel him straining, could see the look on his face as he drew on some inner strength to steady himself.

When at last he looked at her again, when he saw the fear, the concern in her eyes, remorse filled him.

"Oh, Shea, I'm sorry." He tugged on her hands and pulled her up onto his lap. "I scared you, didn't I? That's the last thing I wanted to do."

She lifted a hand to run her fingers along his cheek to the side of his face, cupping it as she looked at him worriedly. "What is it? What is it you have to do?"

"Shh," he soothed, "it's all right. Don't worry about it, songbird. I'll work it out."

"But I—"

"I know you want to help. I wish . . . I wish you could. Just don't give up on me, okay?"

"Never," she said fervently, hugging him.

God, let her mean it, he prayed. When it all comes apart, let her remember that and hang on to it.

"Shea?" he said after a moment.

"What?"

"How about that swim?"

"Now?"

"I turned the heater back on."

"I . . . It's not that."

"Going shy on me, songbird? Don't like the idea of skinny-dipping?"

He could see her blush even in the shadowy lights of the pool. "I've never done anything like that."

He chuckled. "I don't make a habit of it myself." A smile, half teasing, half wicked, curved his lips. "But then, I've done a lot of things with you I've never done before."

"Oh?" It came out a little thickly because of the sudden flare of heat that blazed along her nerves. "Like what?"

He leaned over and whispered into her ear, husky, sexy words that called up even sexier memories, intimate details of the private moments they'd spent discovering how to please each other. Her face was as hot as he was when he finished.

"Maybe I do need that swim," she said shakily.

"Maybe we both do."

He was wondering how this had managed to backfire on him. He'd meant to tease her, and wound up so hot and hard and aching himself that he didn't think he could stand it much longer.

She slid off his lap, and his eyes cut sharply to her face. Was she moving that way, sliding her deliciously rounded bottom over his rigid flesh, on purpose? It didn't matter, the result was the same—a fiery burst of need that ripped through him, clawing his control into shreds. He stood up as she did, his eyes fastened on her face, flicking only briefly to the hollow of her throat where her pulse beat wildly.

She kicked off her high-heeled sandals, her tongue creeping nervously out to moisten her lips. Chance groaned. He'd gone into great detail on that tongue in his whispered discourse, and he was paying the penalty now in the undulating waves of hot compulsion that gripped him.

She reached up and tugged at the off-the-shoulder neckline of the knit jumpsuit, baring the swell of the top of one breast. Chance felt himself unraveling much too fast, and knew he had to slow himself down. With a haste hampered by fingers made clumsy by the throbbing of his body, he tore at his shirt, sending buttons flying.

He sensed rather than saw her move, sliding the sleeves of the jumpsuit down her slender arms. He didn't dare look at her. The sight of her undressing in the moonlight would be the end of what little command he had of himself. He shed his slacks, briefs and shoes in one swift movement, paying no heed to the protest of his aroused body as he dragged the clothing off roughly.

Still avoiding the tempting sight of her, he straightened for a moment as he tossed the garments aside. He was incredibly aware that she had stopped and was looking at him; he felt her gaze as if it were a physical caress on his distended flesh.

The last fragile piece of his control snapped, and he knew he had to grab her now, this instant, or take drastic action to cool himself down. He'd already frightened her tonight, he didn't want to add to it by taking her when he was so out of control. With a throttled groan, he turned and dove into the pool.

Shea watched him go, watched the smooth arc of his lean, muscled body as it cut the water cleanly. She shivered a little, not from cold, but from the undeniable knowledge she had just gained: it happened for him as swiftly as it did for her. His utterly male, totally aroused body had been silvered by moonlight, and the most beautiful thing she'd ever seen.

Hurriedly she tugged the knit jumpsuit down over her hips and kicked free of it. Chance surfaced in time to see her poised there for a split second, the strapless red teddy she wore shimmering. Then she peeled off the thin swath of silk, transforming herself into an ethereal vision of moonlit femininity.

Her hair flowed over her naked shoulders, stopping just above the fullness of breasts that gleamed like some perfect, polished marble in the silver light. The outline of her body was only suggested in the almost ghostly glow, discernible more by shadow and its absence than any true light. Chance swallowed heavily, nearly forgetting to swim as she plunged into the glistening water.

Water that Chance had discovered had only a minimal effect on him. And that had been lost the moment he'd looked up and seen her, first in that clinging silky red thing, and then, incredibly, in nothing at all.

He hadn't really thought she'd do it. He'd never forgotten the night when she'd told him how different she was from most people's perception of her. He knew she was intrinsically shy, and this boldness from her both stunned him and fired his blood to a fever pitch.

She started to swim toward him, and Chance hastily backed up until he could stand on the dark-painted bottom of the pool. He had little faith in his ability to stay afloat with her so close.

She stopped bare inches away, having to tread in the water that only reached Chance's chin. He reached for her, meaning to support her in the water, but the moment his hands slid over her water-slick body he lost all grasp of his good intentions.

She gave a little moan as he pulled her hard against him. Her arms went around his neck instinctively, her head tilting back, her lips parting in anticipation. He cupped her face in his hands, his mouth diving for hers eagerly, needing her honeyed warmth more than he needed his next breath.

She tightened her arms as his lips crushed hers, and when his tongue probed for entry she opened for him willingly. Her tongue met his, twirling, dancing, luring him deeper and deeper. With her arms around his neck, her only support in the warm, caressing water, she was draped against him like a living garment, fitting as if she'd been made only for him. His body knew it and was urgently demanding that he take the last step that would join them so perfectly.

His body may have been demanding it, but his mind still remembered the look in her eyes. He'd frightened her in the moment of weakness, and he wanted to erase the fear more than anything in the world. He had to remind himself of that when his body screamed as one silken thigh brushed against his jutting, ready flesh.

His goal was nearly wiped from his mind when Shea, having felt the shudder that went through him at the intimate contact, moved to capture him between her legs, shifting her thighs in a squeezing caress. The sudden heat that cascaded through him seemed to rob his legs of all strength, and he nearly went under.

He had to stop her, had to turn this around. It wasn't going at all like he'd planned. With a last burst of determination his hands clamped around her slender waist and lifted, raising her body up out of the water. She gave a startled little cry that abruptly changed to a gasp of pleasure when his mouth hungrily found her breasts. He kissed, licked and teased her nipples to exquisitely hard points, making her twist in his hands. Her hands went to his shoulders, bracing herself as her back arched, thrusting her breasts to him in an instinctive movement that played havoc with his knees again.

"That's it, songbird," he murmured thickly against the soft flesh, "give them to me."

He moved to her other breast, licking away the pool water as if it were the sweetest of nectars, then sucking deep and hard as if it had come from her and he wanted more.

When at last he let her slide down his slick body, her head ducked to his chest to return his caress, but he only allowed her the briefest kiss pressed over his breastbone, the barest flick of her tongue across his nipples. Then he was moving, never releasing her as he backed into shallower depths, until the warm ripples lapped at his lean hips. Before she could protest, he had tugged her arms from around his neck, and she found herself floating on her back, sideways to his body, staring up at him in pleasure-fogged confusion.

"You are so beautiful," he whispered, forestalling her instinctive movement. She'd begun to cover herself when she realized she was so wantonly vulnerable to his gaze and touch. The embarrassment receded before it had a chance to take root, and was replaced by a growing heat that made the pool seem cold by comparison.

Then he bent to her, slipping one hand beneath the water to the small of her back, saving her from even the necessity of thinking about staying afloat. She was free to think of nothing but his touch, of his lips that had returned to her breast, and his other hand that was sliding over her body in a slow, sensuous caress that left fiery trails that tingled long after his dexterous fingers had passed.

He continued until she was quivering, shaking with need. She reached for him, but he gently pushed her hands away.

"Let me," he whispered. "Just relax and let me."

He was relentless, his lips and tongue worshiping each achingly hard nipple in turn, his fingers moving in a slow, circular caress that set up an answering motion in her hips that she was helpless to control. She heard the slosh of the water as he moved, heard it quicken as she lifted herself involuntarily to his hand, felt it swirling around her legs as she widened them in total surrender.

Time and again he drove her to the peak, then, just as she was gathering herself for the flight, he drew back, letting the heat churning inside her ebb just enough before he began again. Each time she cried out, past any shame at her begging, knowing only that she would die if he didn't give her what she needed soon.

"Please," she moaned, "Chance, I can't stand it!"

"Sure you can," he soothed in a husky tone that did anything but soothe her tormented body. And then he began again, kissing, suckling, probing, until she was writhing with need, clutching at him blindly, water streaming over gleaming skin as her body bucked beneath his touch.

"Chance, please!" She nearly sobbed with frustration when he stopped again.

"Easy, songbird," he gasped, his breath rattling harshly in his chest as the grip he had on his seething body slipped.

He turned her swiftly in the water, caressing one long, curved leg as he bent it to slip between them. With a little cry of eagerness she wrapped her legs around him, bringing herself up against his belly. She could feel his hardness searing her through the water, prodding the back of her thighs and her buttocks. She reached for him, desperate to have that throbbing strength inside her.

Chance knew his control was splintering, but he held on, refusing to be hurried. One hand went to her hips to steady her in the water, the other, gentle yet merciless, probed the wet tangle of dark and sandy curls for that precious spot yet again. He stroked and caressed, his tortured body screaming at the feel of her slick readiness, a slippery, feminine heat that made the wetness of the pool seem negligible. She was ready for him, and his raging body let him know it had had enough denial. Yet he once more brought her to the brink, then pulled her back, then again, until every gasping breath that rose from her was a plea.

"Now," he groaned, unable to hold back another second. He gripped her waist and lowered her that imperative inch, his swollen, aching body probing frantically for her soft heat, for the sweet, yielding yet coaxing flesh, for the home he'd found only in her. He thrust forward with a violent jerk of his hips that he couldn't control, and when she cried out so fiercely, he thought he'd hurt her. But then he felt it, the rhythmic convulsions of her body around his, the hot, sweet grip and release of satin flesh just as his piercing entry sent her flying over the edge.

He fought a groaning battle not to follow her, to just stand there and savor the feel of her climax without following her into oblivion himself. It was hard, so very hard when her body was stroking him from within, urging him to give himself to her with every fierce ripple of her muscles.

He threw his head back, clamping his teeth on his lip until he was sure he'd fought down the surging tide. Then he lifted her up to his chest without breaking the precious connection between them.

Her eyes opened, then widened as she felt him still full and hard inside her. "Chance...? You...why...?"

He held her close to him as he walked slowly toward the edge of the pool, each step bringing them further out of the water and increasing the delightful weight of her on him. He bent his head to lay a nibbling row of kisses along the line of her shoulder to her throat as he tried to find words to explain.

"I love making love to you, songbird, but you make me so crazy, make me feel so much, so intensely..." He let out a long, shuddering breath. "You blow all my circuits, lady, and I miss what you're feeling. I wanted to know."

"Oh, Chance," she whispered, moved beyond any further words. She hugged him, the small movement making both of them aware that he was still very much aroused and inside her.

"I hope you're not in a hurry to get dressed," he said gruffly, "because I can either pick up our clothes or get us upstairs, but I don't think I have the restraint left to do both."

"What clothes?"

Shea leaned forward and flicked her tongue around the curve of his ear, something she'd learned had an electric effect on him. He let out a groan that was half growl, and started up the stairs to his apartment.

"Good choice," she whispered as she moved to rub her breasts sinuously against his chest. "There's something I want to know, myself."

By the time they reached his bed, he knew she meant to do exactly what he had done. And by the time he finally let go, exploding inside her with a violence of sensation he'd never known before, he knew she'd succeeded.

Shea awoke hours later, wondering in the silence what had roused her. Chance was there, she could feel his heat, but he was strangely removed from her. She usually woke to his arm tightly around her and his legs entangled with hers. She turned her head to look at him, and her breath caught in her throat.

He was on his back, one hand resting palm out on his forehead, as if to shade his eyes from a nonexistent glare of light. His other hand was gripping the sheet, fingers clenched so tightly that even in the dark she could see the whiteness around his knuckles. His eyes were open as he stared at the ceiling, and, incredibly, she thought she saw a trace of wetness on his face.

A horrible shiver went through her, she didn't know if it was pain, fear or premonition. She only knew that it terrified her. She struggled to move but felt strangely numbed, as if fighting off some odd paralysis. At last she managed to pull herself up on one elbow.

"Chance?"

It was a quavery little whisper, echoing how she was feeling inside. His eyes snapped closed as he winced, then turned his face away. Shea felt as though she'd been slapped.

"Chance, please, don't," she begged. "Let me help."

"You can't." His voice was an appalling sound—harsh, dead, hopeless.

"I can't if you shut me out."

She reached for him, but he pulled away at the first touch of her fingers on his shoulder. Shea recoiled, sudden pain tearing through her so sharply she was amazed she wasn't bleeding. For a moment she couldn't move, she could only tremble. She bit her lip as a sob tried to rise in her throat.

It came out as a strangled, barely audible sound, and Chance's head snapped around.

"Oh, God," he ground out, closing his eyes as he strained not to move, every cord and tendon standing out with the effort. Shea stared at him, her eyes wide with pain and fear. Fear for him, he realized with a sudden jolt. The final irony. With a keening groan he reached for her, pulling her hard and tight against him with a bruising fierceness he couldn't control.

"I'm sorry, baby, I'm so damned sorry. I never meant to hurt you. I love you, Shea. I never expected to love anybody again. I never expected to love like this at all. I don't mean to shut you out. I can't help it. I have no choice."

The words were tumbling out like water from behind a dam that had begun to breach. They came in short, choking bursts, each one fought against, each one pushed to release by a pressure too great to resist any longer. The ones that scared her were about even with the ones that gave her pleasure, and she wound up confused and wanting only to ease his pain. Her arms slipped around him.

"What can I do?" she pleaded.

His crushing embrace tightened even more. "Hold me," he whispered in that horrible, desperate voice, "just hold me."

She did, murmuring soft, soothing words that meant nothing except that she loved him, the only thing she could offer him. She stroked his tangled hair, rubbed the tight, knotted muscles of his shoulders, and crooned a litany of peace over and over, lowering her voice to a soft pitch that lulled.

She felt him begin to relax, but she never varied her movements or the sound of her voice until at last she heard his breathing deepen and felt his body slacken against hers. And still she held him, cradling the head that rested on her breasts, stroking the tousled, streaky mane of hair, softly whispering her love even as she held in her fear.

Chapter 11

"Come on, partner. You know my mother'll kill me if you don't show up."

Chance shook his head. "Can't. Like the fine, church-going citizen that he is, de Cortez is closing the club. Shea won't be working."

"So bring her along," Quisto said with a grin. "My mother'd love to get her hands on that girl. She'd have you two engaged by the time the turkey was carved."

Chance went pale. He thought he'd conquered the sick feeling that had defeated him that night by the pool, thought Shea's tender ministrations had healed him, but it all came rushing back at Quisto's careless words.

"You know I can't do that."

"Why? You know I was only kidding. My mother can be the soul of tact when the spirit moves her. And she'd never in a million years hurt you. She says you've already had to carry more than should be asked of any man."

He could hear the tiny dark-eyed woman's phrasing in her son's voice. Celeste Romero might be small of stature, but she ruled her large family with love and an iron hand, and there wasn't one of them who wouldn't die for her. And there had been times, when she had so warmly welcomed his battered soul into her heart, that Chance hadn't been sure he wouldn't include himself in that category. He sighed inwardly, pulling himself together yet again.

"I know she wouldn't," he said softly. "But she's not the problem."

"Then what?"

"Have you forgotten," he said dryly, "about twenty or so assorted nieces and nephews? Each with the subtlety of a tank and absolutely no capacity for keeping a secret? And every last one of them proud as heck of their 'Uncle Quisto'... the cop?"

Quisto looked taken aback, then appalled. "God, Chance, I'm sorry. I completely forgot—man, I was out of line." He shook his head. "It's just that you two seem so right together, I forget how it started, forget that she's even part of this," he finished, gesturing at the ubiquitous papers that nearly covered the table.

"Tell me about it," Chance said grimly.

Shaken, Quisto stared at him. "I feel like a guy who's just had a glimpse of hell ... and you're living in it."

"It seems to have become my permanent address," Chance said, with a touch of bitterness starker than Quisto had ever heard from him.

"My mother was right," Quisto muttered, but said no more as the door opened and Lieutenant Morgan came in, followed, depressingly, by Eaton.

They hadn't been able to keep the one possible break in the surveillance from the federal agent forever, and he'd been furious when he'd discovered how long they had kept it from him. This was Chance's first meeting with him since he'd found out, and the man wasted no time in making it clear who he blamed.

"For someone who preaches cooperation, you seem to have a funny interpretation of the word, Buckner," he fumed.

"I don't find anything about this case amusing," Chance returned coldly, "especially you."

"Can we get on with this, gentlemen?"

Lieutenant Morgan's tone let them know he was nearly at the end of his patience with personal infighting. In impartial tones he covered the last week's work, the one little piece of possible progress—ignoring Eaton's scowl and his furious, darting looks at Chance—and their options from here on.

Chance sipped at a cup of coffee as he stared at the mass of paperwork on the table, more to keep from having to look at Eaton than any hope that by some miracle a solution would occur to him. It was becoming harder and harder to find that line between where the job ended and his personal involvement began, and he knew he was in real danger of blowing one or the other, if not both, sky-high.

Shea had never asked him about the night that had been so horrible and so beautiful at the same time. She had been there for him, giving without taking, holding together with the sheer force of her love the man whose destiny seemed to be to tear her life apart.

"—misjudged Detective Buckner."

Chance's head snapped up at Eaton's smooth words that held just the slightest undertone of sarcasm.

"Ah," he went on, the sarcasm less veiled now, "I see I have your attention at last. I was merely admitting that I seem to have underestimated your devotion to duty, Detective."

"Meaning?" Chance's voice held a warning he realized Eaton was either too stupid to hear or chose to ignore.

"Meaning I find it…admirable that you're so willing to, shall we say, sacrifice your body for the cause?"

Chance bolted upright in the chair.

"Although I'm certain it was quite pleasurable, Ms. Austin being the kind of woman that she is, and no doubt quite…experienced in that area—"

"You son of a bitch," Chance snarled, on his feet with a swiftness that left even Quisto a half step behind. Eaton dodged behind the table with an alacrity that was surprising for his bulk. "You're dead meat, Eaton!"

Chance's fingers curled around the cup of coffee as if he were about to throw it. Eaton eyed it warily but with a smirking expression that turned Chance's stomach.

"Go ahead, Buckner. Throwing food seems to be your style."

"That's enough!" Morgan snapped. "Both of you."

Chance stared at the brown suit, something in his mind trying urgently to break through the anger. He was only vaguely aware of Quisto holding him back, of his partner carefully removing the cup of hot coffee from his hand.

"My apologies, Lieutenant," Eaton said in ill-concealed satisfaction, "but I'm afraid hotshot local cops tend to irritate me."

Hotshot. It hit Chance with stunning force.

"You," he breathed, his voice dripping venom. "It was you, you bastard! Hotshot," Chance spat out. "He said it, too. He picked it up from you, didn't he?"

Chance broke loose from Quisto's grasp and scrambled across the table to grab a handful of suit and shirt. Eaton squealed like a scalded cat.

"It *was* you!" Chance was shouting now, and all of Quisto's wiry strength wasn't enough to hold him back. "Damn it, it was you! You put that tail on me!"

"You're crazy!" Eaton squeaked, but it decidedly lacked conviction. Lieutenant Morgan, who had come to add his efforts to Quisto's, stopped dead.

"I painted your tail with chocolate," Chance said, his grip threatening to cut off what little air the fat man was getting. "And nobody knew it but my partner, and him. But you knew. Because he's one of yours, isn't he? That's why he didn't fit, because he didn't work for de Cortez!"

"I—"

He was choked off. Despite Eaton's weight, Chance was nearly lifting him off the ground in his fury.

"Chance." Jim Morgan touched his arm.

"Oh, no, he's mine. I'm going to harpoon him and skin him, and save some innocent whale somewhere."

"No. He's *mine*. And when I get through with him, he'll ask for the harpoon. Back off, Chance."

It was clearly an order, and only Chance's tremendous respect for the man who was his boss enabled him to get a grip on his temper. Grudgingly, and none too quickly, he lowered the gasping agent to the floor.

"Eaton, my office," Morgan said, pointedly dispensing with any title or effort at politeness. "Your superiors are going to be very interested in this, I think."

Eaton paused only to cast one last glance back at Chance. It was so full of rage and hatred it was almost unbalanced. When he'd gone, Quisto let out a low whistle.

"Man, don't ever turn your back on that guy."

"Yeah. If I hadn't, he never would have gotten away with it for so long."

"I've seen guys you've put away for life that didn't look that mad."

"Should have done what you do to any mad dog. Solve a lot of problems for everybody." He walked wearily back around the table and sank into a chair. "I don't get it. Why the hell tail me?"

Quisto shrugged. "He's got a hang-up, man. We knew that the first day."

"I knew he didn't like me—"

"It's not that, partner. He doesn't like what you stand for."

Chance's brow furrowed. "We're both cops, different kinds, but—"

"You," Quisto said firmly, "are everything he never was. Tall, blond and blue eyed, good-looking, smart, a ladykiller—or at least you could be, if you gave it a tenth of a try. You've got everything he probably never had, and always wanted."

Chance was staring at his partner, stunned by the certainty in his tone. "You sound...awfully sure of that."

Quisto shrugged. "I spent a long time as a kid wanting to be like the fair-haired boys of this country. Like you, and all the others like you, who seemed to have it so easy. The ones who didn't know what it meant to have people look past you instead of at you." He shrugged.

"Then one day I woke up and looked at myself long and hard. And at my family. And I came to terms with what I was, and what I wasn't." He glanced at the door Eaton had gone through. "I'd say he never did."

Chance shook his head, a little dazed. "I...never knew. Did I make you feel that way?"

"No. You've been through enough hell of your own, buddy. Your dues were different, but you paid them just like I did. You're still paying. It makes a difference."

Chance let out a long breath. "I'm sorry, partner. Sometimes it's a rotten world."

Quisto shrugged again. "Yeah." Then he grinned irrepressibly. "Besides, you taught me that you pretty Anglo types have your problems, too. Women always after your body instead of your mind, drooling over your blue eyes instead of listening to what you say, making lascivious comments about your rear end—"

He ducked as Chance, laughing, tossed a pencil at him.

"Easy, partner, it's not me you want to harpoon."

"Yeah," Chance said, his anger gone now thanks to Quisto's diversion. He reached to straighten the papers he'd knocked sideways in his grab for his mock harpoon. "He'd have to smarten up some to be in a whale's class, wouldn't he?"

"He'd have to smarten up a lot."

Chance laughed again, but it had lost some of its energy as he stared at the papers. "I think I'm the one who needs to smarten up. How can we have all this data, every damn move that's been made since de Cortez came to town, and still not have a clue as to when he's going to move?"

Quisto sighed. "We're doing what we can. We've got a watch on the airport, and at the hotels, just in case that little slip was for real and something's coming down the pipe. There's nobody in town now that would handle the kind of action de Cortez is used to, so it's a good bet he'll have people coming in from the outside."

"Did you call the Harbor Patrol?"

Quisto nodded. "Soon as I heard that little piece of tape. No new boats of any size in or out. And they'd notice. There's not much traffic during the week this time of year."

"Winter in paradise," Chance muttered, staring at the log that made his eyes tired just thinking about trying to read it again.

"Let's hope it doesn't snow," Quisto said dryly.

"Remind me to thank everybody in Florida for driving these clowns out of there to California."

He reached down to pick up the pencil he'd tossed, letting out a disgusted sigh as he viewed the now voluminous stack of papers. Pretty soon he was going to need a damned briefcase to carry the stuff around. He grimaced. Maybe he could borrow one of the bookends to carry it for him.

The image formed in his mind again, as it had off and on since that day, of a tuxedo-clad bookend clutching that case like a child protecting a precious toy, or a miser protecting his hoard of gold. He'd looked like—

Gold.

A sudden image of that sign inside the door of the club flashed through his mind.

"Damn!"

Papers scattered as he grabbed at them, tugging out this one, discarding that. Quisto turned, staring.

"Where are the damned bank records we subpoenaed?"

Chance grabbed at another stack, then yanked at the tattered surveillance log. He shoved the rest aside, lined up the three items he'd isolated. Quisto waited, watching warily, knowing better than to interrupt. He watched as Chance's eyes flicked from one page to another, the pencil he'd picked up making quick, impatient check marks on item after item, then scribbling out a list. Minutes passed.

He grabbed for the phone and punched in a number.

"Jeff? Chance. This list of stockholders for the Del Mar Club. You put it together?" A pause. "I need the dates of incorporation on all of them, and I need it yesterday. Thanks."

He went back to the papers, Quisto watching in growing bewilderment as Chance muttered, "I should have paid more attention to that bulletin from the Treasury Department."

"What—"

Chance help up a hand and Quisto fell silent. At last Chance threw down the pencil and looked up.

"It's right there. It has been, only I've been too damned stupid to see it!"

"Make that two of us," Quisto said cautiously. "What have we been too stupid to see?"

"Look," he said, gesturing at the papers.

"I am. What am I looking for?"

Chance ticked off the items he'd scrawled on his list. "The first two weeks the club was open. Deposits to the club account of anywhere from a hundred to a hundred and fifty thousand a night. High, but not impossible for a successful operation that caters to high rollers. Two-hundred-person capacity, three shows, and they run 'em in and out pretty quick. And the most expensive food and drinks in town."

"Ain't that the truth."

Chance jabbed at an entry on the photocopy. "But then it goes up, to over five hundred thou every night. Place took off, right?"

"Right." He stopped at Chance's expression. "But not right, right?"

"Quisto, you or I have been in that place every damned day since it opened. What's it been like?"

"Packed. She brings 'em in, you know that."

"Yes. Some regulars who stay all night, more who come and go. But it's been a full house every night since the opening, right?"

Quisto sighed. "Couldn't squeeze in a sardine."

"Exactly."

"Huh?"

"And that sardine you couldn't squeeze in didn't spend any money."

At last it hit. "So there's no way the profits could have jumped like that," Quisto said slowly.

"No. And maybe he was even padding them at the start with his own money, to make the bigger figures later look less suspicious."

Chance jabbed the pencil at a two-word note circled several times in heavy, angry marks. Quisto leaned over to read it.

" 'Cash Only'?"

"That's one thing I *do* remember from that Treasury bulletin. Retail businesses that regularly collect large amounts of cash can get exemptions from the $10,000 rule."

Quisto's brow furrowed. "You mean the IRS law?"

Chance nodded. "Currency Transaction Reports on any deposits more than $10,000." He grimaced. "Want to bet the Del Mar Club has one of those exemptions?"

Quisto's eyes widened in sudden understanding. He whistled, long and low.

"Yeah," Chance muttered. "And I'll bet if we subpoenaed a full transaction file, we'd find a lot of fat, unreported wire transfers to banks in Hong Kong, or some little island with those nice private banks with no disclosure rules."

"What's the percentage for the middleman these days?" Quisto wondered aloud. "Seven percent? Ten maybe, if the money's really hot?"

"Yeah, quite a profit for running a laundry," Chance agreed sourly. "Look at it. Say the real take from the club is maybe a hundred. Hell, even two. That still leaves three hundred a night, open every day except Monday, that's—" he scribbled some figures down "—over eight million a month."

"And ten percent of that is nothing to sneeze at."

Chance slammed down the pencil, furious at himself for not seeing it sooner. And hurting inside. He'd hoped against hope, even knowing he was being a fool, that for her sake de Cortez was clean. When the phone rang, he jumped at it.

"Buckner." He grabbed the pencil and scribbled down a row of dates. "That's the clincher. Thanks, pal."

He sat back and looked up at Quisto. After a moment, he handed him the piece of paper. Quisto read it and whistled. Chance nodded slowly.

"None of those companies existed three months before de Cortez set up shop here. And I'll bet if you dug a little deeper, you'd find every last one of them is a dummy corporation, owned by another corporation owned by another."

"And when you get to the bottom," Quisto said, "I'll bet you find some very interesting names, getting nice clean checks from their profitable investment."

"And no doubt all using that same little banking paradise—"

They both looked up as Lieutenant Morgan came back in.

"I just got off the phone. What's with you two? You look like you found the answer and it bit you."

"Exactly," Chance said.

Morgan sat on the edge of the table. "Well?"

"He's not running dope," Quisto said.

Morgan's eyebrows rose. Chance let out a weary sigh. "He's running money," he said.

It had taken the greatest effort of his life to keep the knowledge that things were beginning to topple locked inside. But he did it, not wanting anything to disturb the fragile balance of his relationship with Shea. She had responded so sweetly to his torment, giving him a quiet support that tore at him like that merciless trap; he was never quite free of the agonizing knowledge that she was keeping him going so he could bring down the brother she loved.

He found himself looking at every day as possibly the last, and therefore even more precious. He tried to stop short of clinging to her, but it was difficult when she made it so easy. She seemed as eager for him as he was for her, and when they came together the individual flames that never seemed to die joined to become an inferno.

His hunger never eased, he could never seem to get enough of her, and yet he treasured equally the quiet moments when he just held her, soaking up the feel of her with the desperation of a man who knew the memories of this might be all he ever had.

He caught her looking at him now and then with that expression of concern, and tried to assure her that he was all right. And congratulated himself bitterly for finding a woman so trusting that she believed his rather feeble lies.

He'd awakened early this Thanksgiving morning, and lay holding her as she slept peacefully on. She'd mentioned her brother having a party at his house, but when he'd prodded she'd admitted she wasn't going.

"They're not my kind of people," she'd said with a shrug. "I've always thought of Thanksgiving as a...family kind of thing, not an excuse for a party."

That was when he'd decided to forego his usual trip to Quisto's family gathering; he wasn't about to leave her alone. Especially when their days together might be so numbered.

Stop it, he said fiercely. He'd sworn he wasn't going to think about that, not today. One day at a time, wasn't that what they told alcoholics? Well, he was addicted to her as surely as an alcoholic to his drink, but the charm didn't seem to work for him.

Just today, he told himself. They deserved this one day free of the clouds, free of the hovering shadow. He'd give it to her somehow, he'd bury the hell so deep inside she'd never know it was there. Like a knight putting on his armor, he soaked in the strength he gained from just having her there in his arms, using it to build a protective shell around them both. And later, when she began to stir, he woke her gently and made love to her so joyously that she cried out like the songbird he called her.

"Mmm," she said dreamily as she snuggled up to him afterward. "I don't know what got into you this morning, but if I could bottle the way I feel right now, I'd be rich."

He chuckled, a low rumble from deep in his chest, and with a teasing comment about knowing exactly what had gotten into her, proceeded to do it all over again.

They lay in bed until after noon, savoring the new closeness his determined mood had engendered. Chance had succeeded in his goal, but had to smother a pang at how she responded to his new mood. She blossomed, giggling, laughing, until it was only too obvious how much his own strain had affected her. But when he began to make noises about getting up and she pressed him back against the pillows, catching his hips in the silken trap of her thighs while she cheerfully announced it wasn't quite time yet, he gave up thinking about anything except how good she was making him feel.

He was half out of his mind, his hands raised and full of her breasts as, after teasing him unmercifully, she at last lowered her body and took him home, when the rapid knocking on the front door shattered the cocoon that had surrounded them. Shea jumped in startled surprise, looking over her shoulder toward the living room, and a heart-felt groan rose from Chance as he fell back on the pillows.

"Maybe they'll go away," she whispered.

"I wish," he groaned. "But it could only be my land-lord or Quisto, and my landlord has a better sense of tim-ing."

"I guess I'd better let you move, then."

"Yes." Then, as she began to leave him, "No!"

He shuddered as he lost her warmth. She made a tiny sound of protest when he got up.

"Damn," he muttered as the knocking came again. He grabbed the jeans he'd discarded in such haste last night, yanking them on. He reached for the zipper tab, letting out a muffled grunt as he tried to tug it past flesh that was still intent on the activity that had been so abruptly inter-rupted. He settled for getting it halfway and headed for the door. He jerked it open to glare at a grinning Quisto.

"Your timing stinks," he snapped.

Quisto eyed his bare chest and the barely fastened state of his jeans. "Oops," he said, undismayed. "Good thing I don't plan on staying long. Give me a hand, will you?"

Chance eyed the two well-filled grocery bags warily. "With what?"

"The other one of these that's down in my car. Where's Shea?"

Chance didn't bother to deny she was here, he knew Quisto would know better anyway.

"Hiding from you, no doubt."

"Have to fix that," Quisto returned cheerfully. "Get that bag, will you?"

Chance went, grinning as he heard Quisto holler, "Oh, Ms. Austin! It's your favorite Thanksgiving turkey! Come out and say hi."

When Chance returned, she was coming hesitantly out of the bedroom, wearing the pair of jeans and bulky sweater that had, along with several other items, found their way here. The sweater fell off one shoulder in a way he found incredibly sexy, but she had pulled her hair back in a po-nytail that made her look about sixteen. The contrast set up a ridiculous conflict in him. He didn't know whether to rip the sweater off her and take her back to bed, or turn himself in for cradle robbing.

Shea followed him into the kitchen, holding back a little when she saw Quisto was still here. She looked at him a little doubtfully, but he merely set down the dish he'd been holding and threw his arms around her. Shea looked a little stunned when he planted a wet kiss on her cheek. They had met a few more times since the first night in the club, but never had he been so teasingly friendly before.

"There. That's from my mother. Actually, the hug was for him—" he jerked a thumb at Chance "—but I refused to hug that lug, so you get them both."

"Your... mother?" She looked around at the various wrapped plates and covered dishes. "She... sent this?"

Quisto chuckled. "You don't come to the dinner, the dinner comes to you. She sent a little of everything. Good thing we eat early." He glanced at his watch. "Oops, got to go. She made me promise to be back in an hour. 'My boy doesn't need you intruding,' is how it went, I think. See ya."

"My boy?" Shea stared after him, bemused.

Chance grinned. "I told you she wants to adopt me. It's not enough that she has five of her own, she keeps taking in more."

"Are there others? Besides you?"

He laughed. "Not now. I'm the only extra one, currently. She says I take all her concentration."

She smiled. "Why?"

"She worries a lot, that's all."

I understand how you feel, Mrs. Romero, she thought silently. I worry about him, too. Her eyes were troubled when she looked up at him again.

"You would have gone there, wouldn't you, if it hadn't been for me?"

Chance hesitated as the truth he'd been determined to deny all day hovered darkly over him again, then settled on at least a part of the truth.

"They invited you, too. But I didn't want to share you just yet." He grimaced. "Quisto's family is... a little overwhelming."

She seemed to accept it, but her curiosity was piqued. "Are there a lot of them?"

"I lost count at twenty-five. And that's just brothers and sisters and their kids."

"They're all married?"

"Yep. Quisto's the last holdout, much to his mother's dismay."

She looked around at all the food, sniffing the blending odors appreciatively. "She sounds wonderful."

"She is. Not to mention a great cook. You've never had Thanksgiving dinner until you've had a Romero one. It's the craziest combination of Cuban and American I've ever seen." He lifted a bottle out of the last bag. "Including, it seems this time, champagne."

She discovered what he meant as they set out the food, most of which was still warm. He chuckled when her stomach growled audibly.

"Work up an appetite, songbird?"

"Yes," she said simply. "And I think it was awfully kind of Mrs. Romero to send all this."

"And you'd better eat everything, or she'll be on me for weeks." He popped the bottle and got two glasses.

Shea studied him for a moment. "You like her, don't you?"

He smiled. "She's quite a lady."

"Have you always gone there for Thanksgiving?"

"Only since I've known Quisto. Couple of years."

Not with his wife then, Shea thought, and looked down at her plate before he could read the realization in her eyes. When she was sure it was gone, she looked at him again.

"Do you go there for Christmas, too, or do you go see your folks?"

His hand froze in midair as he lifted a glass to fill it. He set it down instead and poured the bubbling wine into it, then filled the second glass. He handed one to her, then sat down, never meeting her gaze.

"Chance?"

He looked at her then, and saw a shadow of the worry he'd tried so hard to banish today. He closed his eyes, steadied himself and at last answered her.

"No. Neither. There's a place up the coast a few miles. Avila Beach. Near San Luis Obispo. A little house on the beach. My parents still own it. I go there."

The words were choppy, oddly tense. She looked at him in concern, but when he turned the question around and asked her what she did for the holidays, she let him. She told him about the small party she and some friends had at a large warehouse every year.

"When the snow is high, there are always some stranded tourists, so we invite them, too. We always have some extra toys on hand for the kids who get stuck because their parents didn't believe the weather reports."

Chance smiled, and she couldn't rid herself of the idea that it was totally without joy.

"A white Christmas, huh?" he said almost wistfully.

"Generally." She eyed him curiously. "Don't tell me. You're a California beachboy who's never seen a white Christmas?"

He shrugged, as if uncomfortable with the subject. "It's not a big deal for me. I prefer to be alone."

"Oh."

He caught the flicker of disappointment mixed with hurt in her eyes before she looked away and said with forced cheer, "Well, I'm starved. Let's eat."

He'd done it again. He'd hurt her, when it was the last thing he wanted to do, and she was determined not to show it. *She's got a hell of a lot more guts than you have*, he thought. *If you weren't so damned selfish you would have dropped out of her life the first minute you saw what was happening.*

He smothered a sigh. *You're going to tear her to pieces in the end anyway, Buckner, do you have to start now? Is she going to hate you any more for having a few more dreams shattered?*

"Shea?"

"What?" She didn't look up.

"Do you think a beach bum like me would like a white Christmas?"

Her head came up then, but her eyes were guarded. He hated that look, and knowing he'd put it there.

"You'll never know until you try," she said carefully.

"Know where I might find one this year?"

Shea stared at him, knowing somehow that there was much more to this than a simple peace offering. This was terribly hard for him for some reason. She could almost feel the effort it took him to speak those words. Gradually the guarded look faded from her eyes.

"I think I might know where to find you a beautiful white Christmas," she said softly.

The meal was, as he'd promised, a fascinating combination of two cultures. The turkey was traditional American, but the side dishes were varied and delicious. Bread and tortillas, mashed potatoes and spicy beans, pumpkin pie and a sweet, flaky, light-as-air fried pastry Chance had to admit he'd forgotten the name of.

"Don't you know?" he asked her.

"No. I'm afraid I know very little of my Cuban background, other than the language. I only know that because Paul always spoke it at home, and my mother would slip now and then."

"Slip?"

She shrugged. "My mother rarely acknowledged that side of her life. I think that's another reason Paul ran away. He was determined to hang on to what traditions and memories he could, because of his father, while my mother was determined to bury them."

"What about your father?"

"He never asked her to, if that's what you mean. In fact, he was the one who wanted to use her name in mine." She picked at the last remnants of the pie she hadn't been able to finish. "Paul's father was...cruel, I think. He was Colombian, and always threatened to take her there. When she married my father she was determined to become completely American. I think she wanted to put it all behind her, and Paul felt she was betraying his father's memory."

"Did they ever make up?"

"No." A touch of bitterness rang in her voice. "She died before he came back. He never saw her."

An image of the routine report flashed through his mind. For the first time he realized that he had listened to her without a single thought about how what she was telling him might relate to the case. He had listened because he loved her, because he wanted to know everything about her, not for any other reason. He was pondering that realization when her quiet words caught him off guard.

"She killed herself, Chance. Pills. And I've never understood why."

"Oh, God, Shea," he whispered, reaching across the table to take her hands. He was stunned that she'd trusted him with this, this deeply personal tragedy. Knowing it long before she'd said it did nothing to lessen its impact. Several moments passed before he could look at the gray eyes that were shimmering with unshed tears, and several more before he could speak.

"I had a...friend once. I worked with him for three years. One day he walked out on the beach south of town and put a gun to his head and fired it."

She sucked in a short breath, and her fingers curled beneath his as he went on.

"I knew every reason why he did it. I'd felt a few of them myself. I understood exactly how he felt. It didn't help."

"I keep telling myself that. That it doesn't make any difference why, only that she...she did it. But it still hurts so."

He couldn't stand it. He got up, lifted her and sat back down with her in his arms.

"I know, songbird. I wish I could tell you it will go away. I can't. It won't ever go away. But it will hurt less and less. All you can do is remember that she loved you."

"I...I know she did. But why didn't she love me enough to stay?"

Her words were a white-hot lance in a wound already lacerated. Would he be saying that mere days from now? Would she be asking how he could have done this do her if he loved her? He held her close, hanging on desperately.

"I wish I had all the answers, songbird," he whispered hoarsely. "All I know is that sometimes people have to do things even when it hurts the ones they love the most."

Those words came back to haunt him with vivid, vicious clarity in the early hours of dawn when, after a night full of Shea's sweet, giving love, the phone rang.

"Yeah," he mumbled into the receiver after grabbing it before it could ring again and wake her.

"Quisto. Sorry man, but things are starting to happen."

He was instantly awake. "What?"

"Got a call from the airport watch. Three very big names in the gray money business have arrived in the last twelve hours."

"Damn."

"They checked into the Mar Vista, the Beachfront, and the Marina View Hotels. Under aliases, of course. And those are only the ones we spotted. We probably wouldn't have spotted them at all if we'd still been looking for a snowfall to come down the pipe. Nice work, partner."

"Yeah, great."

"Anyway, that's just act one."

"What's act two?"

"Every one of them called Paul de Cortez."

Chapter 12

It had to be, Shea thought, something in the water. Everybody was on edge. Chance had been acting like a caged tiger ever since Thanksgiving. Paul had been worse. Even one of the usually unctuous bookends had snapped at her this morning. The only sane person she knew was Eric, who never seemed to let any of it bother him.

"How do you stay so calm," she finally asked him, "when everybody around you has gone Looney Tunes?"

"You haven't."

"You know what I mean."

Eric shrugged. "Everybody's got their own set of problems. Just because I don't see the reasons for what they do doesn't mean they're not there."

Shea shook her head. "You amaze me sometimes. How do you stay in this performing business and stay sane?"

He shrugged again. "You keep out of it because it would take over your life. You're that good, it would just happen. I'm in it, and I'm good, but it's not my whole life." He grinned. "I'm just waiting for the right lady to come along and take me away from all this."

"Someday my princess will come?"

"Something like that." He played a couple of bars of the appropriate song and Shea laughed. "Why should you be the only lucky one?"

Lucky. Shea turned back to the sheet music that was spread over her keyboard. Sometimes she truly felt that way. Most of the time. She'd never felt anything like she felt for Chance. She'd never known she could. She'd known him for such a short time, but already he was so much a part of her life, of the very fabric of her existence, so much a part of her that it frightened her even as it thrilled her. Never had she known what it was like to be cradled in warmth, cosseted with such tender care.

But sometimes she woke in the night in such a shivering, shaking panic that it was all she could to do keep from waking Chance and making him tell her all the things he hadn't. Whether he wouldn't or couldn't tell her didn't matter at those times, all that mattered was the reassurance she was so desperate for.

When he did wake, it came in the form of whispered words of love and the sweet, hot pulse of his body, but she knew in her heart that he'd only staved off the feelings until the next time. Something was eating away at the man she loved, and she seemed helpless either to stop it or ease his pain.

There was so much she didn't know. She wondered what Eric would say if she told him she didn't even know where Chance went when he left her here in the mornings. That she didn't even know where he worked, or really anything about his work, except that he shared it with Quisto.

Somehow Quisto had become a sort of comfort for her. She told herself that anyone with a family like his couldn't be involved in anything unsavory. Besides, Chance had promised her he wasn't into anything like that, and she believed him. He was only secretive because of whatever kind of work he did for his ever-absent landlord.

And in the end, she thought, it didn't really matter. She loved him. That was the beginning and the end and everything in the middle. Nothing else mattered. She trusted him, and that was the bottom line.

Reassured once more, even as she was aware on some deeper level of her mind that she shouldn't have to be reassuring herself at all, she picked up the top sheet of music and went back to work.

Chance stared at the two new additions to the list. De Cortez picked his partners carefully—each one a stellar name in the world of shady money, each one marvelously clean of convictions despite numerous investigations. And each one of them had arrived in Marina del Mar in the four days since Thanksgiving. Spending, no doubt, "gray" money from whatever other laundering sources they had while they inspected their new one.

"They're busy playing tourist," Quisto said, "going everywhere—by limo, of course—but never at the same time. It's like the whole thing was choreographed so they'd never be seen in the same place at the same time. They're pros all right."

"But what are they waiting for?" Lieutenant Morgan asked. "The sixth man?"

Chance nodded. "That's my guess. Six companies on the shareholders list, five men here."

"That bothers me. Why not all in at once, look things over, and a quick out? Fast and smooth?"

Chance looked up from the list. "The tourist ploy, maybe. Easier to claim innocence if a couple of thousand people saw you at the local zoo."

Chance saw Quisto's eyes flick to the much-chastened face of Agent Eaton, who sat in one corner of the room. Because he had set it up, he had been allowed to stay on to complete this operation, but he'd been told to stay out of the way, and been informed he would be recalled to Washington immediately afterward for a "reassessment of his status." All of which did nothing to ease his antipathy toward Chance, who did his best to ignore the man.

It wasn't hard. It was all he could do to concentrate on the essentials right now. Things were starting to tumble, and he was deathly afraid he and Shea were going to be the first casualties. She had trusted him, sometimes blindly, and only he knew how misplaced that trust was. What he had to do was going to destroy it completely; he could only hope it didn't destroy her.

He knew she was feeling the strain as much as he was. He saw it in her eyes when she looked at him, wondering, wanting to ask but knowing he wouldn't tell her. He felt it in her touch, when she would reach out to just put her hand on his arm, as if she were afraid he was disappearing before her eyes and she had to reassure herself he was still there.

But most of all he could sense it when he turned to her at night, could feel it in the eagerness of her kiss as he woke her in the darkness, could see it in the haunted shadows of her eyes as he made fierce, desperate love to her. He knew it, and it was killing him.

"You gonna make it, man?"

Chance snapped back to the present to find the room empty of everyone except Quisto. He started to assure him he was fine, but something in the dark eyes made him give him the truth instead.

"I don't know," he said hoarsely. "I'm hanging on by a thread. And the hell of it is, I'm the one who's got to cut it."

Quisto's hand came down on his shoulder, gripping it tightly. "Maybe...maybe it'll work out—"

"Don't. I can't believe in fantasies anymore. She's going to hate me, and have every right to."

"And what will you do?" Quisto asked softly.

Blow my brains out. His eyes flashed to Quisto's face. He thought he'd said it out loud, but one look at his partner's face told him he hadn't.

"I don't know," he said instead.

That night he made love to Shea for hours in the carved carriage bed of her apartment, sending her on that rapturous flight time and again before he at last sought his own release. She looked at him through pleasure-drugged eyes as if she knew something was dreadfully wrong, as if she knew how close he was to the breaking point, but she was, as he had wanted, too exhausted to ask questions he couldn't answer.

She slept peacefully in his arms as he lay awake most of the night, watching her, saving up the memories against the time he would no longer have the reality. He'd accepted that, although he hadn't let the pain in yet. Soon there would be room for nothing else.

In the morning he waited as long as he could, then eased out of bed and dressed. He went to the cozy living room and picked up the phone. He stared at the picture of the lake, knowing that this was as close as he would ever get to the white Christmas she'd promised him.

Resolutely, his eyes flat and emotionless, he called in as he always did when he spent the night here, out of touch. Quisto answered on the first ring.

"Romero."

"It's me."

"I was about to page you. The sixth man just got here."

"I'll be there in fifteen."

So this is it, he thought as he hung up. The fuse was lit, and there wasn't a damned thing he could do except wait for the explosion. Maybe you'll get lucky, Buckner, maybe it'll go down twisted. They'll start shooting and you can manage to get yourself killed. It'd be easier.

He let out a weary sigh. He'd have to get his gun out of the glove compartment—

"Chance? You have to go?"

He turned around to look at her, his heart hammering so hard in his chest he thought she must be able to hear it. She stood in the doorway of the living room, looking at him sleepily, her mouth still swollen from his kisses, the glint of a totally satisfied female still in the gray eyes. She had on the sweater that drove him to distraction, and it bared one shoulder beneath the mane of hair he'd buried his fingers in so many times last night. The soft sweater was barely long enough to cover the delicious curve of her buttocks, and showed the length of gently molded, sleek legs easily.

Gradually she became aware that he was staring at her as if he'd never seen her before—or thought he would never see her again. She came across the room to him.

"Chance, what's wrong?"

He pulled her hard against him and buried his face in the dark silk of her hair.

"Shea. Oh, God, Shea."

She pulled back to look up at him, frightened by the desperation in his voice. "Chance, please! Tell me what's wrong! Tell me what I can do!"

"You can remember," he said fiercely. "Remember I love you, more than I've ever loved anyone or anything. Remember that, Shea, no matter what."

And then he was gone, leaving Shea sinking down on the couch in a rising cloud of apprehension.

"We've got men at each hotel, one of ours with one of—" Morgan barely glanced at Eaton "—his. Teams are in place at the club and the house. We've got a mobile team standing by if the meet is set up for somewhere else."

"I still think we should have bugged the cars." It was the first thing Eaton had said in days.

"Too risky," Morgan said. "They spot them, and the whole thing is blown. The only reason this has worked so far is because they think they're clean."

"Yeah," Quisto said. "They think we're some little resort-town police department who can't handle anything this size. Probably why de Cortez decided to come here."

"They would have been right if Chance hadn't spotted that pattern," Morgan said, eyeing the detective in question warily. Anyone could see he was on the edge; Morgan only hoped Chance could hold it together long enough.

"I've notified FINCEN," Morgan went on, "but I doubt if they'll be able to help us much at this point."

Chance heard him but didn't react. He'd known the new federal task force had to be notified of any suspected laundering setups, but he also knew that, even with their computer capability of tracking electronic movement of funds, the Financial Crimes Enforcement Network couldn't come up with anything quickly enough. This was unraveling too fast.

"Since we don't know yet when or where the meeting is to be, we'll have to—" Morgan broke off as the phone rang. Quisto picked it up and he went on.

"We'll have to be ready for any possibility, including that it may be somewhere out of our jurisdiction. We will have to notify the local agency of course, but—"

"It's today."

All eyes swiveled to Quisto as he quietly replaced the phone receiver.

"Every stakeout reported in that the primaries are moving. Each one called for his car within five minutes of the others."

"Then we're on." Morgan turned back to talk to Eaton, and Quisto walked over to sit beside Chance, staring at his impassive face.

"I don't know if it matters anymore," Quisto finally said as he pulled out a piece of paper, "but here are those flight records you wanted."

Chance took it, stared at it without really seeing it.

"And those juvenile arrest records you wanted," Quisto added, picking up a folder that had been sitting off to one side. "All prior arrests on both of them are there. Records was pretty thorough for a change." Quisto paused. "I . . . I checked the names. I think I know now why you . . ."

His voice trailed off when Chance didn't answer, but just stared at the folder. Then Chance opened it idly, his numbed brain trying to remember why this had once seemed so important. He lifted a page as if reading it, more to keep Quisto from asking things he had no answers for than because he expected to find anything.

The name leaped out at him, jarring blunted synapses into action. He sat up in the chair, reached for the piece of paper Quisto had given him and looked at the dates again. Forgetting to breathe, he dug through the pile of reports, pulling out the two he'd fastened together, staring at the dates. And then he dropped back in the chair, shivering under the force of the unexpected, unwanted revelation.

"Chance? What the hell's wrong?"

Morgan added his query to Quisto's. "Something we should know?"

"No," Chance answered softly. "It's nothing that matters right now."

Quisto opened his mouth and shut it again as the phone rang once more. The lieutenant answered it, listened, then hung up without a word. When he turned back to them, his eyes were on Chance.

"It's at the club. They're all headed there, and de Cortez just put up a Closed sign for tonight. 'Private party,' it says."

Chance went pale beneath his tan. Quisto snorted. "I'll bet it's a private party."

"My office, Chance."

Chance followed Morgan numbly, terrified at the thought of Shea being in the middle of this. It had never occurred to him that de Cortez would be arrogant enough to do it on his home ground, but now that it was happening, he realized he should have known. It fit perfectly with the man's mentality.

"We haven't got time for discussion on this, Chance. We've got to move fast or we'll lose it all. So I have only one question, and I need a straight answer, emotions aside."

Chance nodded, not at all sure what was coming.

"Is she involved?"

His answer was unhesitating and definite. "No."

"If you're wrong—"

"If I'm wrong, you won't have to ask for my badge. I'll give it to you."

Morgan glanced at his watch. "Twenty minutes, Chance. That's all I can give you."

Chance stared at his boss.

"This could go to hell on us. Go get her out of there. But if you can't, you get out, because we'll have to come in anyway."

Chance didn't waste time on thanks; he realized Jim Morgan knew him well enough to see it in his face. He barreled out the door, barely aware that the man he brushed roughly out of the way was Eaton. In his haste it didn't occur to him to wonder what the man was doing there, hovering near the open door. The only thing on his mind was getting to Shea. No matter how she would feel about him later, right now he had to get her out of a possible line of fire. She would hate him, but he didn't care, not as long as she was alive to do it.

The door in from the alley was locked, but he'd expected that. De Cortez would have every entrance and exit locked or guarded. It took him a moment to disconnect the alarm without tripping it, but mere seconds to get the door open.

The hallway was deserted, but he could hear voices from the main room. He crept down the darkened passage in a crouch, risking only a glance into the room apparently being set up for the meeting. Even if he got caught, he figured he still had a good chance of bluffing his way out. They thought he was only Shea's slightly crazy boyfriend. And at the moment, he wished to hell they were right.

She whirled around the moment he opened the door, happiness sparkling in her eyes when she saw him.

"Chance! How did you know I was trying to reach you? I was going to tell you I was going to be singing for Paul's party, but that we could—"

"Shea, let's go."

"Go? Where?"

"It doesn't matter. But we've got to go now."

Her brows furrowed. "I can't leave. Paul—"

"To hell with Paul!"

She stopped, staring.

"Now."

"But—"

"No questions. And no telling anybody."

He had grabbed her arm tightly, too tightly. She cried out and pulled it free, backing away as she stared at him.

"What is wrong with you?" All the fears and worry of the past few days were in her voice and face. "For God's sake, Chance, tell me! What you said this morning—"

"We don't have time, damn it!"

"Well, you'd better find time! I can't stand this secrecy anymore, Chance! If you don't trust me—"

"Shea, please! We'll talk about this later—"

"It's always later, and later never comes! You scare me to death when you're like this, and lately that's been all the time. I'm not going—"

"You are." He glanced at his watch; he was down to seven minutes. "Now. We don't have time to argue."

She stared at him. This was a Chance she'd never seen—cold, ordering, intimidating. She backed up another step.

"No," she whispered. "Not when you're like this."

He swore harshly and grabbed her. With an unexpected burst of strength she wriggled out of his grasp.

"God, Shea, you don't understand—"

"You're right, I don't. I don't understand why you're acting like this, I don't understand who you've turned into."

It was over. He knew it, and as they had before when the burden was too much, his emotions shut down. He stood back from her, raised dull, dead eyes to her face and fired the fatal round at her.

"I'm a cop."

The delicate brows furrowed even as the gray eyes widened in confusion. "What?"

"I'm a cop. So is Quisto. You've got to get out because they're about to take down your brother."

Confusion changed to bewilderment. "What has Paul got to do with anything?"

"He was a drug dealer in Miami, and he's cleaning dirty money here. That's why the club's closed, and why they're setting up for a meeting here."

"That's crazy! It's just a private party! Paul would never do anything—"

"Paolo Mendez would do anything. He's dealt drugs, ordered murders, and now he's expanded into laundering money. That's what this whole operation is set up for."

"No," she whispered, but his use of Paul's old name had shaken her. "No, he wouldn't."

He glanced at his watch again; they had less than five minutes now. He reached for her again.

"I'll show you all the proof you want," he said wearily, "but now we've got to get out of here before all hell breaks loose."

In a state of shock, Shea let him pull her a few steps, but before they reached the door it burst open with a resounding crack.

"Well, well," Paul de Cortez sneered, "if it isn't my sweet little sister and her charming boyfriend."

"Paul," Shea cried, "tell him—"

"I'll tell him nothing!" de Cortez spat out. "I don't talk to cops!"

Chance tensed, but Shea was too close, he didn't dare risk it. And then the bookends were there, each carrying Uzis close to their bodies, stocks collapsed for use as a pistol. He didn't know how they'd made him, but it didn't really matter now, not with a combined sixty-four rounds of 9 mm ammunition staring him in the face.

"You knew!" de Cortez snarled; he'd been watching Shea's face. "You knew he was a cop!"

Shea didn't bother to say she'd only now found out, she just stared at her brother.

"You brought him in here, and you knew he was a cop!"

He took a step toward her, hand raised to deliver a blow. Chance reacted without thought for the deadly weapons trained on him; he launched himself at de Cortez. They went careening to the floor. Chance rolled, taking them both purposely up against the sofa. He heard de Cortez's grunt of pain as he jammed him against it.

He came up over the struggling man, digging his knee into soft belly to drive out air. With one hand he made a grab for his ankle holster. He didn't want any shooting, not with Shea in the room, but his only hope to control the bookends was to get the drop on their boss.

He felt the smooth wood of the grips under his fingertips, but de Cortez was still struggling as the bookends tried to get a clear shot. Then he had it, the little two-inch revolver sliding into his hand as he tugged it free of the holster.

He never got the chance to use it. Searing pain ripped up his arm as one of the bookends took his hand full force with a well-aimed kick. The little gun went clattering off into a corner. It was the last thing he heard before a bright white light ripped through his head, pain rang in his ears, and he slumped to all fours. That blow was followed by others, feet and fists, raining down on him until he couldn't stop the gasp of pain that ripped from him. He heard Shea screaming, but he couldn't understand what. Then the sound condensed into words.

"Stop it, Paul! What are you doing? Have you gone crazy?"

"Shut up, you stupid little bitch! You bring a cop in here, endanger my entire operation, and you think I'll listen to you?" He turned to the bookends. "Tie him up."

Mercifully the blows stopped, but as he shook his head to clear the mists of pain, Chance felt his hands yanked behind him and tied with something that felt absurdly silky. A scarf, he thought, then wondered why he cared when he was obviously in much deeper trouble. Slowly he lifted his head and sat back on his heels, barely aware of his shirt hanging torn and bloody, and the screaming of his battered body.

Shea was as pale as the moonlight had been that night by the pool. She was staring at de Cortez in stunned shock, and Chance's heart twisted inside him at her pain. That it was his fault she was finding out this way made him ache more than all the blows together had.

"My God, Paul—"

"Just shut up," de Cortez snapped.

"What are you—"

"You little fool!" de Cortez spat out, cutting her off. "Where do you think all that money came from? You think I slaved in some field somewhere for the money I sent you? The money that sent you to that fancy Malibu school?"

"No," she whispered, shaking her head.

"I thought you were different. You were quiet, you knew your place. It's the only reason I didn't make our *beloved*—" he drew out the word venomously "—mother pay for her disloyalty to my father then. You needed her to take care of you . . . so I spared her."

"Oh, God."

"But now I find you're no better than your mother, *puta!* Worse! She only married an Anglo, but you, you spread your legs for a cop!"

"She was your mother, too," Shea moaned.

"Ha! I spit on her. She got what she deserved, just as your father did! Bastard, always ordering me, telling me what to do. No one tells me what to do."

Shea was crumbling, Chance could see it, the shock of his deceit and the realization of her brother's were crashing in on her. She was trembling violently. Desperately he tried to divert de Cortez's attack.

"So you killed him."

The man whirled, staring. After a moment, he laughed. "So, you figured that out, did you? Perhaps I underestimated you a little, pig."

Chance heard Shea's cry but made himself ignore it. "It wasn't that tough. Once I found out that Micky Lopez was Pedro Escobar's cousin, it wasn't too hard to figure out who the shooter was. Especially when I found out you flew here two days before, not the day of his funeral like everyone thought. You set him up, didn't you? You had someone call him, knowing he'd come."

"Paul, no!"

He spun back around. "Quiet, bitch! Haven't you done enough? Your old man got what was coming to him." He laughed harshly. "Along with our sainted mother."

Chance risked a glance at Shea. She was so white it frightened him, her eyes dark and bruised looking in her waxen face. But he had to keep de Cortez going, had to keep him here until Quisto and the others made their move.

"And you came back before she died, too, didn't you? The day before. Did you make her take the pills?"

"No. She did that herself, after I told her the truth about how that *pendejo* she married died. As if anyone could replace my father!"

"You mean after she realized her own son had murdered her husband," Chance ground out.

"Oh, God, the note . . . you're the demon!"

Chance heard Shea moan, saw her shake her head slowly back and forth, like a creature with a mortal wound. Oh, God, songbird, I'm sorry. So damned sorry. I knew it would be hell when it came apart, but I never expected you to have to go through it like this.

He wished he knew what time it was. But it didn't matter, he knew it was running out. The man would never have admitted any of this if he hadn't planned to kill him. As if he'd read Chance's thoughts, de Cortez lifted his wrist and looked at his elegant watch.

"Oh, yes, pig, I know what's happening, and when."

Chance's last hope evaporated. If de Cortez knew the police were on their way, he had no reason to wait and every reason to hurry.

"I have nothing to lose, have I? So we're going to have a little execution, right here and now."

He reached inside his jacket and drew out a chrome automatic pistol. Chance heard Shea's gasp as de Cortez walked over and aimed it at Chance's head.

"Paul, no! You can't!" Shea moved, but the bookends grabbed her, holding her back.

"He'll do it, Shea," Chance said hoarsely. "Get out of here."

"No! No, you can't just kill him!"

"You think not?" He dug the barrel of the gun into Chance's ear. "He is a pig and he will die like one."

Chance heard him work the slide on the automatic to pop a round into the chamber. Then he felt de Cortez's hand on the back of his neck, forcing his head down. He knew what was coming, but all he could think about was Shea. He knew what a shot of that caliber to the head was going to look like, and he couldn't stand for her to see him die like that. He strained to lift his head and look at de Cortez.

"She's your sister," Chance whispered, his fear for Shea clear in his voice. "Don't make her watch this."

"Why not?" de Cortez spat out. "It's her fault that you got this close. She slept with you, she can watch you die."

"No, damn it! Please, don't do that to her!"

"How gallant! You will beg for her, but not for yourself? If only I had more time, it might be interesting to see just how far you would go for the little bitch. But as it is, I have my own plans for her. Plans that befit the traitor she is."

Shea sank down to the floor. The bookends let her go, realizing she was beyond anything more. They turned their attention to de Cortez, watching avidly, waiting. As if wishing to deprive them of a pleasure he wanted to keep to himself, de Cortez ordered them out.

"Make sure all of our guests received our warning." They went reluctantly.

Chance felt the death grip tighten around his neck as de Cortez once more tried to push his head down. He resisted, not sure why, except that he didn't want to die cowering in front of this piece of slime. The pressure increased; he pushed back.

He heard Shea make a sound, a choking, wounded sound that ripped at a heart he'd thought too numb to feel anything. He forced himself up against de Cortez's hand, lifting himself until he could see her. She was staring at him, her eyes wide and stunned, her arms wrapped around herself as she huddled in the corner of the room.

Summoning every bit of nerve he had left, he schooled his expression to calm. Slowly he let his mouth quirk into the crooked grin that made her laugh so. And as she stared at him in shock, he winked, broadly, lovingly.

Somewhere outside of this tiny space in the world, a door slammed. Paul de Cortez swore viciously. Chance felt the hand on his neck tighten fiercely, shoving him down with the full weight of his captor's body. He heard the metallic sound as de Cortez thumbed back the hammer. His nerve deserted him and he closed his eyes as he swallowed heavily, hanging on to an image of Shea the way he'd first seen her.

And in the split second when the boom seemed to rip apart the small room, he had time to wonder that he'd heard the shot at all.

Quisto was halfway across the main room when he heard the sharp report. He froze, waiting, but there were no more. He heard Morgan's shout but ignored it as he headed for the hallway, gun drawn. His goal was de Cortez's office, but when he saw the door of Shea's dressing room open, he stopped.

He held his breath, listening for a few seconds. All he could hear was someone taking gasping breaths and an odd, muffled sound. He darted his head around into the doorway, weapon at the ready.

"No," he choked out, "God, no."

It was a moment frozen in time. Chance, his back to the door, sprawled on the floor with his hands tied behind him with some piece of bright red material. And creeping out from beneath him, an ominous, spreading pool that was even brighter, even redder.

And then, incredibly, he moved. He lifted his head, turned it, and looked at Quisto with a pair of blue eyes that were dazed. When he saw who was there, his eyes closed again on a shuddering breath, and his head slumped back to the floor.

Only then did Quisto see the limp form sprawled half on top of Chance's muscular body, a cocked automatic clutched in dead fingers. And only then did he, with stunned realization, find the source of that odd muffled sound—Shea, huddled in the corner, quivering violently, Chance's small revolver still gripped in her trembling fingers.

"*Dios mio,*" Quisto breathed, seeing instantly what had happened.

"We've got most of them—"

Lieutenant Morgan broke off the minute he got close enough to see over Quisto's shoulder.

"My God."

"I'll handle this. Go wrap it up," Quisto said gruffly, holstering his gun and striding across the room to Chance. There were times, Morgan thought, when the best thing a boss could do was take an order from one of his men. He had no doubts that this was one of those times, and he left.

Quisto knelt beside his downed partner, reaching for his bound hands.

"You all right?"

A shudder went through Chance again; Quisto felt it in his arms as he tried to undo the knot.

"Yeah," he finally croaked out. "Just...get him off me, will you?"

Quisto's first instinct was to shove the limp body off Chance like the garbage he was, but the memory of Shea's presence made him do it more gently. Then he went back to the scarf and untied it. He slid an arm around Chance's shoulders and helped him sit up. Gingerly Chance brought his arms back to normal position and flexed them, rubbing at his wrists.

When he had the tremors slowed, if not under control, Chance tried to go to Shea. He found he couldn't walk, and wound up half crawling. She drew up tighter, shutting him out before he even got close. When he lifted a shaky hand, she jerked back out of his reach.

The last stubborn ember of hope died in him. Like a man feeling his way through heavy fog, he stood up. The shaking had stopped now, the hammering of his heart had slowed. He felt nothing but a vague numbness. He saw Quisto kneel beside Shea, but she turned him away, too. The gun fell to the floor from fingers trembling too badly to hold it any longer.

He let Quisto lead him to the table Shea had used for her makeup. He sat on the edge of it, only peripherally aware that the noise outside had increased.

"Find Eric," Chance said hoarsely. "Eric Carlow. He's with the band. She'll let him help her."

"I'll find him. You sure you're all right? Nothing broken? You look like they beat the hell out of you."

"Nothing's broken."

"What the hell happened, man?"

Chance laughed bitterly. "What happened? He was tipped, that's what happened. He knew who I was, that we were coming in, and when. He knew it all."

Quisto looked stunned, then thoughtful. "Eaton," he murmured.

"What?"

"Eaton. He disappeared right after you left. Never made the raid."

A memory poked through the fog. "He was outside the lieutenant's door. He knew I was headed here."

"The bastard," Quisto snapped, furious. "I'll bet if we dug deep enough, we'd find he's the one who tipped de Cortez to the raid in Miami. Lieutenant Morgan will call them. They'll pick him up, Chance. He's history." Quisto swore sharply. "He must have been getting a hell of a pay-off. And being able to burn you was a big bonus, a sop to his ego."

Chance shook his head, dazed. "He hated me that much...."

It didn't bother him, only surprised him. Then, as the vision formed in his mind of someone else whose hate would hurt as nothing in his life ever had, he lifted his head to look at Shea. And then away.

Quisto had never seen anything like it. Blue eyes that had been dazed with shock and pain went flat and dull even as he watched, as if all the life and soul had left not only the eyes but the man himself.

"Chance," he whispered, "it wasn't your fault. You had no choice but to do what you did."

Chance stared at him as if he were some inanimate object.

"Give her time, Chance."

"All the time in the world won't undo what I did to her."

"She saved your life, man. Even after she knew. That has to mean something."

The last flicker of light in the blue eyes was snuffed out. In a voice utterly devoid of feeling, Chance said flatly, "Yeah. It means I'm a real prize. One woman dies for me, and another one kills for me."

He slipped off the table and walked unsteadily out of the room.

Chapter 13

Shea held her guitar, a blank page scored for music in front of her on the table and a pencil lodged over her ear, but she was spending more time watching the clouds her breath made in the frosty air than committing any notes to paper.

She looked around at the mountains, sadly aware that the snow-covered landscape gave her none of the pleasure it always had. It had been her last hope, coming home, her last chance at regaining any of the joy she'd once had in life. It had failed miserably, and as she sat in the brilliant sunshine and crisp air of a perfect Tahoe winter day, she knew nothing would ever give her back that joy.

After a while she had decided she would settle for the absence of pain. She'd been skating nicely along the surface of life for nearly a month now, never letting her mind stray from the tasks of day-to-day life, rising, working on music that wouldn't come, fixing food she didn't eat, forcing herself to stay awake so the nightmares wouldn't happen. These abnormal things became her normalcy, the anodynes that kept her from thinking of anything else. She'd become very good at it.

She heard the car on the freshly plowed street but paid no attention. Her friends knew of her penchant for solitude since she had returned, and few bothered her. She plucked at the strings again, fretfully. She changed the key and tried again. And again. And at last she dropped the pencil. She couldn't deny it any longer. The music was gone.

She sat hunched over the guitar, staring at the blank page. For the briefest of moments a wish to feel something, anything crept into her mind. She banished it as she had all other thoughts like that, almost all thought altogether. She knew that once she let any emotion in she would be inundated, and she would drown in the flood.

"You look colder than the snow, *querida*."

She went cold inside so fast that he was very close to the truth. Her voice was as chilled as the snowy countryside, her eyes as flat and withdrawn as a pair of blue ones had been weeks before.

"What are you doing here?"

Quisto grabbed the upright post to the porch roof and lowered himself to sit on the top step. "What do you think?"

"Did he send you?"

"No."

She made a wordless sound of disbelief.

"I know you have no reason to believe me, but nevertheless it is true. He didn't send me."

"Then why are you here?" she asked again, her tone flat and empty.

"Has he been here?"

"You came a long way to ask me that. Why don't you just ask him?"

"Because I don't know where he is."

That startled her, but she recovered quickly. "The cops lost a cop?"

The words were flippant, and he would have expected sarcasm, even bitterness, but her voice was as flat and expressionless as it had been before.

"No. He just disappeared. Went AWOL, as it were. The day after you refused to see him, after the funeral."

If he'd meant to bait her, she didn't rise to it.

"Why would you ever think he'd come here?"

"Because he loves you."

He said it simply, as a statement of fact, and for the first time something flickered in her eyes. It was gone so quickly Quisto couldn't tell what it had been—pain, anger or hatred. Any of the three seemed equally likely.

"There's no need to perpetuate the fantasy any longer."

"What fantasy?" Quisto asked softly.

"That he ... loved me."

The break in her voice told him that she wasn't quite as frozen as the landscape, wasn't quite as frozen as she would like to think. And probably not as frozen as she wanted to be. But when she went on, she was once more in control.

"He had a job to do. He used me to do it. It's over."

"If you really think that's all it was, then you're a fool. And I don't think you're a fool."

Shea set down her guitar with exquisite care and much more concentration than the task required. She sat primly on the edge of the chair, her hands tucked between her knees. It was because they were cold, she told herself firmly, not because they were shaking. She took a deep breath.

"I understand he had to do it. I've...come to terms with what my brother was. And I suppose I was a fool for not seeing it." That flicker came and went in her eyes again. "I guess I've made a fool of myself twice, haven't I? Once over my brother, and once ..." She faltered; she hadn't said his name, not even to herself, and she didn't dare now.

"And for the same, stupid reason," she ended in a whisper, hating the way her voice suddenly shook. "I loved them."

"You were wrong about your brother. You weren't wrong about Chance."

"Please." A hint of desperation crept into her voice. "I've told you I understand. That he had to do what he did."

"Yes, he did. But not for the reason you think." Quisto paused, searching for the words to break through the formidable shell she'd built. He'd had no luck with Chance; he prayed he could get through to Shea.

"He was after my brother. What other reason is there?"

"You. To protect you."

She stared at him, then gave an agonized little laugh.

"Shea, listen." He shifted slightly so he could watch her face. "When we began, we all thought you were in on it."

"What?" Her eyes widened in disbelief, but Quisto welcomed it; at least she was listening.

"You were his sister. We thought you had to at least know what he was, and what he was doing. All of us did." His voice went soft as he added, "Except Chance. He fought us all, practically from day one."

Quisto kept his eyes on her. He wanted to be sure she was hearing every word. "We didn't believe him, but he wouldn't budge. He knew even then that he was getting in too deep. Do you remember that week he didn't see you at all?"

Slowly, as if hypnotized, Shea nodded.

"He wanted out then. He told me he was out of control, that he'd lost the line."

"The line . . . ?"

"Between how he felt for you and the job. And which was more important." Quisto moved on the step, edging closer to her. "It may have started out as work, Shea, but it changed almost immediately. He had to lie to you, but he wasn't living a lie. Everything he felt for you was real. More real than anything I've ever seen him feel since I've known him."

Shea shook her head. Quisto wasn't sure if it was in denial or pain.

"He'd been dead inside for so long, Shea. Then you made him come alive again. He hated what he was doing to you. Using you. But he had to come back, Shea. For your sake."

She drew back sharply. "You keep saying that."

"Because it's true. The federal agent who followed your brother here from Miami . . . he wouldn't believe that you were innocent. He swore he'd take you down with your brother, and then we'd know he'd been right."

She took in a harsh, quick breath, shaking her head.

"Chance came back because he was the only thing between you and Eaton. It was tearing him apart, but he knew he had to be there, to protect you. He could have turned it over to somebody else, but he didn't trust anybody with you, not even me. He knew no one else felt the way he did, both about your innocence, and about you personally. Nobody else would go as far as he would to protect you. So he went on with it.''

"And so well," she said bitterly, "I never guessed."

"He may have kept up a good front with you, but he spilled his guts to me, because not telling you was eating him alive. He knew you would hate him for it, but he had to do it. Eaton was crazy. There was no other way to make sure you weren't hurt."

"Why didn't he tell me?" Her voice quivered, but she seemed unaware.

"Because he didn't want you to have to choose, Shea. He felt like he'd betrayed you just as your brother had. You would have had to turn on one or the other, choose one or the other to trust. He didn't want you to have to face that."

She wouldn't meet his eyes, but he saw her shiver, and knew what she was thinking.

"He put his career on the line for his belief in you. And in the end, his life. But Eaton took it out of his hands. He tipped your brother that Chance was a cop, and that we were on the way. And you had to choose after all."

A strangled little sound came from her. "Yes," she whispered, "I did. And how do I live with that?"

"Ask Chance. He's had a lot of practice living with it."

Her head came up then. "What?"

Quisto paused. He was betraying a confidence, but this was his last hand and there was no point in saving any cards.

"About five years ago, Chance busted a crack house. A gang had set it up, trying to get a foothold in town. He stopped them before they even got started. They swore they'd pay him back." He hesitated, then went on. "They planted a bomb in his car. Only Chance wasn't in it when it went off. His wife was. And she was seven months pregnant. It blew up the moment she turned the key. She died instantly, right in front of him. On Christmas Eve."

"Oh, God."

Shea could feel the memories begin to pound in her head, to demand to be let out and be seen. Chance's face when he talked about Christmas. His words as he left her dressing room that horrible morning. "One woman dies for me, and one woman kills for me." She tried to fight them down.

"So every year he leaves," Quisto said quietly, "and every year we wonder if he'll come back, or just become another statistic."

"Statistic?"

"Another cop who bites the bullet, swallows his gun, or any of the stupid clichés. Like his partner did."

"His partner? It was his partner who...?"

"Marty Thompson. Less than a year after Sarah died." Quisto's voice dropped even lower. "Chance said at Marty's funeral that if he had the guts, he'd do exactly what Marty did."

She made a tiny sound that made his stomach jump. He knew he was playing dirty, but he had to give it his best, hardest shot. If he couldn't get her to admit she loved Chance, maybe he could shake her into being scared for him.

"Who knows. Maybe this time he'll find the guts." He got up and stared steadily down at her. "You might just be enough to put him over the edge."

Shea knew she was much too tired to be driving, but she didn't dare stop. She'd waited until almost too late, and now that the decision was made, she had to hurry.

She'd spent three hellish days, the walls she'd so carefully built to hold back her memories ruptured by Quisto's words. The memories had engulfed her one after the other, so rapidly, so powerfully, that she had sat staring blankly for hours under their force. So much made sense now. His odd silences, the moments when she had surprised that quiet pain in his eyes. The night at the pool, the night he had hung on to her as if she were his last hope for life....

"Have you ever had to do something that made you hate yourself?"

His words echoed in her mind over and over, making such painful sense now. And his tears, the tears that had so frightened her, coming from that strong, proud man. For her. For what he was doing to her.

Remember I love you more than I've ever loved anyone or anything. Remember that, Shea, no matter what.

Involuntarily her foot pressed on the accelerator as she did as he'd asked, and remembered. He'd known how she would react, how she'd feel, still he'd had no choice but to do what he did. Yet even in the end he'd come to her, to get her out, though it had very nearly cost him his life.

The pictures shimmered in her mind, one floating to the surface with vivid clarity. That crazy, courageous moment when, fighting Paul's grasp, he had looked up and given her that crooked grin, that broad, teasing wink. Knowing he was going to die in seconds, his last thought had been to try to make it a little less horrible for her. It had been that one gallant act that had sent her over the edge, scrambling for the gun that had skidded into the corner. She gripped the wheel tighter as she drove, the tears beginning again.

When at last she left the city of San Luis Obispo behind her, she barely had time to realize it before the tiny community of Avila Beach, nestled in a protected little cove, appeared to her right. She nearly missed the single off ramp, so stunned was she that she was here at last.

She hadn't thought much beyond this point. Getting here had seemed the most important thing in her life. She glanced at the clock on the dash, realizing with a little shock that there were only three hours left in this Christmas Eve. Quisto's words haunted her, and the weariness she'd been feeling faded. She had to find Chance, she just had to. It didn't matter that all she knew was that the house was on the beach here, she would go to every door in town if she had to.

In the end, it was easier than she'd expected. There were only two Buckners in the thin phone book that covered the local area, and only one in Avila Beach itself. With a tiny prayer of thanks for the Thanksgiving morning when Chance had told her of this place, she scribbled down the address. Then she left the phone booth and walked to the gas station building she'd found. It was closed on this holiday evening, but a map posted in the window told her what she needed to know.

From the road the small house was dark, as were most of the houses here, many of them being vacation homes for people spending Christmas with their families elsewhere. But when she peeked through a window into the garage, she saw the shadowy outline of his Jeep. She went to the door facing the road, then stood there for a moment. He was probably asleep, but she couldn't wait any longer. She had to see him.

There was no answer to her knock, and the doorbell didn't seem to work. She tried again, listening to the crash of the surf on the other side of the house. Still nothing. She remembered what a light sleeper he was, how he would awaken alert and aware while she was still fighting off the fog of sleep, and a chill feathered up her spine. Her shoulders tensed as she fought it off. She knocked again. Nothing.

She left the porch to look through one of the windows. Between the slats of shutters she could see only variations of shadows, and no sign of life. That chill, stronger this time, rippled up her spine again.

She noticed a narrow walkway that ran along the side of the house, dimly lit by the light of a winter quarter moon. She started down it tentatively, then more certainly as she saw stronger light ahead where the thin moon's glow reflected off the rolling water and the sand.

A rectangle of golden light shot out from the sliding glass door on the beach side of the house, but its reach ended where the wooden deck's stairs led down to the beach, deserted on this holiday. She was about to start up the half-dozen steps when something caught her eye. She turned her head to look at the dark huddled shape lying on the beach a few yards away. A seal? she wondered, knowing little about what kind of sea mammals populated this particular area.

Then, as she instinctively moved to get a better look, the faint light of the moon caught and gleamed on tousled hair, blond streaks glinting oddly silver. She started toward him, the chill she'd felt creeping around to encircle her heart. He was lying so oddly, twisted sideways in the sand, as if—

She stopped dead. Her eyes were fixed on the small black shape that lay a few inches from his outflung hand. For a moment a self-protective instinct refused to let her comprehend the implication of what she was seeing. All her stunned brain could think was how odd it was that she who had so little to do with guns had suddenly become so aware of them. And then the reality broke through the protective barrier, along with the devastating thought that she had waited too long. She cried out.

"No!"

She ran, stumbling in the sliding sand, the icy cold tightening around her heart like a ruthless hand.

"Chance, no!" She dropped to her knees beside his sprawled body. "No!"

With a violently shaking hand she reached for his shoulder, terrified of what she would see when she moved him. She pulled him over, tugging on his shoulders to bring his head onto her lap. She wasn't even aware of the tears streaming down her cheeks until they began to drop on his face.

"Oh, God, please," she moaned, searching for any sign of a wound. The sweatshirt he wore was dark, and she could see nothing. His jeans were worn and ragged, and his feet were bare, dusted with sand. His head lolled in her lap, frighteningly slack. And then her heart seemed to lodge in her throat as she stared down at him—his eyes had fluttered open.

"Mmph," he mumbled.

"Chance!"

He seemed to focus on her, and a smile curved his mouth. A smile that was oddly rueful. Then he muttered something she had to bend over him to hear. It was then that the message her nose had been sending got through, and she recoiled. The gleam of moonlight on glass caught the edge of her vision, and she spotted the nearly empty bottle that lay discarded in the sand.

"You're drunk!" Her voice rang out with a relief that left her trembling.

"You bet," he agreed. His brow furrowed as his befuddled brain tried to function. "If I'd known you'd be so real, woulda done it sooner."

"You idiot," she said shakily, "I thought you'd...killed yourself."

"Tried," he said simply, trying a shrug that was beyond his fogged brain to command. He lifted a wobbly hand as if expecting the weapon to still be there. When he saw it was empty, he looked up at her in puzzlement. "Tried," he said again. "Don' know how Marty did it." He grinned suddenly, sillily. "Shot the water instead."

"Oh, Chance."

"Couldn' do it, songbird," he whispered suddenly, the grin vanishing. "Woulda made what you did for nothin'."

With a choking little sound she bent over him, her arms around his shoulders, hugging him to her.

"God, you feel real," he muttered, and she drew back to look at him in surprise.

"What?"

"Hey," he said, the look of utter puzzlement creasing his forehead again, "you're talkin'."

"I...what?"

"How come you're talkin' to me? You always jus' sit there, lookin' at me...so beautiful...then I wake up 'n' remember you hate me...."

Shea thought her heart was going to break all over again at his words and the change in his expression, from wistful to a deep, shuddering pain. She realized then that no matter how hurt she had been by his actions, and by the betrayal of her brother, it was nothing compared to the hell he'd been through.

"Come on," she said softly, slipping his arm over her shoulders. "It's cold out here. Let's go inside."

"'Kay," he said agreeably, and struggled to his feet. Then the deeply ingrained instinct of the cop kicked in, and he looked around the sand at their feet. "Gun," he muttered. "Can't leave it. Could hurt somebody."

Shea didn't know whether to laugh or cry. He'd been on the verge of suicide, yet he was worried about somebody else getting hurt with his gun.

''I'll get it,'' she assured him.

He seemed to accept it, his inebriated brain seeming to forget that a moment ago he was convinced she was nothing more than a recurring vision.

She got him inside, unable to spare more than a glance for the inside of the small house. He muttered something as she tried a door that turned out to be a bathroom. She went to another and found a bedroom strewn with discarded clothes, and drapes pulled tight against the view of the water. The bed was in the center of the room, sheets and blankets in a tangle at the foot. She led him to it.

''Can you help me with your clothes?''

''Could. Won't.''

She looked at him. ''Why?''

'''s when I always wake up. Don't want to wake up.''

''Oh, Chance,'' she whispered, her heart still aching for what she'd put him through. She began with trembling fingers to pull at his clothes, having to stop when she pulled off his shirt, just to stare at him in pained shock. His ribs stood out as if he hadn't eaten at all in the past month. Living on coffee, she thought as she remembered the countless cups scattered all over.

Christmas Eve, she thought inanely as she finished undressing him, cringing at his gauntness. A night that was so joyous to most but only a grim, ugly anniversary for him. The thought kept her from feeling anything but a tender concern as she looked at him. He was out before she got the tangle of covers undone enough to tuck them gently around his naked form.

For a long time she just sat on the edge of the bed, watching him. He looked unutterably weary, dark circles beneath the semicircles of lowered, gold-tipped lashes. Weary, and more vulnerable even than the night he had clung to her so desperately.

She should be tired, she thought. Too tired to be so wakeful. But now that she was here, and knew that he was all right—she shuddered yet again at how close he'd come— she couldn't seem to unwind. She'd had to postpone what she'd come here for, and her body seemed loath to give up the need for movement that had propelled her here.

At last she got up, driven to restore some order to the chaos he'd been living in. Knowing that he was normally neat, if not fanatically tidy, it told her much about his state of mind. He had reached the bottom tonight and survived. She didn't want to take any chances of him sliding back into the yawning pit that had sent him outside with a gun he'd meant to use on himself.

The gun. She'd completely forgotten. She raced outside and grabbed it from the sand. This one was larger, and she stifled a shudder as she picked it up and carried it gingerly inside. She stuffed it out of sight in the first drawer she came to. Then she started on the house, sorting, stacking.

She paused in front of a photo that hung over the desk on the wall opposite the windows. Taken on the deck of this house, it was of a smiling, contented couple, each with an arm around the central figure in the picture—a younger, short-haired Chance. He too was smiling, his blue eyes vivid and clear and unshadowed, dramatically and painfully different than the tormented eyes of the man in the next room. Different, in fact, from the man she'd first met. Only now did she realize how much he'd changed just in the time she'd known him. She'd begun to see glimpses of the man in this picture, or at least she had until things had begun to unravel.

Sighing, she began to shift the papers on the desk. She meant only to straighten them, not to pry, but when her own name leaped out at her from one of the sheets of paper, she couldn't resist looking at it.

"Shea sounds wonderful," it said in a flowing, feminine hand across a sheet of linen-finish stationary, "and we hope to meet her soon. I can't tell you how much it means to us that you've found someone you care enough about to let into your heart, son. We were so afraid you would shut the world out forever. She must be as special as you say to have worked such a miracle. Whatever the problems are that you mentioned, I'm sure you can work them out."

The letter went on to another page, but reading any more would have left her feeling too guilty of snooping. Besides, her eyes were too blurry anyway. She set the pages down carefully, her heart aching poignantly in her chest at this final proof that what he'd felt for her was genuine, and had been all along. The letter was dated the week after he'd come back from those days away from her.

She went back to the bedroom after that, taking a moment to look at him through eyes that wouldn't stop brimming. They were different tears now, not the acid tears of fear and desperation that had been her only companion on her frantic journey, but tears of love and hope, hope that she hadn't hurt him irreparably, that she hadn't destroyed his love for her. She was frantic to know, but she knew she had no choice in the matter. She picked out a spot far enough away so as not to disturb him and sat down to wait.

Shea watched him through the night. He slept unmoving for a long time, and she dozed, but in the hour just after dawn he became restless, tossing, muttering under his breath as if in the grip of some malevolent dream. She knew all too well about that kind of dream, and reached to shake him out of it. But then it subsided and he slept on. Until it began again, the same cycle, the agitation, then the quiet again.

Shea had at last decided, as she sat cross-legged on the bed, that she was grateful he'd drunk so much. If he'd been sober, in cold control as he usually was, perhaps he would have gone through with it. She knew now that living with that would have been the hardest thing she would have ever faced.

He'd been asleep ten hours when he began to show some signs of rousing. His back was to her as he lay on his side, but she heard him let out an odd breath. Then she saw him move, lifting his head slightly. When she heard a low, heartfelt groan, she knew he'd truly awakened, and no doubt to a head that felt the size of the house.

He struggled up to one elbow, another groan escaping as he grabbed at the edge of the bed for support. He lifted his other hand and ran it over his tangled hair, gently, as if even that slight pressure hurt.

"It's a good thing you don't do this often," Shea said softly.

He went rigid, and snapped around on the bed in a movement so swift she knew it had to send arrows of pain through his throbbing head. But he didn't seem to notice, he just stared at her, lips parted in shock. For a long, frozen moment, neither of them moved. Then, with painful slowness, he reached out with an unsteady hand. She watched him, puzzled, until his fingers met her knee and he yanked his arm back as if she had burned him.

"You . . . you're real."

She understood then, and felt the tug at her heart again. She had haunted him as he had haunted her, there the instant she let her guard down. She swallowed tightly, unable to speak.

"What are you doing here?"

He looked so wary, his eyes so shuttered, that she couldn't get out what she wanted to say. She seized on a part of the truth.

"People have been worried about you."

"Where'd you get that idea?"

"Quisto."

His eyes went colder. "I told him to stay out of it."

"He was concerned."

"Then why isn't he here?"

"He didn't know where 'here' was."

He lowered his eyes, hiding them from her, but she saw the distorted twist of his mouth. "But I told you, didn't I?"

He sounded disgusted with himself. Shea's heart quailed; he didn't love her anymore. She'd waited too long, been too involved in her own tragedy when she should have been trusting him, trusting his love for her. And now she'd killed it. She could only watch as he sank back against the pillows.

"Okay. So now you know. You can tell them I'm fine."

Shea gathered her splintering courage. "I wouldn't say sitting on the beach with a gun aimed at yourself and then drinking yourself into oblivion is exactly all right."

His eyes narrowed, his brows lowering ominously. "That's why you're here, isn't it? Quisto gave you some sob story, and you felt guilty, right? Well, you can shuffle your little butt right back out of here."

She winced. "That's not why I'm here. At least, not directly."

"It doesn't matter much anymore, does it? You made your feelings quite clear back in Marina del Mar. I don't see any reason to drag it all out again."

"Chance—"

"Excuse me," he said with exaggerated politeness as he reached for the covers, "I'm going to the bathroom."

The blanket was tossed halfway back when his arm froze in midmotion. He stared down at himself, his hung-over mind only now realizing that he was in his own bed, and naked beneath the covers. His gaze jerked to her face, and Shea saw with amazement that he was embarrassed. He tore the sheet free of the bed, wrapped it around himself and stalked off to the bathroom. At least, he tried to stalk; it was more of a stagger thanks to his muddled head.

Shea stared after him. She knew that body so intimately. She'd touched, kissed and admired virtually every inch of it. She'd seen it dressed, undressed, and at every stage in between. She'd seen it sprawled in relaxed sleep and tensed with a ready alertness. She'd seen it slick with water from the pool, with the dampness of her kisses, with sweat from their passion, and even slick from her own wet heat. And in the quiet darkness of one painful night, she'd seen him weep. Yet now he was acting as if they were total strangers.

Was that what he wanted? Did he truly want her to leave? Had she really destroyed what he'd once felt for her?

Her chin came up. She'd learned a lot in the past month about just how tough she was. She would go, if that's what he really wanted, but he was going to have to convince her of that first. And that, Mr. Buckner, she said to herself with quiet determination, is going to take some doing.

She heard the shower running, and knew he was trying to wait her out. Humming cheerfully, under the theory that if she tried hard enough to feel that way it might catch, she made the bed, then went to the kitchen to start a pot of coffee, sure he was going to need it. Then she went out to stand on the deck, breathing in the salt-tanged air.

She decided to go for a walk on the beach. Let him think she'd given up, gone away. Maybe she'd be able to surprise him into revealing his true feelings, into letting down that wary guard, when she suddenly reappeared again.

It was a crystal winter morning, with only traces of a lingering morning mist lying in the cooler spots. A good omen, she decided, working on building up the strength she knew she was going to need.

When she came back he was on the deck, a steaming cup in his hands as he stared out at the foam-delineated waves marching in to shore. He had the same ragged jeans on, and a different sweatshirt that was cut off at the arms and almost as worn as the pants. He'd washed his hair but hadn't shaved. Shea didn't care, she thought he was beautiful. She walked carefully, quietly, and he didn't look at her until she started up the steps.

Something startlingly alive leaped in his eyes before the wary look returned and he turned his eyes back to the sea. Shea knew her plan had worked. She knew that he wasn't as protected against her as he'd thought. There was still something there, although it was obvious he was fighting it.

Would he stop fighting, she wondered, if he knew that he was wrong? If he knew that she didn't hate him as he thought? That she never truly had, she'd only hated what he'd done? And she wasn't sure any longer that she even hated that, now that she knew why. And what it had done to him.

"If you thought I was going to give up and go away," she said as she sat in the chair next to him, "you were wrong."

"You will." He didn't look at her.

"You'll have a long wait."

His mouth quirked for a split second, then settled back into its impassive line. "I've got time."

"So have I. All the time in the world, now that the music's gone."

His eyes flickered to her, then away. He said nothing.

"I found it won't come, if there's nothing left inside."

He still said nothing.

"Will you at least listen to me?"

He gave no sign that he'd even heard.

"You know," she said with a touch of exasperation, "I'm not sure I don't like you better drunk."

Words came then, sharp and biting. "Stick around then. I plan to get very drunk again very soon."

"Fine. At least then you'll talk to me."

"I talk to...a dream. The reality hates me, remember?"

"No. No, I don't." She meant she didn't hate him, but he took her words as a literal answer.

"Well, I remember. When I came to see you after the funeral, you said, 'Go to hell, you bastard.' I think those were the exact words."

"Chance, I—"

"Look," he said wearily, his knuckles whitening as he gripped the cup he had yet to drink from, "I understand. You have every right to feel the way you do. I used you, and I don't blame you for believing it was all a lie."

"But I know now—"

"I'm sorry you came all the way here because Quisto laid some story on you that I'd come up here to blow my brains out. He should have known I'd chicken out. I won't try it again, okay? So you can leave now."

"That's not why I came."

"Oh, yeah?" He still wouldn't look at her.

"Yes. It was part of it, but only because...because when I thought that you might truly do it, when I thought of you...dead, I remembered the real reason why what happened in my dressing room happened."

She heard the coffee slosh in his cup as a tremor shook him. He didn't speak or look at her.

"I've had a lot of time to think, Chance. I know now that if there's anyone to blame for what happened, it was Paul. He was evil. Utterly, unsalvageably evil. He—" Her voice broke and she had to stop and swallow before she could go on. "He murdered my father. A man who only tried to help him, whose only crime was that he wasn't Paul's father. And he might as well have murdered my mother. He lied, he cheated, he stole, murdered, dealt in drugs and death. And I never saw it. I even—" she shuddered ''—profited from it. My God, I went to school on drug money.''

''You didn't know.''

Hope flared in her at the unexpected words. She wanted to go to him, go throw herself at him and beg him to love her again, but she knew it was too soon. She made herself go on.

''He would never have changed. He would have kept on living as he had, in ugliness and filth. He had to be stopped.'' She took a deep breath. ''And I'm glad it was me.''

That got through to him. His head came around sharply, his shadowed eyes startled as he looked at her at last.

''Why?'' he whispered harshly.

''Because,'' she said, lifting her head to meet his gaze steadily, ''if it had been you, I don't think you would ever believe that I would forgive you for killing my brother.''

He stared at her.

''I made my choice that day, Chance, between good and evil. My true choice. And I paid the price for it in the days afterward. But it was the right choice then, and it is now.''

''But you said—''

''It was the right choice,'' she repeated. ''The only one I could make. But I had to come to terms with it. I'm just sorry that I hurt you so badly in the process.''

''Why was it . . . the only choice?''

It was here at last, the moment she'd been waiting for, wondering how she would handle it when it came. Now that it had arrived, the simple words came easily, without thinking.

''Because I love you.''

Coffee sloshed out of his cup, and she wondered that it didn't shatter under the pressure of his grip. He jerked his head away, staring now not at the ocean, but at the coffee puddling on the boards of the deck beneath his feet.

''Shea,'' he choked out, ''if you're just feeling sorry for me, forget it. I don't want your pity.''

''Pity?'' She left her chair to kneel beside his. ''How could I feel pity for you? You're the strongest man I've ever known. You do a thankless job that everybody needs done but nobody wants to do. You deal with things that would make most people run and hide. You've been through hell and come out alive, and after all that, you still care, even though you try to hide it.''

"You don't hate me?"

It sounded so wistful, so lost that she once again had to hold herself back when what she wanted most was to throw her arms around him and hang on for the rest of her life.

"I never really hated you," she said softly. "I hated what you did. But I see now that you had to do it. It was the only way. I even see that you did it partly for my sake."

"Mostly," he whispered. "I was afraid for you."

"I know. Quisto told me about that man."

His gaze went back to her face. "We might have saved your brother, taken him alive, if Eaton hadn't—"

"Hush. I know. It wasn't your fault. Paul...Paul started the wheels rolling a long time ago, and in the end they crushed him. I was just...the device."

"But—"

"I never hesitated, Chance. It wasn't really a dilemma, there wasn't time. My decision was made the moment I realized he truly meant to kill you." She reached up, risking a tentative touch on his arm. "I couldn't let him kill the man I'd waited all my life for. Especially when, deep down inside and despite it all, I knew that man loved me."

She saw the sudden light in his eyes. "You...believe that?"

"I know it," she said huskily, positively. "My God, Chance, he was about to send a bullet through your brain, and you were still thinking of me. That was the moment when I saw the real man my brother had become. He was the one who was supposed to love me, yet he wanted me to watch your execution. You were on the verge of death, yet you were trying to save me from the horror of it. How could I not see where the real love was?"

"But you wouldn't see me...."

"Oh, Chance, when it really sank in what I had done, I was so confused, I blamed you for everything." She took a deep breath, then plunged ahead. "Have I killed it, Chance? Did I take too long to realize the truth, that you only did what you had to do? That I should have trusted in your love, as you asked me to that morning, no matter what? That I should have known that whatever else you had to keep from me, you never held back your love once you'd given it?''

She saw the guarded look fall away, saw the joy rise in the blue eyes, chasing away the shadows, the exhaustion. His lips parted as he drew in a shaky breath, and he fumblingly set aside the coffee cup and took her hands.

''You're sure?'' he choked out. ''You forgive me for having to lie to you? For... using you?''

''You did what you had to do. And I know that you never lied after you told me you loved me. You just couldn't tell me the whole truth. There's nothing to forgive.''

''Oh, God, Shea...''

''It took me a while to realize that Paul used me as much as you had. And for much more horrible reasons.''

''But, what you did...''

''It wasn't my fault, any more than...what happened to Sarah was yours.''

His eyes closed as he absorbed the fact that she knew what had happened. She tightened her fingers around his, and they opened again. She didn't know whose hands were shaking more, her own or his. It didn't matter.

''Chance? Will you give me back the music?'' she asked softly, baring her heart, her very soul to his gaze.

''I'll give you all of the world I can, if you'll let me,'' he whispered.

''I'll settle for a love song.''

At the instant when she was going to give in to the need she'd been fighting, he took the need away by pulling her up and onto his lap. It was a little fierce, more than a little rough; Shea never noticed. All she knew was that he was holding her tightly against him, that she was in his arms again at last.

''Oh, Shea,'' he murmured brokenly, ''it was real, all of it, I swear. That's why it was such hell. I loved you so much I couldn't stand to lie to you, but I had to, to be able to keep you safe.'' He shivered, and she slid her arms around his neck, resting her cheek against his hair. "I didn't think you'd ever believe it, that I really love you."

"I know."

Her voice was soft, reassuring. She shifted to press a kiss on his still damp hair; it felt like heavy silk beneath her lips. It was her last sane thought, for he leaned back in the chair and dragged her mouth down to his. The blaze ignited as if it had been only moments since it had burned last, yet with all the force weeks apart had given it.

It was much later, as she lay atop him with his ebbing flesh still inside her, smiling as he shifted his hand to more fully cup her breast, that Shea took the opportunity she'd prayed for during ten hours of driving.

"Chance?"

"Hmm."

"Would you mind terribly getting up and dressed?"

One blue eye popped open. "Now?"

She nodded. The other eye followed suit. After a moment of studying her face, he smiled.

"Okay."

She drew back a little, startled. "Just like that?"

He nodded.

"What if I tell you to pack?"

"Okay."

"No questions?"

"Nope."

She got his point, and laughed in delight before she leaned down to nuzzle the hollow of his throat.

"I trust you, too," she whispered. "I just lost sight of it for a while."

"I know." He planted a kiss on her hair. "And I also know that if you don't stop that—" he shivered in response to her tongue's darting flicks over his collarbone "—we'll be in this bed all day. Not that I care, you understand, but I got the idea that you had something else in mind."

Her eyes were sparkling as she lifted her head. "I do." Her smile was almost as dazzling as her eyes. "If we go right now, you can still have that white Christmas."

"Christmas?" Chance looked startled, then rueful. "It is, isn't it?" He let out a short, compressed breath and shook his head wonderingly. "I . . . forgot."

She didn't tell him that she knew just how much of a miracle that was.

"Will you come?" she asked softly.

There was the briefest pause, as if he were turning the last page of a chapter full of both love and pain. The smile that lit his face then was one of release and anticipation.

"Yes," he said simply, and hugged her.

And when they arrived at last at the house she had so hopefully decorated before leaving, Shea couldn't help smiling as if she'd caused it herself when it began to snow.

Epilogue

"Grandma! *Es tio* Chance's car!"

The fractured combination of Spanish and English, common in this house so frequently overflowing with young voices, was delivered with all the considerable power of six-year-old lungs. The chaos of childish voices rising above adult ones echoed as all the one-time occupants of the house, gathered again for this special occasion, poured outside into the front yard. At one sharp command from Celeste Romero, however, quiet reigned.

As he got out, Chance threw a crooked grin at the assembled crowd of Romeros. This Christmas was going to have to go some to surpass last year, the sweet white Christmas that had restored the beauty of the season to him, but as he looked at the crowd of smiling faces, he thought it might come in a very close second. He walked around to the passenger door of the sporty little coupe that had replaced—only temporarily, Shea insisted—the Jeep. He opened it, and leaned down to help his wife out.

A chorus of greetings, subdued by the watchful eye of Mama Romero, met Shea, but all eyes were fastened on the tiny bundle she held. With all the deference and love she had come to feel for this woman who had taken her into her generous heart as if she were her own daughter, who had made space for her in her family as she had for Chance, Shea presented her to Chance's son.

"Tu abuela, mijo," she whispered. "Your grandmother. By love, which is sometimes even better than blood."

"He is so beautiful!" Celeste exclaimed, wiping at her eyes as she stroked a gentle finger over a tiny cheek. The baby recognized a loving, motherly touch and cooed at her.

"Beautiful?" Quisto teased, his eyes dancing with mischief. "Handsome, perhaps."

"Beautiful," Celeste insisted, ignoring her incorrigible youngest son.

Quisto grinned, unperturbed. Chance grinned back. Nothing much bothered him these days, now that Shea's pregnancy was over. It had been hell, he thought. More, she'd sometimes said, on him than her. She had known he was remembering other times, other tragedies, despite his efforts to convince himself that this would be different. She'd done her best to ease his fears, but knew they were only gone for good when he had looked at her with brimming eyes as she held their son out to him.

The children were clustering around her, clamoring for a look. They had long ago decided they quite liked this beautiful new "aunt" of theirs with the lovely voice that could sing them to sleep, or impress their friends with the latest rock and roll; they flocked to her like little bears to honey.

Chance sternly called for calm. He was still, even two weeks later, feeling very protective of Shea. He'd never, he thought, get over the sense of her fragility that had swamped him as he'd watched her fighting to bring his son into the world.

The doctor had told him that the first one was sometimes difficult, but he hadn't been prepared for what she'd gone through. And he'd found it hard to believe when they told him that she'd quickly decide the pain had been worth it the moment she held the baby, but it seemed to be true. Women, he had concluded, were remarkable.

"He has your nose, Shea," Celeste announced positively, "and Chance's eyes."

"And his stubborn chin," Quisto put in with a chuckle. The baby yawned, unimpressed.

"As long as he has his father's heart, I don't care about the rest," Shea said quietly.

Celeste nodded in warm approval, while Chance looked faintly pink and absurdly pleased.

"He will be a big, strong boy," Celeste predicted.

"He'd better be," Chance said with a grin, "if he's going to hold his own with this crew."

"So, partner," Quisto cut in, "you gonna tell us his name now that we've met him at last?"

Shea smiled in anticipation as she looked back at her husband's partner. Then she turned to Chance, and he took the still-yawning baby from her carefully.

"Hey, little one, wake up a second. You're about to be introduced to this madcap clan."

In response to his father's coaxing voice, the clear blue eyes opened and fastened in seeming wonder on the face above him. He cooed happily, lifting a tiny hand toward his father's face. Chance grinned, propped his son carefully in the crook of one strong arm and turned to face the gathered group. His other arm went around Shea. When he spoke, his voice was full of a pride in them both that he didn't even try to conceal. And when he spoke, it was to all of them, but his eyes were on Quisto.

"I'd like you all to meet Sean Rafael Buckner."

There was a second of silence as it registered, then came an uproar from several of the watchers—those old enough to know Quisto's given name. From Celeste came a pleased exclamation, rattled quickly off in Spanish.

Quisto just stared, a little pale. "You can't... Chance, you... you should name him after your father!"

"My old man told me a long time ago that if I ever hung 'Eugene' on a kid of mine, he'd never forgive me. So it's Shea's father and you, partner."

The usually glib Quisto seemed speechless. He blinked rapidly, eyes that were suspiciously bright.

"Besides," Shea added quietly, "if it hadn't been for you, he might not even be here."

Quisto moved then, suddenly, sweeping Shea into a tremendous hug.

"Ah, *querida,* you honor me. And you make me wonder if there isn't truly something to this love thing." He looked over her shoulder at Chance and the baby. "What do you say, *amigo?* Is there another one like her out there?"

Chance shook his head. "She's one of a kind." He gave her a look so full of love and tenderness that Shea blushed. Then he grinned at Quisto. "But you're going to meet your match someday, my friend. I just hope I'm there to see it."

They all laughed, and Quisto bore the teasing with admirable equanimity. Yet more than once Chance or Shea caught him looking at them thoughtfully, and had to smile at the way he tenderly handled his tiny namesake as he carried him around like a doting uncle, whispering silly things about everyone in little Sean's tiny ear.

And later, as Chance rocked the small cradle with a strong, steady hand, Shea sang their son to sleep with the love song she'd written for his father.

* * * * *

TAKE A WALK ON THE
DARK SIDE OF LOVE WITH

October is the shivery season, when chill winds blow and shadows walk the night. Come along with us into a haunting world where love and danger go hand in hand, where passions will thrill you and dangers will chill you. Silhouette's second annual collection from the dark side of love brings you three perfectly haunting tales from three of our most bewitching authors:

Kathleen Korbel
Carla Cassidy
Lori Herter

Haunting a store near you this October.

Only from 🔻 *Silhouette*® where passion lives.

Silhouette Books has done it again!

Opening night in October has never been as exciting! Come watch as the curtain rises and romance flourishes when the stars of tomorrow make their debuts today!

Revel in Jodi O'Donnell's STILL SWEET ON HIM—
Silhouette Romance #969
...as Callie Farrell's renovation of the family homestead leads her straight into the arms of teenage crush Drew Barnett!

Tingle with Carol Devine's BEAUTY AND THE BEASTMASTER—
Silhouette Desire #816
...as legal eagle Amanda Tarkington is carried off by wrestler Bram Masterson!

Thrill to Elyn Day's A BED OF ROSES—
Silhouette Special Edition #846
...as Dana Whitaker's body and soul are healed by sexy physical therapist Michael Gordon!

Believe when Kylie Brant's McLAIN'S LAW—
Silhouette Intimate Moments #528
...takes you into detective Connor McLain's life as he falls for psychic—and suspect—Michele Easton!

Catch the classics of tomorrow—*premiering* today—
only from V. Silhouette

ROMANTIC TRADITIONS

Marriages of convenience, secret babies, amnesia, brides left at the altar—these are the stuff of Romantic Traditions. And some of the finest Intimate Moments authors will bring these best-loved tales to you starting in October with ONCE UPON A WEDDING (IM #524), by award-winning author Paula Detmer Riggs.

To honor a promise and provide a stable home for an orphaned baby girl, staunch bachelor Jesse Dante asked Hazel O'Connor to marry him, underestimating the powers of passion and parenthood....

In January, look for Marilyn's Pappano's FINALLY A FATHER (IM #542), for a timely look at the ever-popular secret-baby plotline.

And ROMANTIC TRADITIONS doesn't stop there! In months to come we'll be bringing you more of your favorite stories, told the Intimate Moments way. So if you're the romantic type who appreciates tradition with a twist, come experience ROMANTIC TRADITIONS—only in

SIMRT1

INTIMATE MOMENTS®
Silhouette®

INTIMATE MOMENTS®

Silhouette®

Next month, don't miss meeting the Rawlings family of New Mexico. You'll learn to love them!

Look for

THE WILD WEST

Linda Turner's exciting new miniseries.

Look for GABLE'S LADY (IM #523), October's American Hero title.

And look for his siblings' stories as the exciting saga continues throughout 1994! Only from Silhouette Intimate Moments.

WILD-G

Silhouette Books
is proud to present
our best authors,
their best books...
and the best in
your reading pleasure!

Throughout 1993, look for exciting
books by these top names in
contemporary romance:

DIANA PALMER—
Fire and Ice in June

ELIZABETH LOWELL—
Fever in July

CATHERINE COULTER—
Afterglow in August

LINDA HOWARD—
Come Lie With Me in September

When it comes to passion,
we wrote the book.

BOBT2

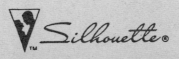